Although this is a fictional novel, where possible I have tried to be historically correct. However, there are some instances in the book where a certain amount of poetic licence has been used.

Acknowledgements.

I would like to thank Sue, my wife, and daughters Emma and Lucy. I would like to…but I'm not going to since not one of them have read a single page of this book. Other than saying that I was wasting my time, they have been no help whatsoever. Still, I love them nevertheless.

Chapter 1 – The World order.

Looking out from his plane, Hans Baur knew that he was witnessing one of the most significant moments in the history of mankind. Perched in the gun turret on the underside of a Messerschmitt Me 264, he had the perfect view of the momentous event taking place some two miles below him on the island of Cyprus. Having watched it drop from his plane and disappear into a tiny spec just a few minutes ago, he could not have envisaged the total and overwhelming destruction that the bomb was now inflicting on the island below.

In a matter of seconds, the might of the explosion was reducing the capital city of Nicosia to dust, with a tidal wave of immense power cascading across the landscape and leaving nothing but charred ruins and devastation in its wake. The most destructive force that the Earth had ever seen was reducing the island of Cyprus to an apocalyptic wasteland and in doing so, was about to change the face of the world.

From Hans' vantage point, it was apparent that this was no ordinary bomb. Mesmerised, he watched as a bluish-green light illuminated the entire horizon. A vast pillar of fire, seemingly coming from the bowels of the planet, rose up into a towering cloud of creamy white foam, seething and boiling away to form the shape of a giant mushroom as it swelled up into the heavens. This was an entity of unequalled power - yet also of incredible beauty, although Hans doubted that beauty would have been an adjective used by those poor souls on the ground. He had never seen anything like it in his life and knew that the implications of this destructive force would be monumental.

The impact of the world's first atomic explosion, sent shock waves of a different kind through the allied forces. With operation 'Overlord' and the 'D' day landings well under way, they had thought that the Nazis were on the back foot and supposedly close to surrender. But now their plans to end the war were thrown in to chaos. Whilst Allied command pondered over what action to take next, the Germans helped focus their minds by inflicting a second, and equally devastating nuclear explosion on the island of Crete. This time choosing to launch it from mainland Europe using a long range V4 rocket in an effective display of the versatility of this horrific weapon. In response, the Americans now had little choice but to bring forward the use of their own nuclear weapons. The launching of their own atomic bombs on the cities of Nagasaki and Hiroshima in Japan left them in a familiar state of total annihilation.

With the Germans claiming to have more nuclear warheads armed and aiming at London and the Americans ready to strike on Munich, there was now a nuclear stalemate. To avoid a full-scale nuclear war, the Americans could see no option but to reluctantly retreat and to leave the Germans unimpeded to re-establish their control over Europe. Without the backing of their American allies and with the threat of a nuclear strike on their capital, Britain, like the other allied countries, had little choice but to capitulate and issue an unconditional surrender. As the German invasion began, there was sporadic fighting and pockets of resistance, but with the British armed forces now out-gunned, they had little choice but to eventually lay down their arms and allow the German army to march into the country unopposed.

The Russians, in refutation of what was happening elsewhere, continued their assault on Berlin from the East, but they too were forced to issue an absolute surrender when Stalingrad was levelled with a further nuclear strike. The Nazis then made it known that Moscow was their next intended target. A new world order was now established, with the globe basically being split in to three: The Americans controlled the Pacific Rim, including Japan, Australia, Vietnam and much of the Far East, while the Germans took Europe, Africa and Russia. The third power was China. They secured a non-aggression pact with the German Republic and have remained insular ever since, not much caring what goes on in the outside world. This new order of global power has remained the case for the last fifty years, with the world existing in an uneasy peace ever since. Both the American States and the German Republic have built up such a huge arsenal of nuclear weapons that both know that any war would see the mutually assured destruction of the planet.

There have, however, been a number of close calls. The biggest came in 1953, when the Germans started to lay waste to entire English villages in retaliation for the acts of resistance that had been going on ever since the ending of the war. Certain fragments of the English population could not accept the rule of the Germans who had taken office in Government. As well as ruling from Whitehall, they also held power in local councils, police and armed forces, education, even entertainment and leisure. In fact every conceivable British institution now had Germans at the helm.

For many years an underground war was waged against the Germans. When in 1953 the resistance started to disrupt the newly commenced national autobahn project by destroying bridges, the German authorities decided that, 'enough was enough'. In retaliation for these acts of defiance, they started having public executions of the men from entire villages and torching the family homes of suspected 'terrorists'. The Americans, unnerved by the reports of what was happening in Britain, flexed their might and threatened retribution if it didn't stop immediately. And so for a short while the World came close to the brink. In the end the Germans backed down and ceased the executions and so the Americans removed the threat of reprisal. The resistance in Britain initially continued, but as the years went on the ferocity and regularity of the attacks slowly subsided. Eventually, realising little had been accomplished by their acts of aggression during the previous twenty years of occupation the underground officially ceased their policy of disruption in 1965. The English have lived in a peaceful coexistence with their German occupiers ever since.

In truth, it wasn't a bad place to live. The Germans held the English in high regard, admiring their work ethic and overall attitude to life. As the years progressed they felt it was more of a partnership than an occupation. In return, the British scientists and engineers excelled in technological advances under German leadership. Output from English factories nearly always exceeded targets. The Germans appreciated the quality of goods manufactured in Britain, and even though they would never admit it, it was secretly acknowledged that Britain produced the best goods in Europe, even better than those manufactured in the great industrial centres of Germany itself. In fact it could be said that Britain had prospered since the ending of the war. Most of the towns and cities had been rebuilt, with many of the slums which had existed since the end of the nineteenth century, being replaced by modern housing complexes. New schools, hospitals and libraries were built with state of the art facilities and modern architecture. The road and rail infrastructure was also vastly improved, with fast autobahns and rail networks now linking all major cities.

The Germans appreciated the beauty in the 'green and pleasant land' that was Britain, and so despite this major rebuilding program, emphasis was still put on keeping England quintessentially English. Many new parks were landscaped and there was an extensive tree-planting program within the inner cities. As part of their efforts in winning over the hearts and minds of the population, a great deal of care and attention was made to ensure that England was a pleasant and safe place to live.

With the redevelopment of the towns and cities came the highest employment levels the country could remember and, as a result, the overall standard of living was far more comfortable than ever before. Through their effective propaganda machine, the Germans also instilled a sense of importance on having both a healthy body and mind into the population. This was accompanied by an exceptional healthcare and education program where partaking in fitness and leisure activities, as well as competitive sport was very much encouraged - if not almost compulsory. Britain had never been so fit and healthy. Admittedly the Germans were rather tough when it came to matters of law and order, but as a result the level of crime was minimal, and thus the streets of Britain safer.

Even though they had lost the war, in essence the English had nothing to complain about. Well, nothing as long as you conformed to the Nazis ideology of a true British citizen. If an individual were classified as 'asocial' or outside normal society, for instance British Jews, Communists, Gypsies, homosexuals, the mentally ill, even an alcoholic or homeless, then they would experience a rather different side to life under German occupation. Let's just say that in 1995, these types of people were no longer 'a burden.'

Chapter 2 – Victory Celebrations.

The year is now 1995 and the preparations are underway for the celebrations to mark the 50th anniversary of the winning of the War. This momentous occasion is the perfect opportunity for the German military to show off its might, with parades taking place across the globe, from Cape Town to Moscow, from Berlin to Birmingham.

There was a knock on the classroom door.

"Enter."

"Excuse me mein Lehrer, I have instructions to escort Karl Smith to the headmasters office immediately." said the prefect interrupting Karl's class.

"Oh shit, what have I done now?" Karl whispered to his friend.

"Karl Smith? Very well. Karl, it appears that you are wanted by der Schulleiter," stated the teacher, as he glanced over to where Karl was sitting.

"Yes sir, thank you mein Lehrer," Karl replied as he rose from his seat.

"And Karl, do not forget that I want your homework on Herman Swartz, on my desk by 8.30 tomorrow morning."

"Yes mein Lehrer, it is already finished, sir."

"Good, then I look forward to reading it. And that goes for the rest of you, half past eight tomorrow morning sharp," the teacher informed the rest of Karl's class.

"Sir, Yes Sir," the glass responded loudly and in unison.

"Now, Mr Smith, you'd better go, you do not want to keep the headmaster waiting - do you?"

"No Sir, I'm on my way, sir."

As Karl gathered his books, he whispered to his friend that he would see him at shooting practice after school. In one motion he stood to attention and gave a courteous nod to his teacher. With a quick click of his heels, he turned sharply and followed the awaiting prefect out of the door.

Karl Smith is 14 years old and goes to the Heinrich Himmler Mittelschule, in Leeds - a prestigious school which, like all schools in England today, was very strict, but this discipline made winners, and this was one of the best. In turn, Karl is one of the school's best pupils. They were almost made for each other and Karl loves everything about the school. He excels both academically and at sports, and with the support and facilities that such a school can offer, he invariably wins at just about everything he participates in. Needless to say, he is quite a popular young man. As the captain of the school cadet team, he has just helped them win the Yorkstein Hitler youth cup for military parading and marksmanship for the first time in their history. And now, because of their achievement in winning such a prestigious cup, Karl and the rest of his team have been chosen to represent Yorkstein in the military celebrations in London this weekend. A great honour indeed.

Karl was very excited about going to London, not only about participating in the celebrations, but because it was going to be the first time that he'd seen his father in three months. Karl's father was a scientist, and in January that year, he had been transferred to a top intelligence unit in London for 'final temporal transfer preparations'. Karl didn't know what this meant or indeed what his father's work entailed at all. In fact, in all of his life, Karl had never really known what his father actually did. He knew that it must be important, since his father was very well looked after by the government. In fact it was because of his father's work that Karl was privileged to attend such a brilliant school. As far back as Karl could remember his father's work had always been shrouded in secrecy and although he had always been inquisitive as a youngster, he eventually gave up asking since he always got the same answer; "Sorry son, it's for me to know and you to find out."

Karl never did 'find out' and was very much kept in the dark about what his father actually did for a living, although he was hoping that he would be somewhat wiser this weekend. When his father had left for London, he was very excited. He had told Karl that his work was on the verge of 'changing the World,' and that he was going to make his son very proud of him; although as usual, and frustratingly for Karl, he refused to elaborate any further. He just added that all should become apparent by the time of the victory celebration weekend. The victory weekend was almost here and Karl couldn't wait to meet up with his father again.

As you already know, Karl is not living in Britain as we know it today - but a very different Britain. A Britain, which 50 years ago surrendered to the Nazis. But this wasn't the case, I hear you thinking to yourself. As we all know, the Germans were not victorious and there was no atomic bomb dropped on Cyrus, Crete or anywhere else in Europe for that matter. It was America and Britain that celebrated victory, not Nazi Germany!

So is this a fictional account of how life might have been, if events had turned out differently back in 1945?

I'm afraid not. I only wish it was that simple.

If I were to tell you that the above events actually happened and this is not fiction but fact, you would be forgiven for thinking that I was stark raving mad. But, at risk of this accusation and my sanity being questioned, I will say it nevertheless.

"The above is a true account of events and Germany did in fact win the 2nd World War. It is the truth, the whole truth and nothing but the truth."

There, I've said it. Whether you believe me or not, is up to you. But I'm telling you now, as God is my witness, that this record of events IS our history, and in fact, may also turn out to be our destiny!

Confused? Then let me take you back to 1945;

Chapter 3 – A National Hero.

"Scheiße," Herman Swartz cursed under his breath, as he banged his knee on the corner of the desk. The laboratory in which he had worked every day for the best part of three years looked so different in the early hours of the morning. In near pitch darkness he stumbled his way around the office, occasionally bumping into a misplaced chair or something not quite where he thought it to be. Even the small narrow windows adorning the top of each of the surrounding walls offered very little light from the moonless night sky outside. He was tempted to fire a quick burst of torchlight into the darkness in order to get his bearings, but knowing that all would be lost if his presence was detected, he opted to continue in the blackness of the night.

Herman had always joked that he spent so much time in the laboratory that he could find his way around it blindfolded. So now, as he moved around feeling each desk or chair in turn, he tried to visualise where his next few steps should take him. Slowly and quietly he continued touching and feeling his way along, until eventually he was confident that he was now standing directly in front of the desk belonging to Kenneth Teller, the lab's assistant director. Straining his eyes, Herman's assumption was confirmed as he could just about make out the silhouette of the familiar large rectangular shape of Teller's desk, and so manoeuvred himself along its edge around to its front. Using his fingers to feel along the top rim of the desk, Herman felt between the top edge of the right hand draw and the thick wooden desktop. As he positioned his finger along the rim he could finally feel the cold metal casing of the lock mechanism positioned a few inches below the top of the draw. Happy that he had now found the optimum position, he cautiously removed a large iron crowbar from the canvas rucksack that was draped over his shoulder. Gripping with both hands he slowly wedged the tip of the crowbar in to the small gap between the draw and the desktop. Then, with his arms fully extended he lent down on to the protruding crowbar and gradually applied his strength, pushing down steadily harder until the wood of the desk started to creak under the strain. Relaxing his grip, he repositioned the crowbar a few inches away from its original position and pushed it deeper in to the widening gap. Once again he began to apply pressure. Encouraged by the evident stress that the wooden draw was now under, Herman began rocking to and throw on the crowbar with almost his entire bodyweight. The wooden panel of the draw creaked and strained even further, until suddenly and with an alarmingly loud snap, part of the wooden panel broke off and fell noisily to the floor.

The silence of the laboratory had been well and truly broken. Terrified that his movements had been heard, Herman stood perfectly still for a few moments hardly daring to breathe. He tried to listen intently over the sound of his own thumping heart for any signs of activity in the long corridors outside the office. He continued to listen, fearful of any indication that the commotion of the panel breaking had been heard by any of the numerous guards that patrolled the complex. The returning silence finally reassured him that his presence had gone undetected and he was in the clear. Taking a deep breath he finally dared to move once again. Fumbling for the top of the draw, Herman was pleased to find that the gap created by the piece of wood now lying on the floor, was just big enough to accommodate his shaking hand. He slowly knelt down and having turned side-on to the desk, cautiously pushed his limb through the accommodating gap in the front of the draw and began to rummage through its contents.

It wasn't there. Pushing his arm further into the hole until his shoulder was pressing against the desk, he fumbled frantically towards the back of the draw. Moving his hands side to side, he shuffled the contents around, carefully identifying each object as it came within reach of his fingers. Finally he breathed a sigh of relief as his hand came into contact with the large cold metal ring that he knew held the keys he'd been anxiously searching for. Teasing the metal ring into his palm with the tip of his fingers, he triumphantly gripped the set of keys in his right hand and with a degree of difficulty pulled it free from the hole - yelping quietly in pain as a large splinter of wood pierced the skin of his forearm.

****

Born in Munich in 1907, his family moved to England shortly after. His initial childhood memories of growing up in England were all very pleasant; however this was all to change in 1914 with the onset of the First World War. Since England now found itself at war with Germany, Herman's father, like most German nationals living in England was interned in a prisoner of war camp, in Douglas on the Isle of Mann. Although neither Herman nor his Mother, Katharina, were 'imprisoned,' the separation from his father meant that they suffered a great deal of hardship and poverty for the duration of the war. Being German meant his mother was shunned by the majority of people in their small Warwickshire town and finding work became all but impossible. Herman now found himself being bullied at school and was completely ostracised by his so called friends. In 1916, Herman's father died during his internment. Although he was only nine years old, this had a profound effect on Herman and even though his father had died from natural causes, he still harboured a deep resentment towards the English for taking his father away from him.

Once the war had ended, Katharina missed her husband desperately and considered taking Herman back to Germany. However she knew that the conditions back in post-war Germany were very harsh and not conducive with trying to raise a young boy alone. Besides, she also knew that she would struggle to raise the fare back to Germany, and so with little option, she took the tough decision to remain in England. It was hard going for both of them at first, but things improved once she secured a job working as a chambermaid for a family on a country estate in Buxton, Derbyshire. The Lord of the manor, a retired professor from Loughbourgh University took a liking to Herman, taking him under his wing and giving him personal tuition. As Herman grew older it was evident that he was a very bright young man and to the delight of his mother and the professor, who by now treated Herman as if he were his own son, he won a scholarship at the age of seventeen to study Physics at Cambridge University.

Although he had spent practically his entire life in England, because of the treatment he and his family had received during the war, especially his father's imprisonment, Herman vowed never to forget his German roots. He paid a lot of interest in what was happening back in post-war Germany and for a long time had been fascinated by the political upheaval that was taking place back in his homeland. In particular he was intrigued by the leader of the National Socialist Party, a certain Adolf Hitler. Having read a copy of Mein Kampf as a young adult he found it to be an inspiration to his own political beliefs and was convinced that this was the man that would eventually put Germany back on the map. Motivated by the doctrine written by Adolf, Herman was quite vocal with his anti-Semitic views during his time at Cambridge and was therefore soon approached by the British Union of Fascists. Joining the BUF was a straight forward decision for Herman, being pleased to find that even in Britain there were people that shared his extreme political views.

Although he had been an avid member of the BUF during his years at Cambridge, having graduated he soon realised that they were never going to be a major political force in England. He longed to go back to Germany and be part of the 'Nationalist uprising' that was now taking place. And so when his mother died in 1932, he decided to move back to Munich and fulfil his desire to follow Adolf Hitler make Germany great once again. On his return, he quickly joined the Nazi party, where his 'enthusiasm' did not go unnoticed. By the time they came to power in 1933, Herman had already been earmarked as an exceptional talent. A bright young man with a science degree, who could speak perfect English without even a hint of a German accent was clearly too good of an asset to waste.

When the Nazis approached him with the proposition of working as a 'reconnaissance' agent reporting directly to the Third Reich, Herman was overjoyed. Especially when they told him that his assignment would be in America. His brief was simply to use his knowledge of physics and intellectual prowess to get in to a position of 'influence,' thus joining the small network of German 'spies' that had already infiltrated many areas of American society.

And so, given the pseudonym of Harold Swift he travelled to the USA. With his newly doctored degree from Cambridge

University and undeniable intellect, Herman found job offers easy to come by. He excelled in every position he undertook and soon found himself working at the University of California. As time went by his roles became more and more influential and he was considered quite an expert in his field. With a war against Germany looking more and more likely, the American government were desperate for decent physicists to work for them and inevitably, Harold's talents did not go unnoticed. He was quickly seconded by the 'Office of Strategic Services,' (predecessor to the CIA) to work on a number of top secret projects. Harold's plan to be integrated into the American establishment had gone even better than envisaged. By the time the war had started in 1939, Herman had managed to manoeuvre himself into a senior role in weapons research. His position gave him clearance at the highest level and through his network of contacts he was able to pass on valuable information to the German hierarchy on a daily basis.

Throughout the war the German military always seemed to be one step ahead of the Allies. Quite simply, much of this was down to just one man – Herman Swartz. With access to the huge American defence budget and the use of other brilliant academics to feed off, Herman Swartz was prolific in the invention and technological breakthrough of military hardware. Unaware of his daily betrayal, 'Harold Swift' was held in high esteem by his American colleagues. They never suspected that Herman was constantly feeding the details of each technical breakthrough to his network of German spies. And so, no sooner had the Americans designed the concept of a particular new weapon - the Germans had uncannily already moved the same new weapon into production. The concept and development of the V1 and V2 rockets emanated from Herman's department in the USA, but mysteriously it was the Germans who somehow managed to produce them first, and wreak havoc and destruction on the streets of London.

So respected had Harold become, that he was eventually transferred to Oak Ridge in Tennessee to help on the American's most secret development - The 'Manhattan Project'- the team entrusted by the President of the United States, Franklin D.

Roosevelt, to beat the Nazis in the race to develop the ultimate weapon - the world's first atomic bomb.

By the end of 1944 their work was all but complete and the existence of the atomic bomb was very close to being a frightening reality. Throughout the bombs development Herman Swartz had continuously updated the German command with the progress of his team. In fact, in the many instances where he had personally been instrumental in any of the technical breakthroughs, he would purposely procrastinate announcing his findings to the Americans. Only after he had updated his German contacts with the data from his results, would he report the breakthrough to his American colleagues. In doing so, he ensured that the German's were at least on a par or even had a slight edge over the American's with the development of their own nuclear weapons. So critical to hopes of a German victory was the information that Herman was supplying, that the Führer himself was kept updated of his progress. Adolf Hitler knew that despite his Nazi forces being in retreat across Europe and defeat looking inevitable, that the blueprint that Herman was about to photograph would be the missing piece of the jigsaw puzzle for their own nuclear programme and would make the German Atomic bomb a reality. To buy Herman the precious time he needed to complete the bombs development and then get the blueprints back to Europe, Hitler had issued a declaration that each and every German must fight to the death in order to delay the advancement of the Allied forces.

****

"Gottverdammt," Herman cursed once again as he pulled the small fragment of wood from his skin. However, the pain could not dampen his delight, for despite the darkness he knew straight away that these were the keys that would get him into the safe in Oppenheimer's office. He paused momentarily to contemplate the enormity of what he now found himself doing and the potential consequences his actions may have on the entire world. He always knew that this day would eventually come and that what he was doing was for the sake of his fatherland. However, he still felt somewhat reticent of his actions, since he had known many of the people he was about to betray for the best part of three years.

Genuine friendships had evolved over this time and Herman wondered what the reaction of these 'friends' would be, when they realised that his whole existence had been a lie. However, he also knew that he was a German and that if successful; his actions could be a pivotal moment in changing the outcome of the war. Failure was not an option.

Oakridge was first conceived back in 1941 and was an integral part of America's plan to build the Atomic bomb. Needless to say, security was extremely tight, with several large fences surrounding the 56,000 acre complex. However, having been here almost since its conception, Herman knew the place like the back of his hand. It was so vast that it was sometimes referred to as the 'Secret City,' so Herman knew that the security was stretched and that the patrols could not guard every single inch of the complex around the clock. And so, with the large ring of keys in hand, his next task was to get to the safe in Oppenheimer's office. Unfortunately for Herman this was situated on the second floor of a separate building on the other side of the complex. Leaving the laboratory, he headed down a flight of stairs and into the network of underground tunnels that connected the various buildings. The passageways were permanently lit with a series of lights running down the centre of each tunnel, suspended by long chains hanging from the ceiling. As Herman approached the final stretch, he knew that this was the tricky part and that once he had entered this section of the tunnel there was nowhere to hide. He knew that he would have some explaining to do if he was to run into anyone at this time of the morning. To keep his time spent exposed in the tunnel to a minimum he ran as fast as he could for its entire length. As he made it to the end, Herman was out of breath but nevertheless relieved to have made it undetected. Through the large metal door at the end of the tunnel and up two flights of stairs, he now found himself in a long unlit corridor, off of which was the door to Oppenheimer's office. There were no windows along the corridor, so Herman felt it safe to use his torch to highlight his way along the darkened passage. Every so often he would turn off his torch and stand in silence to listen for any signs that he had been detected. Each time, when he was confident that the coast was clear he would turn the torch back on and continue along on his way.

Finally he reached Oppenheimer's office and paused for breath as he stood by the door. He carefully inserted one of the keys into the lock of the door and turned it slowly. Unsurprisingly the door opened. There was no doubt in Herman's mind that this would be the case, since these were a set of keys that he was very familiar with. On many occasion he had returned or collected the blueprints from this very office. Such was the trust given to Herman Swartz that he was one of only three people on the entire project who not only had access to Oppenheimer's office, but was entrusted with the code for the combination lock of the safe inside. Obviously the combination was of no use without the key, which up until a few moments ago had been locked safely away in Kenneth Tellers' desk. Equally the keys were no good without the combination – but now Herman had both. Herman turned off his torch and slowly entered Oppenheimer's office. Opposite the door he had just entered was a large window running the entire length of the room. The window looked out onto a floodlit courtyard, some 10 feet below - the light from which lit up the office night and day, meaning that Herman could now put away his torch. This was just as well, since the courtyard was always a hive of activity for the guards and any stray light from his torch would surely give his presence away. Indeed, Herman froze as he could hear guards carrying out their patrols in the yard below. Herman stopped and looked around. Along the remaining sides of the office were a number of blackboards with mathematical equations scribbled all over them. Dispersed in-between the blackboards were a number of large drawing boards, each scattered with an assortment of blue prints and draft designs. However, Herman knew that the blueprints that mattered were the ones in the large safe that now stood directly in front of him.

Herman glanced at his watch. He had chosen this hour since he knew that there was a changeover of the guards and therefore the hole he had cut in the perimeter fence was likely to go undetected for at least the hour - but time was running out. So despite shaking like a leaf, he knew that the sooner he could photograph the blueprints and get the hell out of here - the better his chance of success. Kneeling directly in front of the safe, he slowly turned the large mechanical dial. First three clicks to the right, then several back to the left, and so on from left to right and back again, until he finally felt the clunk of the lock mechanism open. He then repeated the process for the second mechanical dial which was positioned slightly lower and to the left of the main dial. The familiar clunking sound confirmed that the correct combination had once again been entered. He then placed the all important key from Kenneth Tellers' office into the lock - just to the right of the two dials and turned it three times to the left. Herman paused momentarily before pulling at the large metal handle on the right edge. As he felt the heavy safe door open fractionally to confirm that the sequence was now complete he breathed a huge sigh of relief. Fully opening the safe door, he smiled as the precious blue-prints were revealed, neatly folded in a pile at the bottom of the safe. Gathering them in his arms, he placed them on top of the documents already lying on the various drawing boards positioned around the office. Taking his microfilm camera from his pocket, it took all of his effort to keep his hands steady enough to be able to photograph the prints one by one.

Once he had finished, he looked down at the very small camera in his hand and knew that the film inside could be the difference between his country winning or losing the war. The enormity of this thought sent a shiver down his spine. He had always considered himself a far better physicist than a spy, never dreaming that he would have the nerve to do what he was now doing. However, he knew that the task was far from complete and unless he could now escape from the building undetected and hand over the micro-film to his contact, all of his efforts could still prove to be fruitless.

Having photographed the prints, he considered destroying the originals; however he knew that this would be a futile exercise since a second set was always kept in a secret location off-site. Instead, he decided it would be better to try and cover his tracks and hide any trace that anyone had ever been in the office. By putting the blueprints neatly back in the safe and returning the keys back to the main office, he hoped that no one would be any the wiser as to what had happened the previous night. Admittedly, the gaping hole in Kenneth Tellers' desk might give them some cause for concern, but by the time they had fathomed out what had taken place, if at all, the micro-film would hopefully be halfway to the Atlantic Ocean and an awaiting U Boat. If all went to plan Herman hoped he could then return to work the next day as though nothing had happened and remain undercover. There would be nothing to implicate him in any wrong doing, and such was his reputation that it was highly unlikely that he would even come under any suspicion.

Herman began to gather the blueprints to return them to the safe, but as he was doing so, the torch fell loose from the inside of his rucksack. He made a grab for it, but only succeeded in sending it sprawling across the office floor, inadvertently managing to knock the switch to 'on' in doing so. Immediately a beam of bright light shone from the torch and out of the large window at the front of the office into the dark sky above the courtyard. As the torch continued to roll across the office floor, twisting and turning as it went, the beam of light rotated across the sky-line as though it was a floodlight searching the night sky for enemy aircraft. Herman scrambled across the office floor and eventually managed to dive on the torch and smother the beam of light. However, by this time he considered that a lighthouse could not have been more effective in signalling that there was an intruder in Oppenheimer's office. He once again froze and listened intently for any signs that his whereabouts had been detected. This time it was immediately apparent that the light had been spotted since he could now hear heightened activity and commotion in the court yard below.

The sharp sound of a whistle, shortly followed by the intermittent wall of noise from the site's klaxon alarm system confirmed Herman's fears that he had been detected. The continued wailing of the klaxon undoubtedly meant that every single person on the entire site was now also aware of a breach of security. Herman knew that he had just moments before the guards would be swarming Oppenheimer's office and his game would be up. He scrambled himself up from the floor and dashed towards the door and out into the now lit adjoining passageway. The sound of the heavy footsteps of the guards rushing up the stairs echoed down the corridor. Herman had planned his escape meticulously and had always envisaged that his detection was a distinct possibility and so had come prepared. Removing a smoke canister from his bag, he pulled the pin and rolled it towards the top of the stairwell and the advancing guards. He then turned in the opposite direction and headed back along the corridor. As he reached the door to the stairwell he turned to see the blanket of smoke now filling the entire corridor and could hear the sounds of the guards coughing and spluttering coming from the other end. He knew this should buy him enough time to get down the two flights of stairs and back into the network of tunnels. From there he knew all the twists and turns along the labyrinth of tunnels that would get him back outside and to the hole in the perimeter fence that he had made a hour or so earlier. He had calculated that he could get back to the fence, via the tunnels and up through an air vent, a good 10 minutes before the guards would be able to enforce a lock down of the perimeter. He knew it was a race against time, but was confident that he could make it. As the deafening klaxon echoed around the tunnels, Herman sprinted along them, turning left or right at every juncture. Completely out of breath he finally made it to the air vent closest to the fence.

"Come on, come on," he muttered impatiently, as he waited for the mechanised ladder to lower from the vertical tunnel above his head. Finally, it was within reach and so he gave it a helping tug to move it the final three feet or so. As it steadied in front of him he lifted his leg up on to the bottom rung and went to pull himself up, but before he could do so he was startled by a familiar voice.

"Professor Swift, is that you?" questioned a guard, somewhat bewildered to see Herman in such a remote location at this time of the morning. Herman immediately recognised him as being one of the guards that greeted him cheerfully each morning at the gatehouse and actually quite liked him. However, Herman knew that what he was doing was so monumental that he could not allow this single man to jeopardise his success and so without saying a word pulled a Luger 9mm pistol from inside his jacket and in an instant, shot the guard from point-blank range.

The bullet sailed straight through his shoulder, sending the guards own gun spinning down the tunnel as he tumbled to the floor. Herman raised his straightened arm until the barrel of his gun was directly aligned with the guards head. As his finger slowly began to squeeze on the trigger of his Luger the guard instinctively raised his hands and began pleading for Herman to spare his life. Why did it have to be this guard of all people, thought Herman, cursing his luck - could he kill him in cold blood? He had even met this man's young children for Christ's sake. Faced with this reality, Herman realised that he could no longer pull the trigger.

As previously stated, he always knew he was a better Physicist than a Spy, and even though he knew that he would probably live to regret it, decided to spare the man's life. The guard breathed a sigh of relief as Herman lowered his gun - although his joy was short lived. To buy himself some precious time, Herman decided to incapacitate the guard and fired off one more shot. This time, straight through his foot. As he writhed in agony on the floor the guard cursed Herman.

"I'm sorry, but you should be grateful. If you had of been anyone else that second bullet would have been through your head." The guard was hardly full of gratitude as he continued to groan and roll around on the floor evidently in pain. He watched haplessly as Herman turned and finally climbed the ladder.

Reaching the top, Herman removed the turret of the air vent and climbed out. The cold fresh air of the night sky hit him as he stood by the vent. Looking over towards the perimeter fence he thankfully could see that it still looked clear. He knew that just beyond the fence was his contact and awaiting transport ready to take him along the Clinch River to the wilderness and relative safety of the Appalachian Mountains. This is it, Herman thought to himself as he sprinted across the small grass clearing between the turret and the edge of the perimeter. As he carefully prised himself through the cut edges of the fence, Herman turned and looked back at the floodlit Oak Ridge complex.

"Well, I guess that's the last I'll be seeing of you," he said to himself, with the realisation that his decision to let the guard live meant that his days at the plant were well and truly over. Sensing that more guards would not be far away, he decided to keep his goodbyes short and sweet, and so turned and fled at pace into the darkness. Not more than ten minutes later he found himself at the foot of the hills that surrounded the complex and much to his relief, rendezvoused with his escort who had been nervously awaiting his arrival.

"My god, I thought you were never going to make it," exclaimed the contact, who was equally relieved to see Herman. "When the klaxons started going off I began to fear the worst. I'm telling you now, five minutes more and I was out of here!" he declared.

"Let's just say I had a few minor hiccups," Herman told him, somewhat understating the ordeal he had just gone through to get here.

"Do you have the blue-prints?" the escort asked him.

"Of course. Why else do you think I'd be here," replied Herman rather indignantly.

"Good. Then I suggest we get the heck out of here, since you are now America's most wanted."

Herman nodded in agreement, as the pair of them turned and headed off at pace further into the wilderness and to a previously hidden canoe. Once they realised what had taken place, the American Office of Strategic Services were frantic with worry that the secret of the Atomic bomb was about to end up in enemy hands and therefore issued an all states alert to detain 'Harold Swift'. Despite the mandate to capture him at all costs, Herman and his escort were able to evade their pursuers and headed east across North Carolina. Travelling via any means possible, despite the frantic pursuit, they finally made it to the coast at Juniper Bay where a small amphibian craft was waiting to take Herman to a German U Boat sitting some ten miles out in the Atlantic Ocean.

"Auf wiedersehen und viel glück!" the escort told Herman as he boarded the flimsy craft which was to take him to the awaiting vessel. Herman acknowledged him with a smile and a thumbs up.

Once on board U Boat 811, Herman was given a hero's welcome. The crew were fully aware of their passenger's importance and knew that he was potentially their last throw of the dice in the quest for victory in the war and so sailed at great haste across the Atlantic.

In England, the Allies thanks to the Enigma code breakers at Bletchley Park, had decrypted a series of messages and were therefore aware that Herman was on board a U Boat somewhere in the Atlantic and heading to Germany. In an attempt to stop him, the British forces created a blockade of the English Channel and access to the German ports. Unable to take a risk with their precious cargo the Captain of 811 was forced to take a detour around the north of Scotland, through the North Sea and into the Baltic - heading past Denmark to the port of Rostock. It looked like they were going to make it, but as they approached the straits of Ystad on the Baltic Sea travelling just 10 feet below the water's surface their periscope operator spotted the familiar silhouette of a Russian frigate.

'Dive, dive, dive,' was bellowed out through the subs intercom as they tried to put some depth between themselves and the surface. At fifty feet the Captain ordered all engines stop and silent running as they hoped to pass undetected underneath the bow of the frigate. The whole crew, including Herman, held their collective breath as they could hear the hum of the frigates engines directly overhead. With sweat dripping from his forehead, Herman breathed a sigh of relief as the sound appeared to diminish. However, with a huge crash Herman's world was suddenly rocked to the core as the U Boat shook violently from the explosion caused by a depth charge some fifteen feet above the vessel. Herman looked at one of the German submariners standing close to him, as if to acknowledge their lucky escape, but before he could even open his mouth to utter any words a second and far bigger explosion ripped through the side of the submarine. Herman was thrown into metal railings running along the vessel's gangway as thousands of gallons of water rushed into the hold.

Pandemonium broke out as the fuselage filled with smoke and freezing water. Herman felt himself being manhandled and passed from sailor to sailor, before he was abruptly pulled up into an escape hatch by two of the submariners. As the compartment filled with water, one of the sailors instructed Herman to inflate his life jacket and get ready to take a deep breath. Once the pressure in the compartment was equalised the sailor turned the large wheel that opened the hatch to the depths of the Baltic Sea and nodded to Herman that now was the time. As it was opened there was a blast of air and the occupants of the hatch were catapulted towards the surface like a cork from a bottle. The rush of bubbles and noise of the water filled Herman's senses as he ascended rapidly towards the surface. Glancing below him Herman could see the blackness of the doomed U Boat disappearing as it plummeted to the sea bed.

Despite his rapid ascent, Herman felt that he was never going to make it. With his lungs feeling like they were about to explode and his rise to the surface seemingly endless, he was convinced that his life was about to end. It was such a relief when eventually he shot through the surface of the water and was able to fill his lungs with a huge intake of air. Although thankful that he could now breathe once again, the oil laden seawater and acrid fumes from the stricken U Boat, made it an altogether unpleasant experience. Wiping the oily water from his eyes Herman scanned his surroundings and was reassured to see the two sailors that had shared his escape hatch, floating in the debris some ten feet away. He was even more thankful to see that they were in the process of retrieving an inflatable life raft that had broken the surface nearby.

As the two sailors clambered aboard the raft, they quickly turned and paddled with their hands towards Herman. As the bitter cold of the Baltic started to bite, Herman was extremely grateful when they finally pulled him up on to the raft. Once Herman was safely aboard they searched frantically for any other survivors, but managed to pull just two more men from the sea. It was evident that the rest of the ships company had been lost to the Baltic.

As he sat cold and wet in the small lifeboat it was apparent to Herman that so many of the sailors had sacrificed their own lives in the sinking vessel to ensure he was the one who got into the escape hatch. He felt immense gratitude towards them and was humbled by their bravery. This made him even more determined than ever to get the micro-film to his compatriots to ensure that the deaths of the brave submariners would not be in vain. However, his hardship wasn't over just yet. Enduring three more days adrift in the lift-raft on the rough seas of the Baltic, when they were eventually picked up by a German fishing boat they were in a bad way. Indeed, one of the sailors had succumbed to hypothermia and was evidently dead. His cold and lifeless body was dropped back into the sea, whilst Herman along with the three surviving sailors was taken to the port of Gdansk in Poland. With barely any time to recover from his ordeal, Herman travelled from Gdansk across northern Poland to rendezvous with the SS and hand to them in person the blueprints that were to change the outcome of the war.

I'm afraid that at this point history is a bit vague as to what actually happened. I'm sure it has been exaggerated over the years, but it was said that Herman Swartz was ambushed and shot several times. However, despite his ultimately fatal wounds he still managed to hand over the bloodstained blue-print of the atomic bomb to the German intelligence and thus ensure that Germany would win the war and in doing so guaranteed his place in German folklore as a national hero. It is believed that having delivered the Atomic bombs' deadly secret, he collapsed in a pool of blood and died a hero. In fact, as far as heroes went, there were none greater than Herman Swartz.

One would struggle to think of a city in Germany, or England for that matter, that doesn't have a statue of him taking centre stage in their city centre. His actions meant that, despite being on their last legs, the German Luftwaffe could launch one last attack. Only this time their payload was far more deadly. The devastation on the islands of Cyprus and Crete in the Mediterranean and the near total destruction of Stalingrad sent shock waves around the World. The Americans launched their own bombs on Nagasaki and Hiroshima in Japan and so became fifty years of nuclear stalemate.

For most people the occupation is the only way of life they have known. Like Karl and his father, Tony, both were born into a Britain controlled by the Nazis. Karl's Grandfather had told him about life before the Germans and had taught him English; however Karl for all intents and purpose was German. He spoke German and, such was the indoctrination of Nazis ideals - with strict military style schooling and compulsory membership of the 'Hitler-Jugend,' he even thought like a German.

So the Germans had won the war and all was great for the German Empire. However, there was still one cross that the whole of the German empire had to bear. And this was the fact that their beloved Führer, Adolf Hitler, had not lived to see it. Believing that Herman Swartz had been lost in the sinking of U Boat 811 and with him the last chance that Germany had of winning the war, Adolf Hitler had taken his own life in a bunker near Berlin. Hitler had promised the Germans domination of the world and died not realising that he had delivered his promise. This was the biggest burden that all of Germany shouldered. A regret that ate at the very soul of each and every German, especially members of the Third Reich. Many considered their victory too hollow and meaningless without their leader alive to revel in the glory and lead them to greatness. Still, no one could turn back the hands of time, and so this was a regret that they would have to live with for all eternity. Or was it?

Chapter 4 - Operation Sparen der Führer

Karl Smith's father was a scientist. Actually, that was a bit of an understatement. The fact was that Karl's father was probably going to go down in history as the greatest scientist of all time. After ten years of work and unrelenting dedication he had finally made the breakthrough to the holy grail of all inventions - time travel.

Always considered impossible, the dream of travelling back through time had finally become a reality thanks to Karl's father. The German authorities always felt that Tony Smith was an exceptionally talented scientist and when he told them that he thought that it was feasible for a person to travel through time, they listened. Instead of ridiculing him, as you might expect the response to be to such a preposterous notion, they actually gave serious thought to his theory. They concluded that it was worth exploring further and made the decision to give him all the funding and support he needed. They also gave as much time 'as it took' to prove one way or another whether his theory could become a reality.

Ten years on, they were now about to be repaid for their faith and patience in this remarkable man. Against all the conventions of modern science and witnessed by the German High command, Tony Smith had succeeded in sending himself back in time. Needless to say the German hierarchy were overjoyed with his success and the reason why he had been whisked off to London was that they now had a spectacular plan of how to introduce Tony's new phenomenon to the World. The 'powers that be' had always hoped that Tony would make the breakthrough before the 50th anniversary of their victory. To their delight he had delivered the goods, albeit leaving it a little close to the dead-line. With just a few months until the celebrations weekend, Tony Smith had been transferred to London to finalise preparations and to make their audacious plan a reality. The German leaders knew that the best present they could give their people at these celebrations was the Führer himself.

The plan was very simple. To go back in time and to stop Adolf Hitler killing himself. If successful, this would be their crowning glory. The Führer, alive and well, to see his dream of a mighty German republic fulfilled. It was now a possibility, and Tony Smith was the only person in the world who could make it happen. He had spent years coding his own molecular structure into the computer and it was this time consuming process which made the whole procedure possible.

As much as the Germans had admiration for Tony Smith, they would have still liked to have sent 'one of their own' back for such a prestigious honour. However, since they did not have the time to wait while the computer was re-programmed, they had no choice but to give Tony the task of going back to 1945 and saving the Führer from his own suicide. And so it was to be. Tony and his machine were being prepared to go to Germany for operation – Sparen der Führer.

The 'time-machine' could travel in time; although it could not travel in space. Therefore they would have to move it to a precise place where they knew Adolf Hitler would be at a given moment in time. Hitler's movements had been well documented, so they chose a Government building in a small town called Bernau, just to the north-east of Berlin and on the eastern border of Germany. This was in the knowledge that Hitler had held one of his final meetings with Herman Goering there, a short time before his untimely suicide. After a few weeks in London finalising the details for operation Sparen der Führer, Tony and his machine were to move out tonight to Bernau. He couldn't even telephone Karl to explain to him that he wouldn't be able to see him in the military parade this Saturday. Yet if all went to plan, by Saturday he could already be a national hero and be standing next to Adolf Hitler himself at the Anniversary parade.

Tony was confident that he could get the time machine to pin-point his arrival in 1945, however he also knew that he would have to arrive naked, which he wasn't overly enthusiastic about.

From his previous experiments he knew that the molecular structure of two entities could not be combined and that any clothes or weapons would become entangled with his body when he re-materialised in the past and kill him instantly. Without any documentation the authorities were concerned that Tony would have trouble convincing Adolf Hitler of the truth. Tony was given secrets and passwords that only Hitler and senior members of the SS knew. He was also introduced to a man named Klaus Zimmerman. Klaus was a clerk, working in the Bernau Government building back in 1945 and could to this very day still remember the meeting that had taken place between the German leaders some fifty years earlier.

Klaus was a short rotund man with a completely bald head. He wore little round glasses, which were a perfect match for his little round face and he constantly looked hot and flustered, with bright red cheeks giving the false impression that he had just spent an hour or so vigorously exercising in the gym. Klaus was able to tell Tony as much information about the meeting as he could remember. Bearing in mind it was fifty years ago, he was pretty precise in his description of the meeting room and the building itself. He also gave Tony some personal information about himself and the few passwords that he could remember. This, Klaus hoped, would persuade his past self to believe the legitimacy of Tony's mission if they were to meet. In truth, Tony had his doubts whether anybody in their right mind would believe such a fantastical story. He considered that if all went to plan, he should materialise right in front of Hitler himself and therefore concluded that when faced with the bizarre sight of a naked man appearing from thin air, in front of his very eyes, what else could he believe besides the extraordinary?

Needless to say the government building had somewhat changed from 1945, but with the help of Klaus and the original building plans, they were able to reassemble the machine as close as possible to where the meeting chamber had once been.

"Now be careful. People were very suspicious of each other in those days. Remember, do not mention any of these details to anyone but me, if and when we do meet back in 1945," instructed

Klaus as he dabbed the sweat from his forehead with a neatly folded white handkerchief.

"If you do find me, then the following should help convince the young me that you are telling the truth. But you must promise me that you will not reveal it to anyone other than me. If they suspected you of giving away secret information back in those days you'd be shot at the drop of a hat. I don't think my children, or grandchildren for that matter, would appreciate never having existed," he said laughing nervously.

Klaus then proceeded to give Tony a series of meaningless numbers, 'W2543 N1356 25-4-45.'

"These are most important so you must promise to memorise them," he insisted. Tony wasn't sure what he needed them for, but duly promised and wrote them down on a scrap of paper. As good as his word, Tony repeated the numbers over and over to himself until they were indelibly etched into his brain.

The day of reckoning finally came and Tony's machine was assembled in what used to be the meeting chamber of the Bernau Government building, but was now a modern open plan office of the local council. The council workers had been given the day off work so the normally busy office was instead now full of high ranking German officials. Representatives from all areas of the German High Command, from Generals to Politicians and even the German Chancellor himself, were now gathered in the 'waste and refuge management' department of the Bernau council offices, to witness this historic event. In the room, as well as Tony, his machine and the assembled dignitaries, were two glass cabinets. Each cabinet filled with documents, history books and newspapers from the current day and relating to various major events over the past fifty years. Despite not looking anything extraordinary, the first cabinet was in fact another of Tony's ingenious inventions. To complement his time- machine, Tony had created a quantum vacuum to act as a stasis chamber. A stasis chamber had the effect of making all items inside it remain preserved in their own time-line. Therefore anything in this glass cabinet would not be affected by any changes that came as a consequence of Tony's actions while in the past. However, every thing outside the stasis chamber would be subject to the current conventions of time and physics, and therefore be likely to change if Tony created any paradoxical ripples during his jaunts back in time.

Inside the second cabinet were identical copies of the documents, but this time no stasis chamber, just plain wood and glass. If Tony's machine worked and he managed to change the course of history then the documents in the second chamber would change, recording the events in history as they had now happened in this new time-line. The 'stasis chamber' cabinet had a pair of silicone gloves built into the wooden sides, making it possible for the pages of history books, newspapers and other general documentation inside the stasis chamber to be turned over from outside. By constantly comparing the two sets of documents they planned to monitor Tony's progress.

Only Tony's memories of the events in the original time-line and the documents in the stasis chamber would give any clue that anything had ever changed. For those watching, the only memories that they would have would be those of the new time-line and they would be unaware of any changes, however momentous, that may have resulted as a consequence of Tony's actions during his time in the past. Tony had theorised that if he did anything that fundamentally changed history then his own future timeline could be irreversibly altered. For instance, if he were successful in saving Hitler from his suicide, then the assembled dignitaries would not be gathered in this building, since there would be no need to send him back in the first place. Adolf Hitler would already be alive and well, albeit an old man, in 1995. In fact, Tony pondered whether he would have been afforded the time he spent inventing the time machine at all, if it were not for the High Command's obsessive desire to have their beloved Führer back? Tony envisaged coming back to the future as an esteemed and respected advisor to Adolf Hitler, maybe, even his right hand man, with a big house and lots of wealth. He even dared to think that maybe he would still be married to Hannah, since he would not have had to waste the last ten years of his life working on the time machine. Tony had a lot of theories, of what may or may not happen in the process of travelling through time. But he knew that he could have all the theories in the world, but the only way to find out for sure what would happen, was to do it for real. And now was the time.

All the dignitaries were gathered at one end of the office, for a photograph with Tony to record this historic event. Even Klaus Zimmerman managed to get in on the act, standing next to Tony with a big grin on his little round face. Copies of the photograph were quickly printed and placed in each chamber. This would record whether Tony's actions in the past had any paradoxical effect on those gathered.

Finally, the machine was ready and Tony was ushered in to the room, wearing a white bathrobe. He was given a polite ripple of applause as he made his way to the machine. Once there, he removed the gown and handed it to one of the waiting technicians. He stood there naked, nodded nervously to the gathered spectators, before sitting down on a standard office type chair. A number of men in white coats then frantically jumped in to action, attaching a multitude of wires and electrodes from the machine to his body. As he sat there feeling somewhat nervous, the computer screen displayed the words 'Countdown to Temporal Placement ready.' The excitement and anticipation in the room grew as the Chancellor was guided to a rostrum in the centre of the room, which was draped with the black eagle emblem of the Third Reich. He turned to all who gathered and proceeded to make the worlds longest speech on 'the magnitude of what they were about to witness.' Tony's nervousness was not helped at all, as the Chancellor went on and on about just how much greater life would have been if Adolf Hitler had been alive after the war to drive Germany forward and how his vision and guidance would have been fundamental in making the Republic even greater than it was today, and how finally the Third Reich was about to fulfil its destiny.

Much to Tonys relief the Chancellor finally finished. And so to a fanfare of the German national anthem and a hiss of compressed air, a plinth slowly rose from the centre of the rostrum. In its middle was a much larger than necessary red button, almost

33

10 inches across. The Chancellor grinned as he positioned both hands on to the button. To Tony's dismay it appeared that the Chancellor was once again going to break out into a long speech, as he started to thank those concerned for giving him the honour of such a prestigious task, but with the words, 'Just a press of a button for man, but the start of a new era for Mankind,' he finally pressed the button. As he did, a large screen with numbers which filled its entirety, started to countdown from 20.

From his previous exploits Tony knew that time travel was an unpleasant experience. It felt like your body was being turned inside out, as your molecules were separated into a million particles and then imploded back into each other. On his first encounter he had been physically sick and temporarily blinded. Something he sincerely hoped not to repeat when appearing in front of the Führer.

For those watching in 1995, Tony's disappearance was an incredible spectacle. As the countdown reached zero, the numerous electrodes attached to his body were suddenly joined to each other with arcs of fluorescent green light. It looked like an illuminated spiders web spun around his body. As these points established connection, further links were formed, until Tony's whole body was pulsating with a low intensity glow. The light steadily intensified, until it became almost blinding. As the watching dignitaries moved their hands towards their eyes to protect them from the brightness, there was a sudden whoosh as the light seemed to be sucked into a ball of brilliant white light no bigger than the size of a tennis ball. With a final flash and a kind of popping sound, the light was gone and so was Tony Smith. The electrodes that were previously attached to his body dropped to the floor. The spectators gasped at the sight of what they had just witnessed and then broke out in spontaneous applause.

For Tony the experience was over in an instant. From being surrounded by people, machinery and noise, there was a sudden flash of light and then deafening silence. As his senses began to realign themselves to his new surroundings he realised he was alone. The room was how he imagined and how Klaus had described it to him, but with one major difference - no Adolf

Hitler. In fact the room was totally empty and rather cold. Tony was not to know but he had gone back one day too far. In all the excitement and rush to set up the machine, Tony had forgotten to clear the computer's memory buffer from his previous trip back in time and therefore this extra day had been included in the computer's calculations. Tony had no idea about his blunder. He didn't know whether he was too early or too late for his rendezvous. All he knew was that there was no Adolf Hitler and that it was bloody freezing, so his immediate priority was to find some clothes and get warm. Then he could try to work out what had gone wrong.

Chapter 5 - Experiments with T.E.S.S

For his sins Tony Smith was a scientist working for the Central intelligence unit of the German Republic. His son, Karl, was at boarding School in Leeds and his beautiful wife, Hannah is...well, who knows? She left him over a year ago!

She said that he loved his work more than he did her. He didn't, but his paymasters, the German government, were working him harder and harder each day. He had been under increasing pressure to come up with the goods, ever since he had proved to them that he could send objects back in time. Tony had spent the best part of his working life working on a theory of how time and matter could be fused together through the use of a Temporal Energy Separation System, TESS for short. I won't bore you with the intricate details, but the principle was to convert the molecular structure of an object into light signals. These signals would then be sent at such great speeds through an electron pulse generator into TESS, that they would fuse together to form a calculated quantum mass. Not a real object but a fusion of data and numbers in the form of ultra condensed light energy.

Once the energy was forced inside the confines of TESS's quantum stasis field it would be refracted into itself at every juncture, getting more and more condensed, until eventually it would have nowhere else to go but into a 4th dimension. And this dimension was time. The energy should then reappear in the same space, but at sometime in the past. And, not as a mass of ultra condensed light, but as the original molecular structure of the data signal sent. i.e. the object itself. This was his theory in any case.

It could of course just create a nuclear explosion the likes of which the World has never seen before. Admittedly, that this was a worse case scenario and Tony sincerely hoped very unlikely.

He had tried all sorts of things, drawing pins, paper clips, in fact every conceivable inanimate object which had a relatively simple construction. Tony's frustration grew as the objects would glow bright with light, but they didn't appear to move. Then one day while eating his lunch it struck on him to try and send his sandwich back in time. In comparison to the other objects, this was quite complex, taking nearly three weeks to program the molecular structure of a simple ham sandwich in to his computer. But again he was disappointed; the sandwich didn't appear to move. It glowed with intense light, but once the light flashed and disappeared, the sandwich was still there. In his frustration and concluding to himself that time travel was just a silly dream, he picked up the sandwich and decided that all it was good for was his lunch.

As Tony took the first bite he quickly spat it out, realising that it tasted bitter and somewhat stale. He quickly made up another sandwich, but this time doubled all of his calculations. Once again he started up TESS with the new sandwich attached. Once the 'pop' of light had disappeared he picked up the sandwich and gave it a sniff. Yuk, it smelt putrid. Peeling back one of the slices of bread he shouted out loud 'Eureka', since it was evident that this time the sandwich visibly had green mould on it. The paper clip and other inanimate objects had been going back in time, but as the past caught up with the present in an instant it didn't appear to move. His sandwich had not moved, but on the other hand it had clearly aged, therefore he theorised that it could only have done so by travelling back in time.

Tony set to the task of programming TESS to send a multitude of items back in time. Using various fruits, he was able to calculate the rate of decay, and therefore work out how far back in time his calculations had sent them. However, for every new object the process was painfully slow, with the exact molecular details of each item having to be painstakingly punched into the computer to enable TESS to work.

Weeks turned in to months, and months merged into years. Tony's work took over his life. The Government had seen enough to ensure that he was well looked after. Karl was sent to one of the top schools, whilst Tony and his wife, Hannah, were kept in comparative luxury. Hannah was at first understanding about the amount of time he spent immersed in his work, although as time progressed they started to argue more and more. She said she wanted him and not his money and begged him to find another job. Unfortunately, having dangled the carrot of time-travel in front of the High Command's nose, he could hardly turn around to them and tell them that he was now thinking of a career change and wanted to be a dentist or a doctor instead. In fact the Government was becoming impatient and he was constantly working sixteen-hour days to meet the deadlines they were continually setting. What made it worse for Tony was that he was forbidden to tell Hannah the nature of his work and so just fobbed her off with excuse after excuse. Despite coming as a shock at the time, Tony knew that he could hardly blame her when she finally left him.

Without the distraction of Hannah, he now found himself working even longer hours - if that were possible. TESS and all the accompanying gadgetry were cluttered around his apartment, which it could be argued looked more like a mad scientist's laboratory than a home. Hours merged into days and days into weeks. Tony would often go 24 hours without sleeping, but knew that after each experiment he was moving tantalisingly closer to his goal – to send a Human Being back in time!

So ever since Hannah left him, he has led a lonely existence. Programming millions of calculations into his computer and tinkering with program line after program line after program line. To be honest, for the last year or so, he has had little to do with the outside world, other than the odd occasion that he looked after his son, Karl. As far as the outside world was concerned Tony might as well not have existed. He very much wanted to tell Karl why he had neglected him and his mother for so long, but the instructions from his paymasters were very clear; 'Tell no one..''

Reluctantly, he had to keep his work a secret, and since he spent so much time working, he realised that he must seem very distant and an inadequate father to Karl. However, with the success that he had encountered to date he became very single-minded, and knew that he had to press on, even if this meant alienating himself from his family.

On the rare occasions when Karl did stop for a few days he did try and devote his time to him, however if he was honest, even then his mind was still on his work. To Karl's annoyance he would often suddenly stop in the middle of a sentence or whatever they were doing together, to scribble down some notes or 'quickly' amend a few more lines of programming on one of the reams of computer print outs which were invariably strewn around his apartment. On one such occasion when Karl was stopping over for the weekend, Tony was having a bit of horseplay with him when he managed to accidently catch his nose with his elbow.

"For God's sake, now look what you've done" bemoaned Karl as blood started to pour from his nose.

"I'm sorry son, it was accident" Tony apologised. "Here take this."

Karl was no doubt expecting a handkerchief or a tissue, but instead he passed him one of his measuring cylinders.

"What on Earth is this for?" he moaned as he struggled to stem the flow of blood by pinching the bridge of his nose with his fingers.

"Your blood, I need your blood," reacted Tony eagerly, demonstrating for him to put the cylinder to his nose.

"Jesus, Dad. You half-break my nose and all you can think about is your work. I assume you want my blood for work and you're not some sort of bloody vampire?" he quipped as he reluctantly put the cylinder to his nose.

"No I'm not a vampire" Tony laughed, quickly starting a conveyer belt of replacements, as each cylinder became full of his blood.

"Blood is a fantastic thing" he told him.

"Every person's blood is unique and from it you can build a picture of their entire DNA structure. The reason why you have blond hair and blue eyes, the reason why you are good at sport or why you are nearly as good looking as your Dad…..are all here in your DNA," Tony joked. Karl smirked at the idea that his father had the audacity to think that he was only 'nearly' as good looking as him.

"It is your DNA which makes you who you are and all this information can be derived from your blood" he told him enthusiastically.

"That's great Dad, you will be able to make a clone of me, once you have watched me bleed to death" he moaned, as Tony put yet another cylinder to his nose.

Realising that he was getting a bit carried away with his enthusiasm to collect Karl's blood, Tony apologised to Karl and finally passed him his handkerchief.

"So is that the big secret then? You're going to clone me and start a race of superhuman 'Karl's?" he laughed through the handkerchief as he held it to his nose.

"I'm afraid not son. Imagine having to look after dozens like you? Having just the one is bad enough." he smiled, although in reality Tony knew that Karl had never given him a day's trouble in his entire life.

"So why do you need my blood?" Karl asked.

"Just work" Tony said vaguely.

"Which is what?" Karl questioned for the umpteenth time in his life.

"For me to know and you to find out" Tony replied, also for the umpteenth time.

"You always say that – why can't you just tell me what you do?"

"You know I can't son. I wish I could. But you know I have been sworn to secrecy over anything to do with my work. I promise you however, that when the time is right, you will be the first to know. In the meantime please bear with me and forgive me for my shortcomings as a father. "

"Dad, you know I think the world of you. Even though you are a crap father….and have just nearly broken my nose" he quickly added, laughing. "I know your work is important and they have their reasons why it must be kept secret. You do not have to apologize to me" he said with a reassuring smile.

"You're a good lad. Karl" Tony said, almost getting tearful as he gave him a rare hug.

"Please, don't get all mushy on me" Karl said getting slightly uncomfortable by his father's lingering hug and therefore pulled himself gently away. Albeit brief, it was nice for Tony share a rare moment of intimacy with his son.

He wouldn't admit it, but I'm sure that Karl had appreciated the moment as much as his father.

"Here, I have a present for you" said Karl in an attempt to lighten the atmosphere.

As Tony held out his hand Karl handed him his bloodied handkerchief.

"Oh thank you. You're so generous" he said smiling. Karl returned the smile and for once Tony felt like a proper father.

For the first time in years, they spent the rest of the evening playing board games and having lots of fun. Tony's mind did wander a couple of times to thinking how he could now utilise Karl's blood for his experiments, but for once in his life he actually managed to devote an entire evening to Karl without the usual interruptions. It was a real pleasant experience and made him realise just what he had been missing for all these years and the sacrifice he had made for his work.

It made him question whether it had all been worth it, but he knew that the next day he would be back to his experiments, now even more determined than ever to complete his quest. He was driven by the thought that once successful that he could make up for lost time with his son and get back to some resemblance of a family life, yet he still doubted that Hannah would be part of it.

Using the blood he had collected from Karl the night before, his experiments grew in pace. He was able to map out Karl's DNA in digital form and was able to create a blueprint of his entire body structure. The good thing was that he was now never short of blood to use for his experiments, since by using TESS, he could send Karl's blood back in time. The blood would return back to the present time in the blink of an eye, and therefore he could now cultivate buckets of the stuff in an instant. More importantly the process didn't seem to have any adverse effects on it.

With Karl's DNA now completely encoded Tony was convinced that his machine would now work on a Human Being and that he would be able to send Karl back in time. He had felt that the chances of success in sending someone Karl's age back in time would be far better than someone older. However, when it came to the crunch he couldn't do it!

The day that Tony had planned to reveal all to Karl and let him know that he was to have the honour of being the worlds first 'time-traveller' he chickened out. For all he knew Karl's body could be turned in to a quivering mass of blood and guts. He feared that he could be turned into a vegetable or even killed. Therefore, after a lot of soul searching, not to mention a number of horrifying nightmares, Tony came to the conclusion that he couldn't take the risk with his own son.

He decided that there was only one person whose life he would be prepared to risk, and that person was himself.

He made excuses to his paymasters for the delay and again set about the laborious task of encoding his machine, this time with his own DNA structure. Thankfully, with Karl's DNA being so similar to Tony's, it only took a couple of months to replace the calculations of Karl's DNA with those of his own. Besides, the way he looked at it, if this machine did work then he would have all the time in the world. In theory, he had finally done it. All the data had been input and he had checked and re-checked all of his calculations, but for whatever reason TESS would still not work on a human being.

Tony could not see any reason why TESS would not work. It had worked on just about everything else he had attached to it, including Karl's blood. However, for all his attempts to send himself back in time he still couldn't make the final breakthrough. Despite countless attempts he had still not gone back so far as a second. He was convinced that his calculations were right, but each time he attached himself to TESS and activated the computer, nothing happened.

Tony was growing more and more frustrated and then one day – Eureka! It happened. He had just had a bath and sat there naked having made yet another minute adjustment to his figures. More out of habit than hope he attached the electrodes to himself once more and booted up TESS. At 11.02 precisely there was a blinding flash of light. Tony suddenly had the feeling of a wave of convulsions going through his whole body, as he sat there wondering if he was actually in the process of killing himself? It appeared not.

Despite feeling weirder than he'd ever felt in his life and the fact that he couldn't open his eyes due to being temporarily blinded by the flash of light, Tony was pretty confident that he was still alive!

Given this weird and wonderful feeling that he was experiencing Tony was convinced that TESS must have worked.

So what did he do to celebrate?

He was embarrassed to admit it, but he threw up. On what or whom he didn't know but as he sat there trying to focus his eyes he heard a familiar voice.

"You bloody genius.... I knew you could do it!"

Slowly as both his eyesight and senses returned he realised to whom the voice belonged – It was himself!

There he was dressed in his bathrobe with the biggest grin he'd ever seen on his own face. It sounds ludicrous, but Tony and ermm....Tony, danced a jig and whooped with joy like a pair of schoolboys.

"It was the clothes...all the time the bloody clothes," he said excitedly.

"It was obvious really, you have to be naked." he added.

"Why didn't I think of that." the other Tony laughed.

"You did...well in about 10 minutes time, you're about to." he told him.

Tony then felt that he did the stupidest thing - he apologised to himself for puking.

"I wouldn't worry about it; I'm leaving it to you to clean up." The other Tony said smugly. At this, they both fell about laughing.

"So what next?" the 'other' Tony asked.

"I suppose you should get naked and attach yourself to TESS."

"What if I don't? Will all this have never happened?" he asked himself (quite literally).

They were musing about just how ludicrous, yet bewildering this question was, when suddenly and with another flash, the other Tony disappeared and 'Tony' was once again alone in the room. He had set his machine for 10 minutes and Tony guessed that was how long he had spent in the past, yet the clock on the wall now said 11.05. It had worked!

"I'm a bloody genius" he said out loud, affording himself a broad smile. Admittedly, the sense of elation and joy felt a little hollow. Given the enormity of what he had just achieved, it did not seem right that he was all alone in his apartment, cleaning up sick.

Tony Smith would go down in history as the inventor of the Time Machine, he only wished that Hannah or Karl, or anyone for that matter, had been here to share his moment of triumph.

The conversation he had with himself in the past set Tony's mind spinning. Would he have tried the machine naked if he hadn't have gone back in the first place? There were to be many situations where chicken and egg scenarios sprang to mind. Even now, Tony would admit to not fully understanding the complexity of time travel, but he had done it and knew that all the years of effort had been worthwhile.

Realising that he would need proof of his success; his next task was to set about developing a quantum vacuum compressor unit, which he hoped would create a stasis chamber. In theory anything inside it would not be affected by his time travel experiments. He surmised that whatever he placed in it would remain constant, regardless of any paradox that he managed to cause during his visits to the past.

Without wishing to sound too big headed, Tony concluded that creating the Stasis chamber would be a doddle. Well, compared to inventing the time machine it would be.

Indeed, it was finished in less than a week. To test that it worked Tony placed the current day's newspaper in the chamber and kept one on the table besides it. He sent himself back to the previous day and rang the Gazette to place a small ad in their classified section. Returning to the present, to his utter amazement, the paper on the table carried his ad, however the one in the stasis chamber still had the original page layout with no ad in sight.

Eureka!

So Tony Smith could now travel back in time and even had a way of proving that he had altered the time-line. It also occurred to him that his stasis chamber would give him a way of communicating with people in the present, whilst he was in the past. Clearly the communication would only be one way, and he hadn't quite worked out how best to put this in to practice, but at least in theory he now had a means of giving the present day a progress report.

Anyway, like a kid with a new toy, Tony set about learning more about his new-found phenomenon of time-travel. Going back further in time on each occasion, he tried to make more and more radical changes to see if they had any impact on the present. Each time he used the machine, the Tony in the present would disappear. Not materialising again until the time co-ordinates of the Tony in the past caught up with the time in the present. At which point he would suddenly re-appear out of thin air, back to the current time.

He realised that time was moving quicker in the past than in the present. Therefore, however far he went back into the past, the time would sooner or later catch up with the present. When it did, and the time lines eventually merged he would find himself back attached to TESS as though his time in the past had all been an elaborate dream.

Anyone else witnessing his return to 'real' time would see him materialise out of thin air as the time-lines merged. Tony calculated that for every one day that he was in the past, that time moved on just six hours in the present. That meant that, even if he spent an entire year in the past, then when he re-appeared in the present he would only have been gone for just three months.

The whole experience was very disorienting and often confusing. However, as time progressed at least he eventually got used to the temporary blindness and feeling of sickness; although it still has to be said that time travel isn't exactly a pleasant experience.

Tony was tempted while he was back in time, to let the real 'Tony' spend some time with Hannah, while the future 'Tony' continued with the work. But he was getting so close now, and decided that two hands were better than one. The fact that he could spend an entire day in the past and only lose 6 hours in the present, really sped up the process. He was able to go back with the results of experiments before they had even conducted them and if they hadn't worked they didn't bother conducting them. Figure that one out if you can?

One of the more bizarre experiments he conducted was for the Tony already in the past to go back even further, with the other Tony there to witness it. Although spectacular, watching yourself light up like a Christmas tree and then disappearing into thin air was somewhat surreal and rather unnerving.

Part of the reasoning for conducting this particular experiment was to see what would happen if someone unplugged TESS whilst he was in the past. Tony wanted to know if the time he spent in the past could be controlled by someone in the present time.

The simple answer was No.

Despite the fact he turned off TESS, in fact he even dismantled some of the component parts and put the machine in the cupboard under the stairs, the Tony in the past was not affected in anyway and merged back into the current time-line in the usual way, albeit that he found himself contorted in to a rather bizarre position in the cupboard under the stairs.

Tony concluded from this, that once in the past his fate was in his own hands and could not be influenced from anyone back in the 'real world', although it was evident that if TESS was moved that he would return to its new location.

Since there was nothing to stop him going back in time, over and over again, the temptation was to keep on going back to report on the outcome of each experiment and speed up the entire process. The down side of this was that each time he went back to a time that he had previously been back to, there was another Tony in the room. This got quickly out of hand and at one stage there were five Tony's in the room arguing over a particular issue.

Eventually, he came to the conclusion that he had to limit his time travel journeys to one per day, otherwise it became too surreal, not to mention a little disorienting. Sometimes, his impatience still got the better of him, especially if he had made a breakthrough in any of the experiments and was so eager to tell to tell someone of the success – even if this someone was only himself!

It sounds somewhat bizarre, but all the Tony's agreed, that if there were any more than two of them in the past, then the first one back should stay out of the way of the others. Read a book, watch television, anything but interacting with the others.

It came to a head with a big argument between five of them.

Tony would be the first to admit that he is not the easiest of people to get on with, so with so many Tony Smiths in the room, it was inevitable that they would eventually have an argument. He can't even remember what it was about, but it became so heated that they nearly came to blows. Tony appreciated the fact that having a fight with himself would have been stupidity in the extreme, so hence they all agreed on the one per day rule.

Not only was this time travel experience sometimes disorientating, but it also created lots of these aforementioned chicken and egg scenarios. For instance, if Tony went back and stop them conducting an experiment that didn't work, how would he know it didn't work since they never made the experiment in the first place?

He questioned that if he went a long way back in time, for instance to 1945. Would he have to live the next fifty years in the past to find out whether he was a hero or not?

What would happen if during his time in the past, he had an accident or was even killed!?

Or the one that he could never quite get his head around; What if he went back and killed his Grandparents prior to them having children. If that were the case then his parents wouldn't have existed and therefore they wouldn't have had him. If he wasn't born then he wouldn't have invented the time-machine, in which case he could not have gone back in time and killed them. If he didn't kill them, then they would have had his parents after all, who in turn would have had him. Therefore he could go back and kill them after all. But then his parents wouldn't be born....and so on.

What if he did this or made that happen, were questions that went over and over in Tony's mind. Trying to pre-empt the outcome of every possible scenario of his actions in the past started to affect his ability to think straight and also gave him more than his fair share of sleepless nights worrying about the consequences of causing a major paradox.

Could he cause the world as we knew it, to change irrevocably, or could he even destroy the Earth? Or maybe he had just watched too many science fiction films as a youngster!

Eventually, he concluded that the whole concept of paradoxes was one that would drive you insane if you spent too much time thinking about them, and decided to take a more philosophical 'what will be, will be' attitude. But not before he had conducted a little experiment.

Since his task was to stop a man from killing himself, he needed to know for sure what the consequences might be of such a paradox and therefore put his mind to rest.

For days he scanned the local papers waiting for a report on someone to meet an untimely end. At last he read about a child who had been run over the day before by a van in the local High street and had been sadly killed. Tony concluded that if he could pinpoint the time and place of the accident, he could intervene and stop the van hitting him and 'Hey Presto' his life would be saved and a major paradox created. Fortunately the Daily Gazette had painted an accurate picture of the time and place, that the child in question had been hit by the van. So, using TESS Tony sent himself back in time and made his way to the High street. The aim was to simply stop this young lad stepping in to the road and being crushed under the wheels of the van. He knew roughly where the accident had happened and also had a good idea of the approximate time, so all he had to do was grab the boy by any means possible, before he could step out onto the road.

As Tony arrived at the High Street, he anxiously surveyed his surroundings looking for a boy matching the description of our victim. But with the number of people around Tony was having difficulty spotting him, however what he did notice was a white van turning on to the High street. This had to be the vehicle he thought to himself, but there was still no sign of the boy. He scanned the walkway keenly, but it was useless - still no sight of him. Just as he was about to give up hope Tony suddenly caught sight of a lad appearing from between two shops. He headed directly towards the road, evidently in a world of his own. It was definitely him, but would Tony be able to get to him in time? He tried to push past the crowds, but soon realised he was too far away to be able to grab him. As the van veered down on his position Tony screamed out in frustration that his plan was about to fail. But then without even thinking he took his life in his own hands and rather foolishly jumped out in to the middle of the road. Standing only a few feet away and directly in the path of the van he shouted 'Stop' at the top of his voice and held his hand up, like some sort of demented traffic cop.

Tony will never forget the look of horror on the face of the driver as he tried desperately to avoid hitting him. He swerved into the centre of the road and with a huge crash, smashed in to an oncoming car. With a blinding flash and pain like he had never felt in his entire life Tony suddenly found himself back in his research lab. It took a few minutes to recover his senses, but when he did, Tony couldn't believe his eyes! The front page of the Gazette was now reporting that a man had been killed after a head on collision with a van that had inexplicably swerved violently into the path of his car.

The driver of the van had claimed that he had swerved to avoid hitting a man who had jumped out in front of him. Since he had been drinking schnapps all lunchtime in the local Bier Keller, the police didn't believe him. His case wasn't helped, when he told them that as soon as he had hit the car, this mystery man just disappeared into thin air.

I think they were planning on locking him up and throwing away the key.

Tony concluded that if this wasn't a paradox he didn't know what was?

Not only had his actions saved a life, with the young boy carrying on, oblivious to his brush with death. But they had also led to the death of another, with the poor soul in the other vehicle dying as a result of his actions. Furthermore, the newspaper in the stasis chamber was still carrying the original story.

As far as Tony could see nothing had changed. He was still here - the world hadn't ended.

It also answered his question about having to spend the next fifty years living in the past. As long as he created a paradox it appeared that he would immediately return to the present. So all Tony had to do was save someone's life (or kill them.) and he would be back home.

Admittedly this may turn out to be easier said than done, he thought to himself, since he was hardly Arnold Schwarzenegger, and had never harmed a person in his life. Unless you counted the poor soul in the car, but let's face it, that was an accident!

Accident or not, the fact that Tony had played a major part in the death of an innocent person did play on his mind a little. So the next day he went back in time once again and headed to the High street. This time he positioned himself between the two shops from where the boy had made his appearance. He arrived bang on schedule and as he passed Tony he grabbed hold of his arm and pulled him towards himself. The boy was pretty startled and pushed Tony off angrily, muttering a few obscenities before continuing on his way. Tony's intervention, although very brief, was enough to break his concentration and allow time for the van to speed by.

Tony looked over to the roadside and was amused to see the other Tony, with a look of complete bewilderment on his face. He had obviously just witnessed his tussle with the boy and therefore had not stepped out in front of the van. He was clueless as to what was going on, but before he could get an explanation, Tony found himself alone and back in his research lab. The other car involved in the original accident had sped by in the opposite direction and since the other Tony had no longer stepped out into the road, there was no longer a van for him to collide with. As soon as the car passed the original point of impact the paradox was complete and once again there was a blinding flash and Tony was back in his lab.

Returning back to the present through causing a paradox was a painful experience, but at least now he knew it worked and that by causing the paradox, he had a way home. Furthermore, he also knew that consequences caused paradoxically by himself in the past were not irrevocable and if he went back again he could at least correct any mistakes that he had made. Tony actually felt quite pleased with himself that he had now saved two lives, admittedly the second one was never intended to die in the first place, but nevertheless, he had still changed two individuals future without them even knowing. Just for reassurance he checked the newspaper once again, only this time there was no mention of any accidents, just a story about some old lady who swore that she had witnessed two identical men disappear in front of her very eyes, while shopping in the High Street. The rubbish some papers print!

Tony decided that his experiments were now complete and informed his bosses that TESS was now ready to be shipped out to Germany. The rest, as they say, is history, since here he was freezing his nuts off, standing in an empty meeting room in Bernau Town Hall.

Chapter 6 - I have a message for the Führer

As Tony stood there contemplating his next move, it quickly became apparent that his first priority was to find some clothes - He was bloody freezing. Besides, as and when he needed to explain his presence here in Bernau Town hall, his incredible story might just be a little easier to swallow coming from someone with clothes on.

The room itself was large and echoey, with a rather high ceiling. A large polished table, surrounded by sixteen chairs, sat in the middle of a cold stone floor. Around the room were a couple of writing cabinets and more chairs. On the walls on each side were a number of large and very impressive paintings of the Führer. At one end was an enormous, but sadly, unlit fire. At the other end was a big double door draped with two huge swastika flags.

'If I don't find some clothes soon I'll freeze to death', he thought to himself, standing naked and shivering in the middle of the town hall.

He could hear that the building wasn't empty, with voices coming from down the corridor. The question was 'what should he do next?'

He could hardly go and walk up to them naked shouting "I have a message for the Führer." But then again, why not? After all he had come to save his life! On second thoughts though, maybe it would be more prudent to err on the side of caution. After all he was now in the middle of a war zone and therefore decided that it would be sensible not do anything rash.

Tony tried the cabinets, but not surprisingly they were both locked

Looking around, it soon became very apparent that he was not going to find anything that resembled clothing. Reluctantly, he decided that one of the flags would at least preserve his modesty and give him a little warmth.

Back in England the Swastika was given huge importance. In the early fifties the English considered it a huge show of defiance to burn the Swastika in public. Needless to say, such acts were dealt with swiftly and ruthlessly. Many of the English who couldn't come to terms with the Nazi rule, used the burning of the Swastika, as an almost ritual suicide; knowing that their final act of defiance would usually only have one outcome. Instant execution!

The Swastika became very symbolic.

To the Germans it represented their glorious victory and was an emblem of German nationalism, whereas the English saw it as a symbol of their repression. Although over the years its significance has waned, it is still almost sacred. Tony was therefore mindful that what he was doing would be considered disrespectful, if not almost sacrilegious back in 1995, but still, what choice did he have?

Tony pulled the flag from its horning and draped it over his shoulder. Using the cord from the flag he managed to make quite an impressive Swastika toga. Rubbing his hands to keep warm he sat down at the table to gather his thoughts. He knew where he was. But when was he here? If the meeting had already taken place, then Hitler could already be on the way to his bunker. If so, the chances of reaching him would be slim. On the other hand, if he was here before the meeting, he knew that he could hardly hang around, dressed as he was, waiting for the Führer to arrive. Tony decided that his best course of action would be to find Klaus Zimmerman. If he was going to convince anyone of his story then he was his best chance.

There were no windows in the room and from his conversations with Klaus back in 1995 Tony knew that the meeting room was near the centre of the building. The only way out was through the double doors and along the main corridor. The prospect of this did not appeal to Tony; in fact he was extremely nervous. This was wartime and wars made people suspicious and unpredictable.

Tony's trump card was the fact that he was going to materialise right in front of the Führer and he would have had to believe what he saw with his own eyes. But since that did not happen and he was now stood in a meeting room, in the middle of a high security Government building, wearing nothing but a Swastika and a rather worried look, Tony knew that his story might not now sound so plausible.

One thing for sure, was that he couldn't stop here all day. Tony decided that he had little choice but to get out into the corridor and see if he could find Klaus. He walked over to the double doors and took a deep breath before warily turning the large door handle. With an alarmingly loud creaking noise the door slowly opened. Tony glanced out of the doorway and up the corridor.

There was nobody in sight.

'Here goes', he thought to himself, as he stepped out of the doorway and in to the corridor. He cautiously edged along the wall, ducking into each door recess as he went.

'This is ridiculous. Why am I so scared?' Tony questioned himself.

Heading gradually along the corridor to where most of the noise was coming from, Tony could now make out of sound of clanking dishes and pots and pans. It must be the kitchen he thought to himself. Maybe they were preparing for the Führer's arrival he surmised - well at least he hoped that was the case.

Tony suddenly felt a little more confident. The prospect of explaining his story to a chef seemed a little less daunting than to a German guard. Chefs are usually pretty friendly chaps and with a little luck, one of them might even know Klaus, he hoped. Tony approached the kitchen door, and with his new found confidence decided to walk right in. As he turned to open the door, it suddenly burst open and before he could move, a Waiter carrying a silver tray and huge pile of plates crashed straight in to him. I don't know who jumped out of their skin with fright more, the Waiter or Tony?

To Tony's consternation, the Waiters high pitched shriek and the sound of crashing plates hitting the floor now echoed around the building.

"Help.," "Help." he yelled.

"Ssshhhh" Tony vainly tried to gesture to him.

But it was too late.

"Schnell, schnell" Tony could hear the voices and commotion of the guards rushing from the front of the building.

"For God's sake please be quiet - I'm not going to hurt you" Tony told the now trembling waiter. "I have a message for....," but before Tony could finish his sentence he felt a huge crack on the back of his head. Tony turned briefly to see a rather plump and red-faced chef holding a large frying pan in his hand.

Chapter 7 - Tony's Interrogation

"Wake up."

If time travelling was an unpleasant experience, then this was like having the mother of all hangovers. As Tony slowly tried to open his eyes, he was rudely awakened with a jug of freezing water being thrown in his face, quickly followed by the back of a gloved hand to his left cheek.

"Wake Up."

"Vot is your name?"

"Vot were you doing in the Government building?"

"Who sent you?"

"Whom are you working for?"

"Why were you dressed in a swastika?"

As he saw that Tony was coming around, his questioning quickened, hardly giving time for, or expecting an answer. Tony's worse nightmare had come true. As he came to his senses he quickly realised that he was in a cell, stark naked and bound to a chair. In front of him was a German soldier dressed in the black uniform of the SS.

Even in England back in 1995 the SS were still to be revered. They were in essence the law and so if they said jump – you jumped. It was widely acknowledged that only a fool or those with suicidal tendencies would dare to argue with them. Tony knew that he would have to be very watchful of his next few words, if he wanted to live, let alone save the Führer.

"My name is Tony Smith, I have a message that is a matter of life or death for the Führer," he blurted out.

"You are English spy?"

"No...I'm errr German; I must speak to the Führer." Tony responded hesitantly.

"You are English spy. Who sent you?"

"What were you doing in the Government building?"

Another slap quickly followed to his right cheek.

Tony had spoken German all his life and although raised in England, he almost felt like a German. 'Why would he think I was an English Spy? My German was as good, probably better than his' Tony mused. Then it occurred to him. Although naturally fluent, he spoke with a Yorkstein accent. Back in 1995 it was barely noticeable, but to his SS man it no doubt made his accent sound very strange and was enough to convince him that Tony was an English spy.

'And why had I told him that my name was Tony Smith? It was hardly a name common in the Fatherland.' Tony reflected.

"Please I'm not a spy; I must speak to Adolf Hitler."

"For the last time English pig, what is your mission?"

How could Tony tell him the truth? If he did, would he believe him?

Tony assumed that the answer to this was probably not, but there was only one way to find out.

"OK, yes I am English, but I work for the Germans...in fact I am a German Spy.... I have returned to Germany with some vital information that will win us the War and stop the Führer from committing suicide."

"Suicide? The Führer would never commit suicide!" the SS guard bellowed, and gave Tony another whack across the face for being so insolent.

"Look, if you get a man called Klaus Zimmerman, he will be able to confirm that I'm telling the truth.," blurted out Tony in frustration, not really giving it much thought as to exactly how Klaus Zimmerman could in reality verify anything.

Telling him that he was a German spy, seemed far more feasible than the truth, although no sooner had Tony said it, he regretted mentioning Klaus's name. Even if they summons Klaus, how on earth would he convince him of his story, since Klaus had never even laid eyes on Tony. Not in 1945 in any case.

"Do you think I am stupid? I know of this Klaus Zimmerman – He is a simple office clerk whom I have known since before the war. I can tell you now that he is incapable of being involved in such things as spying or espionage."

"So tell me - If you are a German Spy, what is your unit, who do you report to?" demanded the SS man.

Tony remembered some of the secret passwords briefed to him before he travelled back in time and started blurting them out. This had the opposite effect to what he had hoped, and his captor became even more aggressive and agitated.

"Where did you get this information?"

"Who is your informant?"

It didn't matter what Tony now said, as each word he muttered seemed to make the guard angrier. And the more angry he got the harder and more frequent his blows to Tony's face became.

One particular blow knocked him cold and he felt himself drifting in and out of consciousness.

As he slowly came around, Tony gradually opened his eyes, half expecting a further blow in process. However, to his relief, the room, which was little more than four filthy walls and a reinforced steel door, was now empty.

Tony realised that he must have passed out and struggled vainly to get free, but soon conceded that his binding was too tight and that he was going nowhere in a hurry. He now concluded that he had to tell him the truth. His tormentor was running out of patience and so Tony felt that he had nothing more to lose by telling him the truth given the next opportunity.

Although he was left on his own, Tony's torture continued. He could hear screams coming from a cell not too far away from his own. Judging by the ferocity of the screams Tony guessed that this poor soul was getting an even worse beating than he had. It made Tony believe if anything, things were likely to deteriorate even further for him, rather than get better.

He was left alone for about an hour, but to Tony it seemed like ten.

Finally his door opened again and he braced himself for further torment. However to his surprise instead of the SS officer there was a Civilian, which Tony instantly recognised as Klaus.

Although fifty years younger, there was no mistaking who it was. In front of Tony stood a short, balding man, wearing a familiar pair of little round glasses and with his unmistakable little round face and red cheeks. Although somewhat slimmer, it was definitely Klaus Zimmerman.

"Thank God it's you...I have..." but again before Tony could finish his sentence the SS officer followed Klaus into the room.

He then manhandled Klaus, to position him directly in front of Tony.

"Do you know this man?" demanded the SS officer to Klaus.

Klaus looked at Tony, long and hard. Dabbing the sweat from his forehead with a neatly folded white handkerchief, he finally shook his head.

"No" he said truthfully.

"Then why does he claim to know you?"

"I have no idea; I have never seen him before in my life, heir commandant."

Tony contemplated giving Klaus the code he had made him memorise, but he remembered what Klaus had told him back in 1995 and did not want to do anything that might jeopardise his life.

"Well?" reiterated the SS officer.

"I do not know, honestly I do not know" pleaded Klaus.

"Well, we will soon find out. Take him away" commanded the officer.

Two more guards appeared and led Klaus forcefully out of the room.

"Right, Englander, for the last time, what is your mission?

"If you do not tell me the truth then we have clear rules for enemy soldiers out of their uniform. Do you understand?"

Quite frankly Tony didn't understand, but he nodded nevertheless.

So he wanted the truth, did he? Tony concluded that he had nothing to lose, and so that was exactly what he gave him.

"My name is Tony Smith, I am a scientist from the year 1995, and I have travelled back in time to save the Führers life...."

Tony looked at him and waited for a reaction, but he just gestured for him to continue.

So he told him his story. In fairness to him he listened intently to every word Tony said.

He told him about Herman Swartz, about how Germany had been victorious and all about life in England in 1995, how he had built the time machine and therefore how he had met a future Klaus Zimmerman.

When he had finished there was a long silence. Then the SS officer started to laugh. "You are about to be shot for being a spy, yet your English sense of humour can concoct such an unbelievable and elaborate story. You English are so funny." he said laughing half-heartedly.

"Do you take us as fools Mr Smith?" sneered the officer.

"No. But you asked for the truth and that is what I told you" reiterated Tony.

"Now you listen - it is my turn to tell YOU a story. If you do not tell me the name of the person who gave you the passwords, you will be taken away at dawn, have a blindfold put over your eyes and be shot for being a spy. Only, this time Tony Smith, my story is not fiction. It is fact!"

"Look I have told you the truth, and if you do not take me to Hitler, the history books will show you as the simple minded moron who cost the Führer his life."

This little outburst got Tony a couple of cracked ribs, as the SS Officer smashed the butt of his revolver into his chest.

"The only thing the history books will show is that you were shot for being a spy. Now for the last time, are you going to tell me where you got this information?" the officer bellowed.

"I already have - it came from Klaus Zimmerman in 1995" repeated Tony.

"You are no longer funny, Mr Smith. If Klaus Zimmerman is involved, which I doubt very much, then thrust me – we will find out. In the meantime, enjoy what is left of your very short life - auf wiedersehen."

With this he abruptly left the room, slamming the door shut behind him.

The sound of screams, including those of Klaus, continued throughout the night. Needless to say Tony did not sleep. It had all gone horribly wrong. Not only had he failed to save the Führer but had also managed to implicate poor old Klaus. Tony considered that Klaus was such a meek and unassuming man and did not deserve to find himself in this predicament. Tony very much regretted mentioning his name and dreaded to think what torment was now being inflicted up on him. To be honest, Tony very much regretted even inventing the bloody time machine in the first place and resigned himself to the fact that in all probability that he was going to end his time in 1945 by getting shot for being a spy!

In his previous conversations with himself, Tony had often argued about what would happen if he was killed whilst in the past. Although they agreed in theory that he should be catapulted back to present, it was one theory he had hoped not to have to verify. However, the way things were turning out, unless there was a major change of attitude from his captors and something of a miracle, it appeared that this theory was about to face the ultimate test.

Chapter 8 - Tony's Liberation.

When the morning arrived, four guards came in to the cell and untied Tony. Throwing some dirty stained trousers and a shirt that was barely rags at his feet, they instructed him to put them on. Tony dressed slowly, since the bruising on his ribs made any movement very painful. Despite his obvious discomfort he was constantly hurried along by one of the guards and no sooner was he dressed in these rather malodorous garments he was ushered out of the building.

"Come on, move" the guard instructed, emphasising his command with the occasional prod in Tony's back from his rifle.

Tony was eventually manhandled into the back of a waiting truck. Thirsty and hungry he sat on one of the wooden bench seats that ran the length of the vehicle, however having a decent breakfast or even something to drink were the least of his worries. He was now more concerned about the likelihood that he was about to meet an untimely death at the hands of his German comrades.

In the back of the jeep were four guards and two more prisoners. From his uniform, one was clearly an English soldier and the other he guessed was a civilian, although there was no clue as to his nationality. Both looked like they had had the misfortune to meet the not so friendly SS Officer. The Englishman in particular looked like he had taken one hell of a beating, with eyes that were barely two slits peeping through swollen and badly bruised eyelids. The front of his shirt was also ripped and covered in blood. Tony knew it was futile but nevertheless asked him in English, if he knew where they were taking them. The Englishman could barely manage a shake of his head. The Civilian, who was unshaven and had black hair swept back behind his ears, just looked at them suspiciously, but didn't say a word.

Tony supposed that his accent hardly made them warm to him. It was ironic that his German captors had noticed his Yorkstein accent, yet when he spoke in English to his fellow prisoners Tony realised that he must have sounded very German. Although his father had taught Tony English and had always preferred him to speak it at home, at school and later in life at work he had always spoken German. In fact German always felt more natural to him, and once his father had died he didn't speak any English at all. As for his accent, it was a bit of a mess. Not true German, but certainly not the Queen's English.

He mulled over asking one of the guards if he knew their destination, but since the last time the civilian had spoke he received a sharp dig in the ribs from the butt of a rifle, Tony deemed silence to be the most prudent approach.

'Why did war make people so angry?' Tony questioned himself.

As they pulled away, Tony pondered what misery the day had in store for him. They drove for about an hour, stopping just briefly to pass through a checkpoint. Tony guessed that they were now no longer in Germany, but since his memory of post war Europe was pretty jaded, he wasn't sure which country used to lie to the east of Germany.

Many of the European countries were renamed after the war, with most of them being absorbed into the Greater German Republic. Therefore Tony wasn't to know that he was now in what was once called Poland.

"At least I get to die in my homeland." said the civilian risking another dig in the ribs.

"Which is where?" Tony asked quietly, not wishing to draw any attention to himself.

"Polska" he said. "God bless my beautiful country." he added loudly and defiantly.

"Silence!" screamed the German guard, giving him the expected dig in his ribs.

Tony wondered why the need to take them on such a long journey and across the border to Poland just to kill them? He supposed that if you are going to blow someone's brains out, then doing it in someone else's country leaves them the inevitable mess to clear up. In truth the Germans still followed the Geneva Convention and since they were about to execute an English officer in cold blood, they wanted it to be as far away from their base as possible. If they were to be in a different country altogether; then even better. If there were any awkward questions later, they could deny any knowledge of the murder and therefore avoid any potential repercussions.

Suddenly they came to an abrupt stop.

"OUT. OUT."

One of the guards gesticulated with his rifle that he wanted them out of the truck. With the barrel of a gun staring down at his face, Tony did exactly what he was told, and jumped from the back of the jeep onto the gravelly road.

They were seemingly in the middle of nowhere and, under better circumstances, Tony might have considered their surroundings to be rather pleasant. Once the dust from the vehicle had settled he could see that they were in a meadow, surrounded by an abundance of trees and fields of resplendent green grass. The smell of fresh air was as sweet as any that he had ever experienced in his life. Not a bad place to die, he morbidly thought to himself.

"Stretch your legs, rest a little" instructed one of the German guards.

'Oh well, it looked like this wasn't going to be the place after all', Tony concluded to himself.

But no sooner had the feeling of relief registered with his bruised and battered body, when he heard the click of a rifle being cocked. Glancing over to the German soldiers he saw that in unison they were raising their rifles in his direction.

'Jesus, this is it.' thought Tony, resigning himself to the fact that he was about to die here after all.

As anticipated, the air suddenly exploded with gunfire. With the loud swish of bullets whizzing through the air, Tony braced himself for the inevitable impact.

Standing there haplessly, waiting for the shot that would either kill him or hopefully send him back to 1995, he heard a voice shout "get down you blithering idiot."

Assuming this instruction was directed at himself, he instinctively fell to the ground. Tony lay there motionless as the gunfire continued to clatter around him.

As the deafening sound of an explosion shook the ground, he again waited for the flash of light or waves of convulsions, which he had become accustomed to when leaping back to the present. But still nothing happened. After what seemed like an eternity, the gun fire and explosions eventually subsided and all fell silent again. The only noise now was the ringing in Tony's ears.

Lying there, on the grass of the meadow, it was obviously apparent that he was still in 1945. 'Why had I not been hit?' he contemplated to himself.

Could the German guards really be that bad a shot or maybe there was some force of nature, which he hadn't previously considered, somehow protecting him, he pondered.

As he slowly looked up to survey his surroundings, Tony was shocked to find that around him were the dead bodies of numerous German guards scattered on the floor. The driver of the truck was also slumped over his steering wheel, either dead or dying. One remaining guard was trying to run off in to one of the surrounding fields, but as a final shot rang out and a spray of blood blasted out the back of his head, he too slumped to the ground with a sickening thud.

The sweet fresh air was now replaced with the smell of smoke and burnt flesh.

Tony did what he could to get up, which wasn't easy since his hands were still tied behind his back. As he struggled, he was suddenly and unceremoniously hauled up to his feet, by the Pole.

"If you want to live you must follow us" he said as he gestured towards Tony's apparent saviours, who were now emerging from the bushes and trees from where they had laid their ambush.

This had not been any force of nature protecting Tony, but a band of Polish resistance fighters, who had thankfully coordinated an attack on the German guards at the very moment they were about to execute their prisoners. As Tony steadied himself on his feet and watched his liberators walk towards him, his thoughts turned to his fellow prisoner.

"What about the Englishman" he asked the Pole.

"I do not believe he will be coming with us" he replied, as he pointed with a gentle nod of his head to where the English prisoner lay.

As Tony turned to see, he realised what the Pole meant, since the Englishman was staring blankly at the sky. Much of his chest was now a bright red gaping hole. He had clearly been shot in the back and was evidently dead.

As the rescuers approached their position, the Pole walked towards them and as they met, was embraced enthusiastically by each and every one of them.

"Kapitan, I thought I'd never see your ugly face again" said one man as he embraced the Pole.

"Nor I yours, Aleksy." replied the Pole.

Breaking their embrace and standing back from him, Aleksy looked his comrade up and down.

"You've let yourself go a bit, haven't you?" he joked, seeing that the Pole was unshaven, dirty and looking somewhat bedraggled.

"Very funny" replied the Pole.

"I think I look rather good, considering where I've just spent the last few days" he laughed. "You left it a bit too close for comfort this time didn't you?" he complained, looking accusingly at the man Tony now knew to be called Aleksy. "I thought for one minute that I was going to be an ex freedom fighter." he added.

"You very nearly were, Jakub. You very nearly were!" exclaimed Aleksy.

"Klaus was arrested by the Gestapo and if it had have been two minutes earlier he'd never have got the details of your route to us."

"What have they got on Klaus? He's normally so careful" asked the Pole, who Tony also now realised was referred to as 'Kapitan', but called Jakub.

"I'm not sure, my friend, all I could find out was that they had captured an English spy, who had given KRealising they were referring to him, Tony blurted out that 'I am not an English Spy'.

Both men turned to look at him.

"Who is this?" asked Aleksy.

"I'm not sure, but he certainly isn't a friend of the Germans, since he was about to meet his maker at their hands" replied Jakub.

"I'm not an English spy" Tony repeated.

"With an accent like that I would be more likely to accuse you of being a German spy," said Jakub accusingly.

"I'm not a German spy either" he replied.

"I am English, but not a spy. It's a long story" he added, not wishing to explain himself further.

"I would be very interested to hear your story and, since you have managed to get one of our best undercover agents arrested, it had better be a good one. But for now we must get the hell out of here" said Jakub.

So Klaus was working for the Polish resistance, Tony concluded to himself. 'I supposed he just happened to forget this fact back in 1995. Then again, he could hardly admit to being a traitor during the war', he contemplated. It occurred to Tony that he could make life very uncomfortable indeed for Klaus, if and when he got back to 1995!

At least Tony knew that Klaus had lived through last night's interrogation, otherwise the effect of the Paradox would have surely sent him back to the future.

The rest of the men continued to take it in turns to embrace Jakub.

$$******$$

Jakub Przewoznik, was relatively tall and slim, just under 6 feet tall, with a darkish complexion and jet black hair, swept back behind his ears.

Although he was looking a little worse for wear, having spent the last three nights in a dirty prison cell, in normal circumstances he was considered quite debonair. Despite the hardship of war, he prided himself on his appearance and had an unwritten and ongoing competition with Aleksy, the man who had greeted him and who was previously a RAF pilot, as to whom looked the most Sauvé and sophisticated.

Jakub was born in the polish town of Lodz, in 1920, and just two days previously had 'celebrated' his twenty fifth birthday by being beaten by his SS captors. During his interrogation he had resided to himself, that he was not going to see his 26th birthday, and if it were not for Aleksy and his colleagues he most certainly wouldn't have.

From the age of 15, Jakub had been a soldier in the Polish army. Prior to the capitulation of the Polish forces to the German invaders he had just been promoted to the rank of captain. Jakub was proud to be Polish and despite the disbanding of the Polish army, he refused to surrender his arms to the advancing German troops. Instead he led a number of his regiment into hiding. Avoiding capture they eventually joined up with the remnants of other units to form part of the Polish Home Army.

Although, ostensibly a resistance organisation, the Home Army still constituted an integral part of the 'new' Polish Armed Forces and remained under the overall command of the Polish Commander-in-Chief who now resided in London. Jakub and his team were one of a number of special combat units known as a 'Kierownictwo Dywersji' (Diversionary Directorate) – Kedyw for short. Their chief task was to prepare and execute a general uprising in Poland coordinated with the Allies. The on-going struggle concentrated on self-defence (freeing prisoners and hostages), and striking at the occupant's apparatus of terror (the physical liquidation of Gestapo and SS functionaries), or as Jakub put it, to reek bloody havoc with the German bastards.

Although, Jakub's unit was voluntary and therefore operated far more democratically than the normal rank and file of the army, he was very much respected by the others and fondly referred to as the 'Kapitan'. He was a good leader and a brave fighter. His bravery had gotten his men out of trouble on many an occasion and in return they gave him their unadulterated loyalty. Without doubt each and every one of them would have laid down their life for him. Sadly, many already had, with his 'Kedyw' now down to just a handful of men.

✶✶✶✶✶✶

Jakub started giving orders to the rest of them.

"Get rid of those bodies, take what weapons you can" he shouted. "Aleksy you and I will take the jeep, the rest of you get back to the truck and take our English, or is it German, spy with you. Make sure he is blind folded, I do not trust him. We'll meet back at the farmhouse. Now let's go."

Tony was impressed with the immediate response by which his orders were met, as he was led quickly by his arm, across the field to an awaiting truck.

"Come quickly," shouted the driver. "We must leave now."

To his surprise the driver's voice was that of a female, but before he could see her face a blindfold was slipped over his eyes

71

and tied tightly around his head. Tony was then bundled rather forcefully into the back of the truck, although compared to the German guards earlier, this was kid's glove stuff. Tony sat on a hard wooden bench next to and, judging by their voices, opposite his liberators, come captors: at the moment he wasn't sure which, although, at least they had the decency to untie his hands. With a swish of air Tony felt a sheet of canvas being strewn over the top of the canopy of the truck. By the sound of the engine, which started on the third attempt, he thought it would be a miracle if they got out of the field, let alone to their destination, wherever that may be? The only consolation was that it couldn't be any worse than where he'd spent the previous night.

The journey was something Tony didn't wish to experience again in a hurry. The noise and the fumes from the engine were bad enough but, God, was it bumpy. The knackered suspension of the truck exaggerated each bump in the road and made him wince with pain as it jolted his bruised ribs. The fact that he was blindfolded also added to the unpleasantness, although at least he was given occasional sips of water.

The engine had a rather rhythmic tune to it as it chugged along and every so often the crack of a loud bang made Tony jump out of his skin. 'A back-firing engine was one of the last things you needed when you had just been involved in a shoot out', Tony thought to himself.

It was during the journey he started to contemplate how he had managed to get in this mess and more importantly how he was going to get out of it. Tony was very mindful that although the people he was now sharing his journey with were his rescuers, in essence they were still his enemy. He had after all come back to save the Führer. Given the chance, Tony guessed that each and every one of them would gladly save him the trouble of committing suicide, by putting a bullet of their own in his head!

Tony was not sure that if he told them the truth, whether they would appreciate knowing that their resistance efforts were destined to be futile and that the Germans were going to win the war and rule Europe for the next 50 years at least. He was also concerned that they were going to want an explanation of how he knew Klaus.

With all this going through his head it occurred to him that he might have been better off being shot and 'killed', back at the meadow. At least in theory he surmised that he would have been catapulted back to the comforts of 1995, although on second thoughts, he still had his reservations about this hypothesis and hoped that he could get back to 1995 without having to put it to the test.

'If I could get back, all I would have to do was work out why I had not ended up face to face with Adolf Hitler, make the adjustments, clear the buffer and go again', he deliberated.

"Clear the buffer! For God's sake, what sort of idiot am I?" he found himself questioning out-loud.

It had suddenly dawned on Tony what he had done wrong. In all the fervour building up to his historic trip to save Hitler, he had neglected to clear the memory buffer from the last time he had gone back in time.

'As a result of saving that sodding car driver from being killed in the collision with the van, and clearing my bloody conscience, I now find myself in all this shit', he reflected as he let out a deep sigh and buried his head in his hands.

'Because of this extra excursion back in time, TESS already had one day's calculus in its memory buffer. And I had bloody well forgotten to clear it!' he muttered to himself in utter frustration. If he had a wall he would have gladly banged his head against it.

"How could I, a bloody genius, make such a fucking elementary mistake?" he found himself swearing out loud.

"Keep your mouth shut, German, we are nearly there," came a voice from opposite Tony.

"Then maybe you will have something to curse about," added another one of his fellow passengers.

So, at least Tony knew when he was, if not where. He was exactly 24 hours early. That meant that Hitler was going to have his meeting this afternoon. Although being blindfolded and probably heading in the opposite direction didn't exactly fill Tony with confidence that he would be getting his message to him.

Even if he was to escape his new captors, he hadn't had much luck so far convincing the Germans of his story.

Tony decided his best bet was to at least try to escape. If he got killed or better still, killed someone else as he was escaping then he hoped that the paradox would have him safe and sound back in 1995.

'Whatever happens I have no intention of spending any longer than I have to, in this God-forsaken mess of a time-line' he concluded as he pondered his escape.

Chapter 9 - The Beautiful Kaska.

The truck came to an abrupt stop.

"Right, everyone in to the house. Ludwik, you hide the truck in the barn. Damek, you bring in the prisoner." It was the female voice again, this time giving out the instructions. Tony was helped out of the back of the truck and led, still blindfolded, into the building. Once inside, his blindfold was removed. Tony squinted as his eyes became accustomed to the light. As his vision returned to normal he could see that he was in the kitchen of a dilapidated farmhouse. What furniture there was appeared very sparse and basic and the décor gave the impression that it hadn't been lived in for many years. There were cobwebs hanging from the rafters of the ceiling and the whole place had a musty damp smell about it. As he stood taking in his surroundings the female driver walked in and closed the door behind her.

"Congratulations everyone," she said smiling broadly. "We have successfully rescued Jakub, without any fatalities and we also seem to have captured a German spy," she added, glancing over to where Tony stood.

"I'm not German nor a spy," he protested.

"In that case you have some explaining to do," she said, as she moved across the room. Pulling up a chair, she sat at the kitchen table, beckoning Tony to do the same. "Please enlighten us," she said, looking towards Tony and encouraging him to speak. As he collected his thoughts to answer her, Tony was suddenly taken aback by just how good looking this woman was. Although her attire could only be described as grubby, underneath the dirt was clearly a very attractive woman. In fact, with her long dark hair and her naturally tanned body she was probably the most beautiful woman he had ever seen in his life, with the exception of Hannah of course.

Back in 1995 they didn't much go for tanned bodies. The Germans felt that the true Aryan race consisted of blonde hair, blue eyes and white skin. In fact, the whiter the skin the closer to the perfect being you were considered to be. Therefore, people tended to avoid the sun, since to tan yourself would only make you appear inferior. Tony always felt that the reason he had progressed so well in his work, other than being a bloody genius, was the fact that with his blonde hair, blue eyes and pallid complexion, he fitted the bill perfectly. Hannah also had bleached blonde hair and bright blue eyes, which made them the perfect 'Aryan' couple. This beautiful stranger was the complete opposite. Her dark completion, jet-black hair and piercing brown eyes, gave her an air of mystic. He had never seen anyone quite so dark in all his life, although instead of making her inferior it made her the most beautiful thing he had ever seen, and yes, he supposed that did include Hannah.

"We are waiting," she snapped. Tony suddenly remembered where he was, as his concentration was broken by her softly accented voice.

"I errrm, errrr," Tony nervously mumbled something incoherently. He didn't know if it was the situation he found himself in, or the fact that he was in awe of this beautiful woman sitting in front of him, but he had suddenly become a blithering idiot, hardly able to string two words together.

"Let's start at the very beginning," she said, trying to help him out. "My name is Kaska, what is yours?"

"Tony Smith," he answered back in a low voice.

"Tony, we know you're not a friend of the Germans, else why would they want to fill you full of lead? But we also know that you implicated one of our best men with your story. God knows what they are now doing to poor Klaus or whether he's even still alive," she added with obvious concern.

"He is still alive," Tony assured her.

"Tony, unless you have a crystal ball, you cannot possibly know whether Klaus is dead or alive, although I hope for your sake that he is. Everyone here is very fond of Klaus, and not to mention the fact that he is a critical part of our unit. If anything has happened to him, you will not be a popular man," she said sternly.

*****

Klaus Zimmerman was indeed a critical part of Kakas' team. As a clerk on the 'Combat Service Support' section within the Bernau government building, his team was responsible for the military logistics of the region. Their responsibility was to ensure the continued supply of food and munitions to the frontline troops. Because of his position Klaus was often privy to the movement of troops and supplies, sometimes even before the troops knew themselves. Klaus was Austrian, with a Serbian father and although he gave the persona of being a staunch member of the Nationalist Party, deep down he despised what the Nazis had done to his country. He was also sympathetic to the plight of the Jewish people, since his best friend from childhood, Herbert Güttermann, was a German Jew. Although Klaus had moved from Austria to Bernau in 1937, he still kept in touch with Herbert and his family. As nationalistic fervour took hold of Germany and Klaus witnessed the harsh treatment of the Jews first hand, he spent months begging his friend to get his family as far away from Austria as possible. Herbert dismissed Klaus's concerns and told him he was overreacting. However, as the brutality against the Jews intensified, the warnings also became more and more desperate. Eventually, Herbert conceded that he could no longer ignore Klaus's warnings, when his friend told him in tears, that the large Synagogue in the centre of Bernau was in flames and that Jews were being beaten to death in the streets. Herbert finally decided he had no choice but to move his family out of Austria.

Despite making the decision to leave, Herbert was still dithering, trying to get his affairs in order before leaving. Only when Klaus frantically called him to warn of a huge deployment of troops on the Austrian border and that it was a case of either leave now or die, did he finally heed his advice and hastened his departure. And so, thanks to Klaus's forewarning, Herbert Güttermann and his family headed west to Switzerland just hours before the German Anschluss of Austria, and in doing so, had undoubtedly saved their lives. Only Herbert's Grandparents refused to leave, stating that they would look after the family home until it was safe for the rest of the family to return. Sadly they both perished under Nazi occupation. Saving Herbert and his family gave Klaus a great deal of satisfaction and he soon realised that the information he handled on a daily basis put him in a position to perhaps save many more lives. Initially he leaked snippets of information to a 'friend of a friend' who he knew shared his dislike of the Third Reich. However, he was never sure whether this information was getting to the right people or indeed, whether he could ultimately trust this person. A short while later his fears were realised when this so called friend turned out to be an informant who then started to blackmail Klaus in to giving him money in return for keeping his mouth shut. Having handed over one envelope of money, Klaus found the situation to be intolerable. So, on their next liaison, Klaus once again gave the blackmailer his money, however this time, as soon as he turned to leave, Klaus grabbed him in a headlock from behind with his left arm, whilst thrusting the blade of a large knife under his ribcage and into his heart with his right. He was surprised at just how easy it had been to kill a man and although he was glad to see the back of the blackmailer, he gleaned no satisfaction from the killing - considering it to be a necessary evil.

The betrayal by this so called 'friend' made Klaus more cautious and resolute not to be caught out again. It also made him more determined to get his information to those that mattered. To create a smokescreen he became a party activist, attending Nazi meetings and other party gatherings, but at the same time keeping up the façade of being a rather meek and unassuming man. At the meetings he ostensibly kept himself to himself, happy to sit in the background, but at the same time contributing just enough to make sure that his attendance was noted. Klaus liked the idea of keeping his friends close, but his enemies even closer and found these meetings to be invaluable. Not only did it divert any suspicion away from himself, but he would often gleam gems of information from fellow party members, that were priceless in the hands of the resistance. In fact it was as a result from one such meeting that inadvertently brought him into contact with Kaska and her team. Throughout most meetings there was always a lot of finger pointing and shouting, and a general air of mistrust. Accusations were often aimed at non party members of being traitors, communists or Jewish sympathisers. These often resulted in arrests or the brutal beatings of the accused. In one such meeting Klaus knew of the man who was being vilified, having known him prior to the outbreak of the war. His name was Ludwik Fleischer, a baker in the town. He was being accused of being a communist and of treachery against the State. By the time the meeting was coming to an end, the party members were building up quite a frenzy of hatred towards Ludwik. From his experience of these meetings, Klaus sensed that a lynch mob would no doubt gather afterwards and seek out Ludwik, intent on immediate retribution. So, despite the obvious risk to his own safety, Klaus slipped out of the meeting room unnoticed as it was drawing to a close and headed straight to Ludwik's house. Once at the house, he told Ludwik that if he wanted to live that he only had minutes to leave Bernau. Ludwik was understandably a little reticent as to whether to believe this sudden bombshell from someone he only knew as an occasional customer in his bakery. But when he heard the commotion of the mob advancing up the street, he realised that Klaus was telling the truth, and therefore they both made a hasty exit out of the back of the building and into the dimly lit cobbled streets of the town.

Once out on to the streets in the cold night air of Bernau, Klaus doubled back round to the front of the house, slipping in with the gathering crowd unnoticed. Once part of the baying mob he slowly pushed his way to the front, ensuring that his participation was noted by the other party members by throwing a brick rather violently through Ludwik's window and enthusiastically joining in with the anti communist rhetoric. In the meantime, Ludwik continued away from his house in the opposite direction, stealing a pushbike to help him get as far away from Bernau as possible. For a few days Ludwik cycled aimlessly around the East German countryside, believing that he did not have a friend in the world and fearing for his life. As his welfare started to suffer in the cold of the German winter, he was fortunate enough to be found by Jakub. Realising his predicament, Jakub took him back to the farmhouse where he was introduced to Kaska and her team. Despite being German, Ludwik hated the Nationalist Party and what they were doing to his country and was therefore only too pleased to pledge his allegiance in the fight against the Nazis. Once he had settled in the group, he recounted how he had been forewarned of his 'arrest.' They quickly realised that they had a friend in a very strategic position with Klaus, and so took no time in contacting him.

The rest, as they say, is history, with Klaus very quickly becoming a critical source of information to the unit and in doing so becoming pivotal to their success. In fact, Klaus's main reservation was that they were becoming too successful. The command were beginning to believe that the regularity and success of the attacks against them were too much of a coincidence and were beginning to home in on his CSS department, as a likely source of the treachery. Klaus got wind of their suspicions and so decided to implicate a co-worker. Planting a note with troop movements and allied codes (albeit out of date) in the pocket of another man, he then informed his superior that he believed his work colleague was actually a spy and that he had overheard him plotting against the regime. The worker was arrested and once searched, accused of treason. Despite the obvious protests of his innocence he was summarily executed.

This had two benefits to Klaus. The man in question was a fanatical Nationalist who was always stirring up hatred against non-party members. Klaus befriended this man, attending most of the party meetings together. In doing so, he ensured that he never had any reason to suspect himself of any wrong doing. In fact this 'friend' even confided in Klaus his suspicions of treachery that he held against others. Maintaining this friendship meant that Klaus's loyalty was beyond reproach, however Klaus was always wary of him and knew that he always had to be so careful in his company. He knew that one word said out of place could easily alert him to

Klaus's true beliefs and put his life at risk, so to rid the workplace of this man was a bonus in itself. The other benefit was that Klaus was now revered within the party membership. Since he was prepared to inform on his friend for the good of the party, his standing within the nationalist movement was now exemplary and therefore he was above suspicion. To look at Klaus, with his rotund face with red chubby cheeks and round glasses, you would be forgiven for thinking that he would not be capable of harming a fly. But behind this façade was the reality of a man with a ruthless determination to do whatever necessary to succeed. If that meant killing a man or double crossing a colleague, so be it.

*****

The conversation continued. Tony apologized for the fact that he had seemingly implicated Klaus and once again tried to reassure her that he was still alive.

"Look, I'm sure if the Germans wanted him dead, he would have been in the back of that truck with the rest of us," he told her.

"We will pray that you are right?" stated Kaska unconvinced.

Tony nodded in agreement, without wishing to elaborate as to why he was so confident that Klaus was still alive. His concentration was broken by the clunk of the large wooden door of the farmhouse closing as they were finally joined by the remaining two members of the team. The men joined Jakub and Aleksy, whose names Tony already knew, at the table. Ludwik, who had now parked the truck, was ordered upstairs to keep lookout by Kaska, who was the sixth and final member of the group.

"So, Tony, please tell us your story and I suggest you make it a good one, since your life may depend on it." Tony sat there silent for a moment, contemplating what to say. He could hardly reveal his mission, but then again he wasn't very good at thinking on his feet. Given that they were waiting with bated breath for him to speak, he concluded that the chances of making up a plausible story in the next ten seconds were nonexistent. Tony knew that as

81

soon as he started lying he would probably dig a bigger and bigger hole for himself, which he could never get out of. So, with little choice, he decided to tell the truth. Although, in all probability, he knew they wouldn't believe him. He was already too late to complete his mission, so to be honest, he had gone past the point of caring. They had two choices. Whether they believed him or not, was pretty irrelevant. Whatever they decided wasn't going to change history, he concluded to himself. 'What was the worst thing that they could do to me, even if they didn't believe a word I said?' he thought to himself. He supposed they could probably shoot him. But what the heck, he decided to burden them with the truth.

"Come on, Tony, we are waiting." said Kaska, growing increasingly impatient with his slowness to respond. "We are intrigued as to why a person who can speak perfect German, with hands that look like they have never done a day's work in their life, was in the back of that truck, being driven to the killing fields of Lubuskie along with our Jakub here?"

"I will tell you," he said hesitantly, "but you must promise to listen with an open mind. I know the chances are that you will not believe me, and if I was in your shoes, I'm not so sure I would either, but what I am going to tell you is the absolute truth."

"Good, if you tell the truth you have nothing to fear from us," Kaska responded reassuringly. So Tony told them his story. Most of it was met by derision and fits of laughter, but each time Kaska told the rest of the men to shut up and encouraged him to continue. He explained how the war was won, about his time machine, about Herman Swartz, how he knew Klaus and therefore why he was confident that he was still alive. He told them how he had ended up on the wrong end of a fat chef's frying pan, and therefore interrogated by the SS. In fact he told them everything they could possibly need to know about himself and what 1995 had in store for them. In fairness, other than the occasional derisory comment, they listened intently to every word he said. As he finished speaking they sat there bewildered without saying a word. Finally Kaska broke the silence.

"Wow, that was some story, Tony," she exclaimed.

"What proof do you have?" questioned Jakub, from across the table.

"It's bullshit," retorted one of the men who Tony had not yet been introduced to.

"Olek, you wouldn't know bullshit if you were standing up to your knees in it," Kaska quipped, much to the annoyance of Olek, but to the amusement of everyone else. "Tony, it is a fantastic story, but you must admit a bit farfetched," she stated not wishing to sound sarcastic. "Jakub has a fair point. Where is your proof?" she asked, reiterating his question.

"Why would I tell you such a story, when it basically makes me your enemy?" queried Tony. Jakub responded by shrugging his shoulders.

"I've yet to work that one out," said Kaska answering for him.

"I do not believe an Englishman would work for the Germans - they have too much pride to do such a treacherous thing!" added Aleksy angrily.

"But I was born fifteen years after the end of the war, I have only ever known the one way of life. I can remember some of the resistance troubles when I was very young, but could never understand why they were fighting. By and large the Germans are good people - if you work hard, you are rewarded well," stated Tony rather foolishly, given that these people despised the Germans and had been fighting against them for the past five years or more. Whether they believed him or not, his response had them up in arms. Each of them were shouting and gesticulating at Tony as though he had just offended their own mother!

"Quiet," Kaska shouted, in an attempt to calm the situation. "Quiet now." she repeated loudly as the commotion continued. Slowly the noise abated and Kaska spoke once again.

"Tony, how can you defend the Germans and call them good people?" she questioned. "They are evil and have committed crimes against humanity."

"The Germans are inhuman pigs, how can you live amongst them at their beck and call?" added Olek, almost spitting venom.

"What about the way they have treated the Jews?" shouted Jakub from across the table. The noise level started to rise again, as they started to bombard Tony with questions, come accusations, all at once.

"Enough." shouted Kaska again. "Let Tony speak." Unsure of what to say next, Tony repeated the question from Jacob.

"What about the way they have treated the Jews?" he asked in all innocence, but before Jacob could respond Kaska interjected.

"Tony, the Germans have massacred thousands, if not millions of men, women and children, for no other reason than for being Jewish. Those not killed are treated so appallingly that death is a blessed relief. I have seen it myself. My best friend and many, many other good people that I knew, were killed by your so called 'friends,'" she said with her voice also reverberating with hatred.

*****

Kaska Galinski was born in Warsaw in 1918. She had grown up in an affluent suburb of the city and had received a rather privileged upbringing. Her father was a banker and her mother was a local councilor. Given the poor economic state of Poland during her childhood, Kaska had not really wanted for much. It was only when she had started her University studies at Krakow, did she realise just how fortunate she had been. During her stay at University, she forged a strong friendship with a young Polish Jewish girl called Olesia Slonimski. Olesia opened Kaska's eyes to the real world and to some of the inequalities of 1930's Europe, which they planned to travel once their studies had finished. However, they never did quite manage to complete their social economics course, with the onset of war cutting it short. Although not Jewish herself, Kaska was horrified at the treatment of Olesia and the hundreds of thousands of Jews in Warsaw. Kaska vowed to her friend that she would do everything in her power to help them.

The Jews were soon ostracised from the rest of Warsaw and a large Ghetto was created. This was effectively a large prison camp with movement in and out of it almost impossible. The thought of not being able to see her friend again was too much for Kaska to bear and she knew that she had to find a way to get in and out of the ghetto. A friend told Kaska that it was known that there were a number of German guards that would turn a blind eye to virtually anything - in return for certain 'favours'. The thought of this repulsed Kaska, however she was convinced that without her help that Olesia would perish. Kaska reluctantly befriended a couple of the guards and as it was suggested, they pretty much let her come and go as she pleased, so long as she kept them 'satisfied'. Kaska loathed each and every one of them and hated every second she spent in their company. However, if it meant the difference of her best friend surviving or not, then Kaska considered that what she endured was a small price to pay to save her life. Kaska knew that Olesia would be furious if she found out and would rather die than subject her best friend to such a nightmare and so Kaska kept her liaisons with the guards a secret - never giving Olesia any indication of her ordeal. Even then, despite this 'friendship' with the German soldiers, it was still extremely dangerous, with Kaska risking her life every time she entered the Ghetto. Random acts of violence and the indiscriminate killing of Jews for 'fun' were a daily occurrence and once inside Kaska knew that she was just as likely to be singled out for retribution as any of the inhabitants of the Ghetto.

During her visits, Kaska always tried to avoid one guard in particular - Rolf Friedrich. Kaska despised this man. He did not like the fact that Kaska was friends with the Jews, but could not resist what Kaska offered him, in return for giving her access. He had a fearful reputation for being particularly cruel to the inhabitants of the ghetto and had the blood of many Jews on his hands. Kaska hated him with a vengeance, and always hoped it would be one of the other guards on duty. She also knew that her relationship with Rolf Friedrich was at best precarious, and that he would not think twice about shooting her in the back if she no longer kept him happy. Kaska considered him to be a sadistic evil bastard, but despite this, she still visited her friend as often as she could. Without a thought for her own safety, Kaska did everything in her power to make sure that Olesia's life was just that little more tolerable.

For the rest of the Jews in the Ghetto, the horror of having to live there was almost unimaginable. Daily beatings and killings by the Nazis happened all too often. Many more died of starvation or disease. Those that did survive were slowly and systematically rounded up and deported out of Warsaw. No one was sure where to, but none of the three hundred thousand or so that had gone so far, had ever returned. Rumours started to circulate that they were being deported to Treblinka, where they were being mass murdered in horrific conditions. The young Jews left in the ghetto, blamed themselves for offering no resistance against the Nazis and therefore a number of them, including Olesia formed an organisation called the Z.O.B. (for the Polish name, Zydowska Organizacja Bojowa, which means Jewish Fighting Organisation.) The Z.O.B issued a proclamation calling for the Jewish people to resist being taken to the railroad cars and declared a policy of resistance against the Nazi occupiers. Although not Jewish, Kaska, became a radical supporter of Z.O.B Her friendship with Olesia had grown over the years of hardship under the occupation and given any opportunity Kaska would do whatever she could to help not just her friend, but the Z.O.B fighters as a whole.

At first, Kaska had purely been taking in food and clothing to Olesia, but as time progressed and the plight and hardship suffered by the Jews became more evident, she knew that she had to do more to help them. So, at great risk to her own life, she began to help organise the smuggling of weapons into the Ghetto, as well as communication from the outside world. In January 1943, with the help of the information and weapons received from Kaska, the Z.O.B were able to orchestrate an attack on their German oppressors. With the effective use of Molotov cocktails, several hundred Warsaw ghetto fighters attacked the German troops as they tried to round up another group of ghetto inhabitants for deportation. The Nazis retreated and although they were soon to retaliate, this small victory of the Warsaw Ghetto uprising inspired other resistance fighters across Poland to stand against the Germans. The ghetto fighters were able to hold out for nearly a month, but half starved and disease weakened, they eventually succumbed to the superior weaponry of the Germans, who laid waste to the entire ghetto. Many were burnt to death, and of those that were captured, many thousands were shot. The rest were rounded up to be deported and faced the horror of the Nazi death camps. There were a small number of survivors, including Kaska, who had helped a group of the Z.O.B fighters, including Damek Konecki, another member of the team, escape from the ghetto using the network of sewers under the Warsaw streets and out to the Lomianki forest.

One person who didn't survive was Olesia. To the heartbreak of Kaska, she was shot in the back when helping patients escape from the ghetto hospital. She had heard that the Nazis were shooting patients as they lay in their beds and rushed, with a number of friends, to try and help them. Despite the fact the Nazis had started to torch the building, Olesia bravely aided a number of patients to safety. Her friends told that her that it was now too dangerous, but Olesia insisted on going back in one more time and although she managed to help two more patients to safety, saving their lives, she was shot in the back as she left the building. Kaska, had rushed to help her friend, but found her dying on the steps of the hospital. Although hardened by the many grotesque sights that she had seen in the Ghetto, Kaska still sobbed as she cradled her dying friend in her arms. Olesia had always said that she knew she was going to die. Z.O.B was not a question of saving Jewish lives; she knew this was hopeless. It was a question of what kind of death the Polish Jews would select for themselves.

Although of little consolation, as Kaska returned to help Damek and the others escape to the Lomianki forest, she came across Rolf Friedrich. He was clearly reveling in the death and destruction that he was now inflicting on the inhabitants of the ghetto. As he approached her with a satisfied grin on his face, Kaska pulled a small pistol from beneath her tunic. Before he had time to react, she shot him from point blank range, plumb between his eyes. As Rolf slumped, bereft of life to the ground, it was now Kaska, although shaking like a leaf, that afforded herself a satisfied grin.

"That was for Olesia, you dirty German bastard," she shouted at the dead soldier. Rolf Friedrich, was the first Nazi that Kaska had killed - but he would not be the last. After escaping from the Ghetto, Kaska never returned to Warsaw. Instead she vowed to continue to avenge her friends' death, going to wherever she was needed to inflict as much damage as she could against the Germany military.

*****

"I didn't say they were my friends," continued Tony. "I just said that the one's I know in the future are good people."

"Good people? How can you call these monsters 'good people'? Take it from me, the only good German is a dead German!" snapped Jakub. "I can't begin to tell you what it was like for Damek here, living in Warsaw," he said, introducing Tony to the final member of the team.

"Damek is Jewish and lost his entire family in the Warsaw ghetto," stated Kaska in a sympathetic tone.

"Yes, and if it wasn't for Kaska, I too would have perished," he said, acknowledging Kaska with a nod of appreciation.

*****

Damek had been born in Warsaw and had helped in his Fathers' hosiery business up until the war. Once the occupation started, the premises of his father's firm were burnt to the ground and his family, like most in the ghetto, suffered terrible hardship. The years of prolonged adversity and malnutrition during his time in the ghetto had, even now, left its mark on Damek. He looked far older than his age of 35. His face was gaunt and his overall demeanour was cadaverous. After his parents were sent to their death in the camp at Treblinka, he had blamed himself for not standing up for them and had felt worthless, almost inhuman. After that, the only things that kept him going were his acute hatred of the Germans, who he despised with a vengeance, and the benevolence shown to him by Kaska. During their time in the ghetto, his parents had been betrayed by an informant, whom Damek, thought was a friend. Since then he had treated everyone with suspicion. He had also become very withdrawn and shunned company. Seeing this, Kaska had befriended him and had made it her mission to restore his faith in humanity and to help him regain his self esteem. She had just about succeeded, but Damek still remained apprehensive of strangers.

*****

"Look, I'm sorry about your family, but this is war time and people die in wars," said Tony. "I heard stories that the Germans were quiet ruthless after the war, but that was because some of the English refused to accept their occupation and pushed them to the limit. However, in my lifetime there have never been any problems with them. Admittedly, they can be rather strict with law and order, but they would not kill innocent people without provocation."

"Provocation? Provofuckingcation! Screw you, Tony Smith. You're full of shit," shouted Damek as he rose aggressively to his feet. "You know absolutely nothing about these Germans and what sort of atrocities they are capable of! My parents were exterminated. They did not provoke this. They had done nothing wrong. Their only crime was being Jewish and being in the wrong place at the wrong time. I have a good mind to rip your fucking head off, you German loving piece of shit," he snarled as he lunged towards Tony. Jakub held him back by his arm. Kaska, sensing that the situation could easily get out of hand, gave the now very agitated Damek some reassurance and tried to calm him down.

"Damek, I'm sure Tony did not mean to accuse your parents of provoking their own death. His words were not well chosen. Were they Tony?" she asked, raising her eyebrows to demand an answer.

"Erm, no, I am sorry, I did not mean to offend you or your family," Tony apologised nervously, "you must understand I have never seen the Germans in the same light as you have."

"Very well, but choose your words more carefully in future, or I will not hesitate to slit your throat," said Damek, with an unnerving amount of menace.

"Ok," Tony replied meekly, and offering a nervous smile as he again apologised. Jakub, sensing the opportunity to draw the conversation away from Damek then asked the next question.

"So, say you are telling the truth, Tony, how then are the Jews treated in 1995?"

"I wouldn't know, since there are no Jews in England," he replied.

"No Jews in England! How can that be so? There are hundreds of thousands of Jews in England, many fled from Europe at the start of the war. What of them?" questioned Jakub.

"I have no idea," responded Tony. "As far as I know the Jews, like all foreign nationals, were rounded up and repatriated back to their homelands shortly after the war," he told them.

"Where is their homeland Tony, where? Where were the sent?" shouted Damek, once again getting involved and even more agitated.

"I don't know; I've never actually met a Jew. It all happened way before I was born. I assume it has to be somewhere in the Middle East, but admittedly I haven't a clue where. We are not encouraged to get involved in foreign affairs in 1995 and very few of us are allowed to travel abroad. In fact this is the first time I've ever travelled outside of England. I am sure however, that wherever they were sent, they would have been looked after. The Germans are not inhuman - it is only the war that makes you hate them." Despite his efforts to choose his words more carefully, Tony had once again managed to inflame Damek.

"Bullshit! The reason you have never met a Jew in 1995 is because they have all been exterminated - wiped off the face of the Earth as though they had never even existed. Can you really be so dumb to believe that they were sent back to their homeland to live happily ever after?"

"I'm sure they would not have been exterminated. You are just speculating on future events -events that did not happen," responded Tony. "Why would the Germans want to continue killing people after the war had finished? As I have said, after the war the Germans are just people like you or me, they are not these demons you describe."

"Fuck you Tony Smith. You are either very stupid or very naïve. The Nazis have utter detestation towards the Jews and will not be satisfied until the very last one of us is dead. Mark my words, the killing will not stop just because the war has ended. You know fuck all about what it is to be a Jew under German occupation, so shut that dumb mouth of yours before I shut it for you," exclaimed Damek spitting across the table towards Tony.

"Stop this now!" demanded Kaska. Whether they believed Tony's story or not, the fact was that they were arguing with him passionately about events that were yet to happen or as far as Damek was concerned were never going to happen and were nothing more than bullshit. Either way, Tony had managed to provoke a vigorous and heated argument amongst the men.

"Look, you are arguing over something that hasn't yet happened," interjected Kaska trying to defuse the situation. "Besides, as long as I have blood in my veins it never will!" she added trying to return their thoughts to their fight against the Nazis. "We need to stop all this arguing and get some sleep," she urged. "We must rest well tonight and be ready to step up our efforts against the German pigs starting tomorrow morning. We have a war to win," she reminded the men.

"Damn right we do," snarled Damek, "to rid the world of arseholes like him," he added.

"Damek, enough now," scorned Kaska "Save it, for the real enemy," she told him abruptly. But before Damek could protest that Tony Smith was the real enemy, Kaska quickly added, "anyway no more arguing, we need to rest. Aleksy, please tie our prisoner up against the boiler pipe in the other room - we will decide what to do with him in the morning." Her command was quickly carried out, as Tony soon found himself sitting on a chair in the corner of a dark and dusty room, with his hands bound behind his back and around a large pipe that came out of the floor boards and disappeared up through the ceiling. It was apparent that a number of them wanted to continue his 'interrogation,' but Kaska insisted that they get an early night. Although Jakub was their leader by rank, Kaska, was clearly the one they listened to, and such was her command over them that one by one they reluctantly settled down for the night. Kaska had a quiet word with Damak and she was satisfied that he had calmed down she bid him goodnight and came in to the room where Tony was tied up.

"Do you mind if I join you?" she asked him, rather politely given the circumstances.

"Not at all," he answered, giving her an encouraging smile, not that he really had much choice. She smiled back, as she positioned herself on the floor besides him. Her softly accented voice spoke in almost a whisper.

"Tony, I didn't want the questioning to continue as I could see it was starting to upset Damek. He's had a very hard life you know, and it has taken such a long time for me to bring him out of his shell. I thought it better we stop before he got too upset. Too many bad memories for him you see."

"I understand," said Tony sympathetically.

"Besides, they have had a long day and need their rest," she added, almost like a mother justifying putting her children to bed early. She paused for a moment before continuing. "I doubt whether he would slit your throat, but it is not wise to push him too far since he does have a very short temper."

"Yes, I'm sorry, it was careless of me. But it is difficult for me to comprehend these Germans you talk of, since they are unrecognisable from the people I know in 1995."

"Listen Tony, I'm not saying I believed a single word of what you said in the kitchen, but I must admit some of it was fascinating. Please tell me some more about this supposed life that you have in this future of ours," she requested, as she positioned herself to get as comfortable as the floor would allow. So Tony told her of 1995 and covered just about every aspect of life back there. He told her all about Karl and how proud he was of him and that if he had not have chickened out then it could have been Karl here in 1945, instead of him. He told her about Hannah, and how he had neglected her for so long to concentrate on his work, and how she eventually left him for another man. Kaska laughed and said that she would have done the same. Tony also told her of the arguments he had with the numerous 'other' Tony's, during his visits to the past and how he had nearly come to blows with himself. This she found very amusing and chuckled to herself as he told her of some of the other predicaments he had managed to get himself into whilst medaling with time travel.

The conversation turned to Kaska, as Tony asked her how she came to become the leader of such a group of men. Kaska, told him of her life before the war and of her plans to travel Europe. She told him how the fighting had put an end to her hopes and ambitions and how the Nazis had turned her beautiful Warsaw into a hellish ghetto. Tears filled her eyes as she recalled the end of the ghetto and the death of her best friend, Olesia. She gave a satisfied smiled however, as she told Tony how she had shot dead Rolf Friedrich and warned him that if she did have to shoot him in the morning that she was very unlikely to miss.

They both laughed and continued to share stories into the night. Tony still found it difficult to comprehend that the German soldiers could be as cruel and evil as she described them to be, whilst Kaska didn't necessarily believe a single word Tony was saying. But as the night wore on they clearly warmed to each other, laughing and joking and enjoying each other's company. Kasha found Tony to be intriguing and far more intellectual than anyone she had ever met, whilst Tony simply found Kaska to be mesmerizing. She was beautiful, intelligent but above all courageous.

Tony sensed that Kaska was now starting to warm towards him, so he decided to tell her that the one thing they didn't have in 1995 was anyone quite as beautiful as she was. Kaska laughed hesitantly.

"What about your wife, Tony, was she not beautiful?"

"Of course - with blonde hair and bright blue eyes, but not like you" he told her.

"My wife is beautiful, but in 1995 we do not have anyone as brave, courageous, or dare I say it, as wonderful as you" he exclaimed.

"Thank you, Tony, but let's leave it there shall we, before you get carried away?" Kaska said, rising to her feet.

"I'm sorry, I didn't mean to scare you off," said Tony, disappointed at the way things were turning out.

"Look, Tony, no offence, but I'm sure you'd say that to any women who held your life in her hands."

"Not at all," he tried to argue. "You are astonishing," he still insisted.

"Listen, in the morning I will have the rest of them insisting that we shoot you through the head and as you know, if that is the case the chances of me missing are pretty slim" she said, once again smiling. "I admit that I find you intriguing and I have enjoyed tonight. In different circumstances I could even be attracted to you, but I still find your preposterous story hard to believe. Even if you are from the future, and I admit you give a fascinating account of how life could be, however I cannot believe that we are about to lose the war to a,…what did you call it, an atomic bomb? No one could invent such a thing! Besides, I have good intelligence that the Germans are on their last legs. It is only a matter of time before the Allies liberate us from this evil. When you first started to tell this story, you said I needed an open mind. Well, I have believed in the impossible all my life - how else do you think we have managed to inflict such damage on the Germans with just a handful of men? I have lived by believing the impossible and succeeding against all the odds. But what you are asking me to believe is beyond my imagination. In the morning Tony, you need to tell me the truth or something more believable otherwise I may have no option but to shoot you through the head."

With that she bent forward and kissed Tony gently on the lips and without saying a word went off to the other room.

'Shit…I had just fallen in love with a woman who is intending to blow my brains out!' lamented Tony to himself.

Unless he could now think of a more believable story during his sleep, which let's be honest, there wasn't the remotest possibility. Or, for some reason she has a miraculous change of heart during the night, then Tony concluded that the prospects looked pretty bleak for him come the morning. Strangely though, he felt somewhat at ease. She had asked him to tell the truth and he had. As far as he was concerned there was little more he could do and resided himself to the thought, 'what will be, will be.' He didn't even contemplate trying to come up with an alternative story, instead he was just happy to grab some much needed sleep and fill his mind with thoughts of this fascinating lady.

Chapter 10 – Take every day as it comes.

When Tony eventually awoke, it was to the sound of arguing coming from the kitchen. From what he could make out they were debating what should become of him. After a while Kaska came into the room.

"Ah, I see you're awake. Sleep well?" she asked smiling.

"As well as anyone could, given the circumstances," Tony responded.

"I'm sure you've slept in worse places," she laughed. To be truthful, he almost certainly hadn't, but he still acknowledged her statement with a nod and a wry smile. If she was about to kill him then she was certainly a cool customer, Tony thought to himself.

"Tony, some of the men think it might be easier just to kill you right now. And I agree that you are a complication that we could do without - but I've managed to convince them that we should drive you away from here, blind folded of course, and let you go. I'm sure you will be able to fend for yourself." Tony was relieved, to say the least, that he wasn't going to get his brains blown out. At the same time he was surprised and somewhat confused by her change of heart.

"Not that I'm complaining, but why the change of heart? I thought you said I would die this morning if I didn't tell the truth," he added, rather pushing his luck.

"So, are you going to tell me the truth?" Kaska asked.

"I already have," he replied.

"I somehow knew you would say that," she said, shaking her head slowly, but with a smile on her face at the same time. "I don't believe your story for one minute, but I'm convinced that you do. My guess is that the Gestapo have somehow brainwashed you in to believing what you are saying," she surmised. "Why they would want to do so, I do not know, but whatever the truth is, I do not think you pose a threat to us," she added. "Even if your story were true, then it is too late to warn Hitler. Besides, the Germans didn't seem to believe you the first time, why would they now? And if, as you say, the Germans do win the war, then maybe you will put in a good word for us when we are your prisoners," she laughed. "Besides, we can't afford to waste good bullets!" she laughed again, as she untied him. "Come on in to the kitchen. Ludwik has cooked some eggs for breakfast and I bet you're starving," she said, leading Tony in to the kitchen. Tony was indeed starving and soon found himself tucking in to the tastiest scrambled eggs he had ever eaten in his life.

"These are delicious," he said complimenting Ludwik.

******

Ludwik Fleischer was the old man of the team and was actually German. Born in 1896, he was now nearly fifty years old. He had short greying hair, which was also starting to go rather thin on top, and he sported a neatly trimmed, although rather dirty grey beard. He was the patriarch of the group, looking after their welfare and doing the majority of the cooking. However, behind this rather fatherly figure, also lay a strong and brave fighter, who was a complete madman when it came to dynamite. Ludwik had seen active service, fighting for the Imperial German army in the First World War - specialising in explosives. He now made it his mission in life to blow up just about anything that moved. Despite his age, Ludwik was still pretty fit, and his skill and knowledge of explosives made him invaluable to the team. He did have a tendency to overestimate the amount of explosives needed, often blasting his intended target, including German soldiers, into far more pieces than necessary. However, there was no denying that much of the success of the unit had been down to Ludwik's technical expertise with a stick (or two) of dynamite.

After the First World War he had settled down in Bernau, where he had been a baker. He despised the inequality of life in Germany between the two wars. He hated the decadence of the privileged few and so became a member of the Communist Party. As the Nationalist Party began to take hold of Germany, and the Communist Party became vilified, many of his political comrades were rounded up and arrested. If not beaten or killed outright, the rest were shipped off to become some of the earliest occupants of the newly built concentration camps. Seeing what was happening, Ludwik tried to keep his political views to himself once the war had started. However, it was relatively well known within the community that he was not a great fan of the Nazis. He therefore suspected that it would only be a matter of time before they eventually got to him. As luck would have it, when the 'Brownshirts' of the Nazi party marched on his house he had already been forewarned by Klaus Zimmerman of the imminent attack. With seconds to spare he had escaped out of the back of his home, just as the fascists were literally kicking in his front door. Fleeing east on a stolen pushbike to the edge of the Polish border he was eventually found and befriended by Kaska and her team.

Ludwik considered that it was a sad indictment of the current state of the world, which meant he had to fight and kill his fellow countrymen purely because of his political beliefs. However, he knew that as long as the Nazis were in power that it was a case of either kill or be killed. He was therefore as committed to the fight as each and every other member of Kaska's team, and knew that the sooner Germany could be rid of the Third Reich the better it would be for everybody. The years working as a baker in Bernau also meant that he wasn't a bad cook. Not that the men would let on, preferring to constantly tease him about his culinary skills. Although they often accused him of trying to poison them with his cooking, in reality they really appreciated what he managed to produce with such limited supplies and, to a man, they were all exceptionally fond of Ludwik.

During breakfast, Tony's inquisition continued from the night before, and he was once again bombarded with questions. Since none of them apparently believed Tony's story, it was strange how interested they were in his account of what their future held. Maybe they were just trying to catch him out, but they still listened to every word, with an intense fascination.

"So you are telling me that a man has actually walked on the moon?" Jakub asked skeptically.

"Yep, lots of them. But the first was Sepp Muller in 1968," confirmed Tony.

"And so the English are all driving around in 'Beetles' and 'BMW's?" laughed Olek.

"Correct, the Germans make very good cars - in fact they make good everything."

"Especially time machines!" Jakub added with just a hint of sarcasm in his voice. They all laughed - all, except Damek. Tony still got the distinct feeling that Damek wouldn't consider it a waste of a bullet to blow his brains out. From his glare it was obvious that he remained very suspicious of Tony and had not forgiven him for insulting the memory of his family. Tony decided to avoid eye contact with Damek as much as possible, so as not to antagonise him. Although the atmosphere was far more amiable than the previous night, Tony knew that his position was still precarious. After breakfast Tony was offered a jug of cold water to give himself a much needed wash. He was also given a change of clothes, which were a great improvement on the rags he had previously been wearing. Having washed and dressed, Tony felt far more optimistic about the day ahead, although in reality he still had no idea how he was going to get out of this mess.

"Right Tony, it's time to go," instructed Kaska, as she entered the room. "Sorry, but you will also need to put this on," she added, as she handed him a blindfold.

"Thank you," replied Tony, taking the blindfold from her.

"For what?" she asked.
"Believing in me and saving my life."

"Don't kid yourself. I've already told you bullets are hard to come by and Damek makes such a mess when he tries to slit throats," she said, smiling as she beckoned him to hurry with his blindfold. Once the blindfold was securely on, Kaska escorted Tony outside and to a waiting jeep. From the conversation taking place, it appeared that it was going to be driven by Olek.

******

Olek Glowacki was a Polish Roma gypsy. He had a general dishevelled appearance, with greasy black shoulder length hair. He was usually unshaven, with a dark complexion, made even darker by the thick black hair that appeared to cover most of his body. He had a very muscular physique and was as strong as an ox. Olek had joined the unit after they had inadvertently 'rescued' him, by killing his captors' convoy, during one of their missions. Since the day his family had been lined up by a ditch and massacred by the Germans, he had waged a one man war of vengeance against the perpetrators. Operating on his own, his favourite trick was to sneak up behind lone soldiers and slit their throats with a single swish of his knife. He was so successful, that he was a wanted man. Eventually he took on more than he could chew and was captured trying to take out an entire tank crew. Because of the fact that he was a 'Roma' the Nazis were particularly brutal towards him during his interrogation. The Germans felt that the gypsies were asocial or outside of normal society. They believed that they threatened the biological purity and strength of the superior Aryan race, and treated them with distain.

Olek was barely alive and was on his way to be 'disposed of,' when Jakub and his team destroyed the convoy taking him to his execution. His treatment by the SS made him more hateful of the Germans, and when offered the chance to join the team, he recognised that he could inflict more harm on them as part of an organised unit, rather than acting solitarily. He jumped at the chance, although principally, he always considered himself to be a loner. When he first joined the unit he very much kept himself to himself, and didn't socialise much with the rest of the team. He also had a frightful temper, which made the others wary of him. However, once they understood his dry sense of humour and just how far they could push Olek, they started to warm towards him. They also appreciated his courage and bravery when it came to engaging the enemy. He was a ruthless and skilled fighter, especially with that knife of his.

******

As Tony stood by the jeep Olek eyed him up and down.

"See, I told you the clothes would fit him," he boasted to Aleksy, who had now joined them in the courtyard. Aleksy just smiled and nodded to Olek.

"From a dead German you know," Olek exclaimed. As he did, he also ran his finger across his throat to indicate that the German in question had undoubtedly had the misfortune to be on the end of his knife. Although dramatic, this gesture was rather pointless, given the fact that Tony was blindfolded.

"Not that you probably mind wearing the clothes of a dead German, since you love them so much," he added.

"Olek, leave it out," intervened Kaska, "Let's try and make this journey as pleasant as possible, without any snide remarks," she instructed. Olek reluctantly nodded in agreement. "Jakub, you stay here and look after the rest, Aleksy you're in the jeep with me and Olek. Right, let's get moving," instructed Kaska, as she guided Tony into the back of the jeep. Olek was joined by Aleksy in the front, whilst the beautiful Kaska sat alongside Tony in the back. With an almighty wheel spin and cloud of dust, they were soon navigating down the very bumpy track leading from the farmhouse and then away in to the open countryside. With the sun shining and the wind blowing in Tony's face, he was actually enjoying the experience, except when there was an occasional bump in the road, which reminded Tony that his ribs were still rather tender. They had been travelling for about twenty minutes when Tony felt a soft hand brush against the side of his face. With a single tug the blindfold was pulled away.

"I don't think you will need this anymore," said Kaska, smiling broadly at Tony as she put the blindfold away in a pocket of her jacket.

101

"Thank you," said Tony, returning the smile as his eyes became accustomed to the bright sunlight.

Although Tony had been enjoying the journey previously with the freshness of the wind in his face, this was so much better as he could now also take in the beautiful view, although it wasn't just the resplendent Polish countryside that he found himself admiring. Kaska looked stunning. He sat mesmerised by her beauty and could not help but eye her up and down. Her knee length skirt showed just enough of her long brown legs to make him long to see more, whilst her white blouse was tantalisingly undone to the third button, revealing just enough flesh to get the pulse racing of any red-blooded male. He was just starting to let his mind run wild, when his thoughts were halted.

"Tony, do you mind?" said Kaska abruptly.

"I'm sorry," stuttered Tony, as he felt himself starting to blush intensely. Tony was embarrassed that his roving eye had been noticed by Kaska. The fact that his usually pallid complexion was now going bright crimson made Kaska start to chuckle to herself.

"May I remind you that you are still my prisoner, and prisoners should not be looking at their guards in such a manner," she said trying to control her laughter. Tony smiled, appreciating the fact that she was joking. Well, he hoped she was.

"You know that last night, I meant every word I said," he whispered, trying to keep this moment private and out of earshot of Aleksy and Olek.

"What, about man walking on the moon and driving around in 'Beetles'?" she said teasingly.

"No, you know what I mean. About you being the most beautiful…" but before he could finish the sentence Olek screeched the jeep to an abrupt stop engulfing them in another cloud of dust.

"For God's sake Olek, do you always have to stop so dramatically?" complained Kaska. Olek just smirked, as he jumped from the jeep. Kaska also climbed down from the jeep, and once out, turned and beckoned for Tony to do the same. As he clamoured down Tony grabbed Kaska's hand and pulled her slightly towards him.

"I was referring to the bit about telling you that you were the most beautiful woman I had ever seen in my life," he continued to whisper.

"Tony, I knew what you were going to say, but it is irrelevant. I'm afraid this is where we say goodbye and I doubt whether we will ever meet again. So whatever your thoughts and feelings are, you might as well keep them to yourself since they will come to no good," she added, almost apologetically.

"I know, but I didn't want you to think that I only said what I did because you held my life in your hands. It was the truth," he promised her.

"Thank you Tony. I appreciate the sentiment, but I'm afraid romance and war do not mix. Besides, you are still my prisoner and you know my feelings on that," she laughed. "Anyway, my only concern right now is that we are doing the right thing in letting you go. I just pray that it doesn't come back to haunt me," she said, letting go of his hand. Tony assured her that she wouldn't regret it and that she was doing the right thing.

"So this is goodbye then?" Tony said, not wanting this moment to end.

"I'm afraid so, Tony. Good luck" she added, as she motioned forward to embrace him.

"Does this mean I'm no longer your prisoner?" Tony questioned.

"I suppose not, you are free to do as you please," she affirmed.

"Good," Tony replied, as he grabbed her waist with both hands and pulled her towards him. Before she had time to complain, he had given her the most passionate kiss he'd ever given anyone in his life. For a brief moment all his cares and worries disappeared, as he was lost in the tenderness of her lips.

Unfortunately, Tony's moment of tranquillity was cut short as Kaska gently pushed him away.

"Thank you Tony, but in war-time it doesn't pay to become too close to anyone. All too often, it only ends in tears," she said. Disappointed that their embrace had ended prematurely Tony gave her a reluctant smile as she turned to leave. But then to his surprise she turned back to face him and without warning grasped him passionately around the neck. Pulling his head towards her own, she gave him a truly intense and but beautifully delicate kiss. Tony naturally responded, and once again, he found himself lost in the arms of this stunning woman as they kissed passionately.

"I thought you said it would only end in tears?" Tony said teasingly, once they had finished their embrace.

"In war-time you also learn to take every day as it comes, since you don't know if you will live to see the next sunset. Life is too short to play games. I like you very much, Tony, and if we both live through this, maybe we will meet again one day after all," she said hopefully. Tony told her that there was nothing in the world that he would look forward to more. He promised her that the war would be over soon and that as soon as it was that he would find her wherever she was. She smiled saying that she looked forward to that time.

"For now I have the rest of the men to care for and as I have said, you are a complication I do not need at this moment in time," she told him as she climbed back in to the jeep.

"Goodbye and take care," she said, as she settled into her seat. She nodded at Olek and he instinctively started the engine. Aleksy also wished Tony luck as he too climbed up into the jeep.

"But, where am I?" Tony asked, wary of the fact that he was about to be abandoned in the middle of nowhere.

"There is a village about a mile over there," Aleksy informed him, pointing to the far side of a field and beyond some trees.

"I'm not sure how pleased they will be to see a German, so tell them that you are an English pilot and they should help you. So long, my friend," he added, as he acknowledged with a nod to Olek that he too was ready to depart. With that Olek put his foot on the accelerator and with a skid of wheels they disappeared in the customary cloud of dust. So Tony was now alone in the middle of nowhere and without a clue what to do next. Although, instead of planning his next move, all he could think about was Kaska.

He contemplated that one of the wonders of time travel is that you can do it over and over again. So as long as he could get back to 1995 he could easily correct his error and then, this time come back in front of Hitler as planned. Although he had to admit that the stories by Kaska and the rest, about the plight of the Jews were somewhat playing on his mind and made him feel uneasy. Although, even if it were true, it happened before he was born and therefore he concluded that there was not much he could do about it in any case. The more he thought about it, the less he believed that the Germans would mass murder a whole race of people.

'At the end of the day, war is full of propaganda. No doubt someone spread this sort of story to make the resistance hate the Germans even more. And from a few being killed the story gets exaggerated each time it is told. That's what it is,' he convinced himself. 'Anyway, I have enough problems of my own to worry about at the moment,' he thought to himself. Getting the hell out of this mess and back to 1995 was his priority and only concern right now.

Tony was in the middle of nowhere, somewhere in the Polish countryside with nothing but lush green fields, trees and rabbits as far as the eyes could see. Although desperate to get home, when he surveyed his surroundings he conceded that his current location was actually rather pleasant. He took in a deep breath of the sweet fresh air to savour the moment.

"OK, so what now?" he said out loud to himself. Tony knew the only way of getting back was to cause a paradox, but how? Tony contemplated that maybe if he killed one of the rabbits or something small it would count as a paradox. He knew that he was probably clutching at straws but still spent the next two hours running round the field chasing rabbits.

Tony was convinced that they were teasing him. The rabbits would seemingly ignore him as he edged ever closer to their position. Then as he crouched in a goal-keeper's position with knees bent and arms stretched slightly out in front of him, ready to pounce, they would stop their grazing and stare him straight in the eyes. Neither Tony nor the rabbit would move an inch, waiting for the other to make the first move in a battle of wills. Invariably it was Tony that cracked first, but each time as soon as he made his leap towards the rabbit, it would jump left or right, or even straight towards him, darting underneath his diving body to evade capture. Each time the outcome was the same, with Tony laying prone on the ground with the rabbit a few feet away, once again ignoring him. Occasionally Tony would lose his temper and just start chasing them in all directions scattering rabbits throughout the meadow. Needless to say, this tactic also proved fruitless as the rabbits basically had him running around in circles.

By the time he gave up, Tony was convinced that there were now twice as many rabbits as when he first started. He considered that the whole rabbit population of Poland had come out to witness him making a complete arse of himself. Eventually, tired and hungry he decided to concede defeat to the rabbits. Although disappointed that they had won on this occasion, Tony had actually enjoyed the last couple of hours. He smiled, as he warned the rabbits that they may have won the battle, but not the war. It was starting to get dark and colder, so he decided to head towards the village to see if there was a barn or somewhere suitable to sleep. Tony didn't much fancy trying to get friendly with the locals just yet and so waved goodbye to the rabbits and set off to find somewhere to settle for the night. After walking what seemed like miles Tony finally found somewhere vaguely suitable. It wasn't quite a barn; in fact it looked more like a pigsty, but at least it had four walls, a corrugated tin roof and a couple of holes that resembled windows. With some hay from around the field he managed to make it pretty cosy. At least in comparison with how he had spent the previous two nights, he considered this to be five star accommodation and so made himself comfortable for the night.

Chapter 11 - I would rather die a thousand painful deaths.

"Kaska, where have you been?" Jakub questioned, relieved at their return.

"We ran into a convoy of Germans heading West - there were too many for us to tackle, so we had to lay low until they had passed," answered Kaska.

"We were starting to get worried," added Ludwik.

"Worried? You should know better than that. It would take more than a convoy of Germans to stop us returning. Your cooking might do the trick, but never a few hundred Germans," she laughed.

"Anyway, you had better come in. I've got something to show you that will blow your mind!" said Jakub, hurrying the returning trio in to the house. As Kaska entered the kitchen the others sat staring blankly, as though in a state of shock.

"You lot look like you've seen a ghost," Kaska laughed.

"We have received a communication from headquarters. You need to read it," said Jakub. Kaska took the piece of paper from Jakub and read it out loud.

German Spy last seen at Gdansk. STOP

Likely to be heading to Berlin across Northern Poland. STOP.

Must be stopped at any cost. STOP.

Will be carrying technical drawings. STOP.

Must be destroyed. STOP.

Will be carrying ID papers under name of Harold Swift. STOP.

Top Priority. STOP.

The outcome of the war may depend on your success. STOP.

End message. STOP. # # # #

"Right, we have our orders let's ship out," responded Kaska with a level of urgency.

"But Kaska, the message!" exclaimed Jakub.

"What about it?"

"It's what Tony Smith told us. This is the Spy from America!"

"No, he said his name was Herman Swartzzer or something like that," added Jakub.

"No...it was Herman Swartz," responded Kaska. "And if he had infiltrated the American OSS, he would hardly use his real name would he? But Harold Swift, that's another matter! We must find Tony Smith and quickly."

"Nonsense, utter nonsense," snarled Olek from the other side of the room, having just come in from parking the jeep.

"Tony Smith, or whatever his real name is, was full of bullshit."

"All this crap is nothing more than a coincidence," he argued.

"I'm sorry, but it's too much of a coincidence for me to ignore. We're moving out."

"Pathetic...this is absolutely pathetic. The only reason you want to find Tony Smith is because you fancy him, with his girly blonde hair."

"Olek, I didn't have you down as the jealous type."

"I'm not jealous, but we could hear you laughing with him last night and could hear you in the back of the jeep."

"I also saw how you kissed him back there by the side of the road. I'm not blind you know. It is obvious, that you have fallen for him," said Olek. But then Kaska turned on him angrily.

"Look here Olek, if you don't watch your mouth you will be staying here permanently. Whatever my feelings for Tony Smith , they are irrelevant. If there is the slightest chance that he can lead us to this spy, then we must take it."

"You read the message - the outcome of the war may depend on us finding him. Besides do you really think I would have abandoned Tony Smith in the middle of nowhere if I had feelings for him?"

"Kaska, you know damn well that if you didn't have feelings for him that he would have been dead by eight o'clock this morning," continued Olek, intent on carrying on the argument.

"Olek, I'm not arguing with you. If Herman Swartz is heading to Germany from Gdansk, then the chances are that he will go through Koszalin. Where we abandoned Tony is on the way. Therefore, we have nothing to lose by picking him up. So keep that big mouth of yours shut, gather the equipment and let's move out." Olek muttered something inaudible under his breath, but grudgingly carried out her orders. Although he was strong willed and ostensibly a loner, Olek was also very loyal, so if Jakub, or Kaska told him to jump, he would ultimately jump, even, as on this occasion, he didn't entirely agree with her commands. So Olek grabbed a couple of boxes of ammunition and loaded them on to the truck.

As night closed in, Tony settled down in his 'Pig Sty'. At the same time Kaska and her troops, in a convoy of one truck, one jeep and one rather knackered old motorbike, headed back towards where they had earlier dropped Tony off. With the first light of daybreak Tony's sleep was broken by the sound of motor vehicles coming to a halt.

The realisation of where he was quickly brought Tony's dreams of the beautiful Kaska to an abrupt end. Hardly daring to, he poked his head out of one of the holes. He could just about make out the truck and the jeep and could hear faint voices.

"Right this is not far from where we dropped Tony off. The village is just beyond those trees. Jakub, Aleksy and Damek, you need to rest. Olek and Ludwik you come with me," instructed Kaska, once again giving out the orders.

"Kaska, you need to take a break like the rest of us. If Tony made it to the village, he will not be awake yet; it is only just sunrise. I suggest we all rest for a couple of hours," argued Jakub.

"Our sleep is not important, we have a top priority mission and the sooner we find Tony the sooner we can go after Harold, or Herman or whatever his name is," insisted Kaska.

"I still think you should rest" argued Jakub weakly.

"I agree." interrupted Tony, as he walked towards the group.

"Tony!" Kaska said startled.

"Kaska," he replied, rushing towards her and embracing her like a long lost friend. To his surprise she responded with a kiss of unequalled passion. As they parted lips, Kaska informed Tony politely that he stank.

"Sorry, but my accommodation last night was hardly the Ritz!" he said defending his poor state of personal hygiene. They both laughed and kissed again.

"How come you did not head to the village?" Kaska asked.

"I did, but it was further than you said. I walked miles last night, but I eventually gave up and decided to settle here instead." Kaska burst out laughing.

"Tony you are about 100 yards from where we dropped you off yesterday."

As Tony looked around, he realised that it did look a bit familiar.

"So I am." he exclaimed, much to the amusement of the rest of team.

"I can't believe my crap sense of direction, I must have been walking around in bloody circles," he said rather sheepishly.

"I must have got disorientated chasing the rabbits." he added.

"Chasing rabbits?" Kaska giggled.

"Don't ask, it's a long story." said Tony, not wishing to appear even more useless than he already had.

"If it was a rabbit you wanted you should have asked," laughed Olek, pulling a large knife from his jacket and with one swift movement launched it through the air and straight into the grass some fifteen feet ahead of them. As Olek retrieved his knife, to everyone's amusement, now attached to it was a dead rabbit. Pulling the bloodied knife from his kill, he wiped the blade on the rabbit's fur, and put it away in his jacket.

"Here," he said, tossing the dead rabbit in Tony's direction, "Let's see if you can catch it now?"

To his embarrassment, but to everyone else's hilarity, Tony once again failed to catch it. Instead it sailed past his shoulder and landed at Jakub's feet. With everyone making quips and having a joke at Tony's expense Kaska abruptly came to his rescue.

"Men...enough now! Remember why we are here," she said sternly, "we have a mission to complete. Tony, we have important news..." she said, turning to him.

"Yes, I heard you mention 'going after Herman'. What has happened?" he asked, pleased that the attention was now going to be diverted from his own ineptitude.

"Listen to this. We have received a message instructing us to stop a German spy at all cost."

"Herman Swartz by any chance?" Tony asked inquisitively.

"No, a man called Harold Swift." Kaska replied.

"It's the same person. Harold Swift was the name he used in the States."

"Bullshit!" interrupted Olek. "You've just made that up."

"No. It was part of our history studies. Harold Swift is the same person as Herman Swartz."

"What else did your history studies tell you?" she questioned.

"That he will successfully hand over the blue-prints of the atomic bomb and that Germany will win this war," Tony informed her.

"Then you must help us kill him," demanded Kaska.

"Why would I want to kill him? In my past Herman Swartz dies anyway, killed by......oh Jesus....ooh no, please no!" Tony stuttered, as his blood started to run cold.

"Tony, what is it?" Kaska demanded.

"Kaska Galinski?...you are Kaska Galinski!"

"Tell me something I don't know." said Kaska.

"You have never mentioned your surname to me have you?" Tony now demanded.

"I can't recall" she said apologetically.

"You haven't, I know you haven't!" he repeated.

"Then how do you know it, Tony?" she asked somewhat puzzled.

"Because you are part of my history book."

"I am?" she said rather intrigued.

"You are the person who killed Herman Swartz!" he exclaimed.

"That's great then, I succeed in our mission," she said jubilantly and with a big smile on her face.

"No, you don't see, you can't kill Herman Swartz, please you can't."

"Tony, if what you are saying is true, then I have already killed him or will kill him soon. As you say, if it's part of your history, then it is inevitable that it will happen."

"But you fail! You may kill Herman Swartz, but the Gestapo still get the plans, and Germany still wins the War. And you will still be…" but Tony could hardly finish his sentence.

"Be what Tony? What will I be?" she questioned.

"They will hunt you down like a pack of rabid dogs. Your men savagely beaten and then killed, and you…" at this point tears filled his eyes as he struggled to get out his words. "You will be nailed alive to the gates of Berlin. There you will survive in agony for many weeks. They will feed and water you. Just enough to keep you alive. Passing Germans will spit or urinate on you. They will go out of their way to ensure that you suffer as much as humanly possible. They will prolong the agony as long as they can, until you eventually die from blood poisoning caused by the rats which fed nightly on your flesh. Your decaying body and, once stripped by the rats and birds, your skeleton, will be left there for many years as a reminder of what you had done to their national hero - Herman Swartz. Many more Poles will be made to suffer in the years to come because of your actions. A picture of your decaying body is one of the most vivid images of the war and was even on the front cover of one of my history books."

"Oh, I see," laughed Kaska nervously. "I hope the photographer caught my good side," she joked.

"It is not a laughing matter," Tony told her, like a school teacher disciplining one of his pupils.

"But surely history can be changed?" she argued. "Why else did you come back to 1945 if you can not change history? You intended to stop Hitler killing himself, so instead you can now make sure I complete my mission. Not only will I kill Herman Swartz, but this time, with your help I will also destroy the blue prints!"

"You can't do that," Tony warned her.

"If you do that and Germany loses the war my past will not have existed. I might not have existed!" he exclaimed.

"But Tony, we can make history better for all of us," she responded like a politician rallying the people.

"I have a good life in 1995, why would I want to destroy it?" he argued back. "I came back to save a life, not to change the entire future of the world. The effects of the paradox could be devastating. No, I have a better idea. You don't kill Herman Swartz. I will then go back to 1995 a hero for creating the paradox that saves his life and you....well you won't be nailed to the Berlin gates. - it's perfect," he said excitedly.

"It's not perfect. I would rather die a thousand painful deaths than let your future exist," Kaska shouted angrily.

"Look, even if I were to help you, the chances are that you would still fail, and still end up being crucified," he said starting to get angry with her. "I'm sorry, but I can't help you. I do not want you to die at all, let alone the horrific death you have in store if you insist on going after Herman Swartz. You just don't understand how horrendous it was," said Tony defiantly.

"Then we have nothing more to say to each other," replied Kaska turning to go back to the truck.

"Kaska, please listen to me," Tony shouted, trying to reason with her. But it was to no avail, as she stubbornly continued to walk back to the truck, without as much as a glance back at him. Tony was about to shout again, but instead he suddenly heard the voice of a German trooper.

"Actung, Actung...Lay down your weapons and put your hands in the air," he demanded. They had been so engrossed in their argument that a German patrol, had inadvertently landed right on top of them. In an instant and before the German guard had the chance to speak again, Olek, who was standing just two feet away from Tony, pulled the knife, that moments before had been used to kill a rabbit, from inside his jacket and, in the blink of an eye, had thrown it with great speed and accuracy in to the chest of the soldier. The German guard looked down at the knife now protruding from his body. His face was expressionless as he dropped to his knees and then, in one movement, fell face first to the ground.

Instantaneously, pandemonium broke out and the air was suddenly filled with the crackle of gunfire. Olek gestured for Tony to get down as he reached for his gun. However, before he could set his sights on a new target, he too was laying on the ground devoid of life. He had taken a fatal shot to the back of his head. In an instant his face exploded in to a thousand pieces, splattering Tony with his blood and other lumps of grotesque flesh and fragments of bone. A bullet had ripped through the back of his head and came out through his eye socket, quickly followed by the majority of his brains. Olek fell towards Tony, almost knocking him off his feet as he dropped to the ground. This once proud man now lay lifeless in front of Tony, with his long black hair, red with blood and draping into the hole that was once his face. With the sight of Olek and the smell of burnt flesh, which was now filling his senses, it took all of Tony's strength not to be physically sick.

Not wanting to end up like Olek, Tony quickly took his belated advice and hit the deck. Using his dead body as makeshift cover, he nervously and very cautiously looked up to see what was happening around him. Although the German patrol had surprised them, Tony thought it likely that it was now the German patrol that were being surprised at the speed and voracity at which Jakub's unit were now engaging them. Although grossly outnumbered he watched in awe at the speed and ruthless efficiency of how the men despatched guard after guard. Aleksy, especially, was seemingly firing his gun randomly in all directions, but each time a shot rang out another guard dropped to the ground.

Ludwik had also sprung in to action, which was no mean feat for a fifty year old. As if in one motion, he was lighting and throwing sticks of dynamite in all directions. Tony was amazed at his precision, as the explosion from each and every stick had the same result; with the limbs of German guards being strewn all around the Polish countryside. Kaska's troop quickly took control, and must have killed at least twenty German soldiers. The few that were left now tried to scatter, but they too were picked off one by one. The air was still again and all was quiet, except for a German soldier gargling blood, which was gushing out of a massive wound to his throat. Jakub put him out of his misery with a bullet through his head. As Tony got to his feet he noticed Aleksy was in pain. By the look of it he had taken a bullet through his shoulder.

"Here, let me help you," Tony said as he walked towards him.

"Never mind me, help her," replied Aleksy pointing to Kaska, who was laying face down on the grass. Please not Kaska, Tony thought to himself, as he rushed over to where she lay. His heart sank as he reached her. Nervously he slowly turned her over. Her white blouse was now red with blood. It was evident that she had been shot in her chest. She was alive, but only just. Tony sat down besides her and pulled her tentatively into his arms.

"Tony," she said, managing the faintest of smiles as she looked into his eyes.

"Please say that you will help us…the Germans cannot win this war." she whispered, as she panted for breath.

"Ok I'll help, but please don't die," Tony pleaded.

"You must go to Auschwitz, and see for yourself," instructed Kaska, as her voice grew weaker.

"Get Jakub to take you, it's not far from here, please say you will," she asked faintly.

"Anything, but please don't die…" he pleaded once more.

"We all die eventually, Tony. I just don't want my death to be in vain," she said, insisting once more that he help them defeat the Germans.

"I will, I promise," he told her.

"Thank you Tony," she murmured, as she raised the back of her hand to wipe away the tears that were now starting to roll down Tony's cheeks.

"I know we come from worlds apart and that we have only known each other for such a short time, but I love you so much," Tony told her, as he cradled her in his arms. Despite struggling for breath, she still managed to smile once more and said in the faintest of whispers,

"Never get too attached, not in war time...it always ends in..." but before she could finish her sentence her eyes closed and she slipped away.

"Kaska, please, don't do this to me, you're not meant to die, not here, not now," Tony cried out to her, but it was hopeless, she was indeed dead. As Tony held her tightly in his arms, with his tears now dripping on to her beautiful black hair, Jakub put his hand on his shoulder.

"There is nothing more you can do, we must leave quickly. Where there's a patrol, there are usually many more Germans. They will be on us like a swarm of wasps if we don't get out of here now."

"We can't just leave her here like this," Tony argued.

"We must or we will die too," and with that Jakub helped him to his feet. "She always knew that one day this bloody war would be the death of her," said Jakub. "We all do." he added rather coldly. "When you have seen as much death as we have, you shut it out of your mind. You have to, or you would go mad. Now let's get out of here," he said directing Tony towards the truck.

Ludwik was already helping Aleksy, whose shirt was covered in blood, into the back of the truck.

"I will follow on the bike," Jakub informed them.

"Let's move," he commanded. Ludwik turned to face the scene of carnage and calmly threw a hand grenade in to the back of the Jeep. As they pulled off it exploded with a huge bang.

Chapter 12 - What becomes of Tony's future?

They sat silently as they drove north. Tony wasn't sure where they were going or what their next move was, but one thing was for sure and that was that he was still here. Why hadn't he been zapped back to 1995?

'I had caused a major paradox. Kaska wasn't meant to die here, and since she can no longer kill Herman Swartz, then my being here must have saved his life. So why am I still here?' he contemplated.

On the journey Tony tried to bandage Aleksy's wound, but he was in a great deal of pain and clearly in a bad way. His condition was not helped by the extremely bumpy road and far from adequate suspension on the truck. Seeing the distress that Aleksy was in, Tony asked Ludwik to stop on a number of occasions, but Ludwik insisted that they press on. Each time stating that they were nearly there and that Aleksy would be better off once at the safe-house where they were heading.

******

Aleksy, was the only non-pole in the group, having been born in 1916, in a town called Havlíčkův in Czechoslovakia. Despite the ravages of war, Aleksy always managed to look well groomed. He kept his hair short and was always clean shaven, which probably stemmed from military training with the Czechoslovak Air Force. He was 18 when he joined the Czech air force, and clocked up some 2,200 flying hours before the Germans occupied Czechoslovakia in 1939. They immediately disbanded the armed forces and Aleksy knew that he had to get out of the country. Three months after the invasion, he managed to travel from Czechoslovakia into France by hiding in a coal train. Together with many other Czechoslovak pilots, he was drafted into the French Foreign Legion to await the imminent outbreak of war. When war came, Aleksy flew with the French Air Force in the fierce but brief Battle of France. He was a formidable pilot and was credited with a number of 'kills.'

As with the battle, France's resistance was short lived and when France fell, Aleksy, once again found himself fleeing a country. This time he managed to reach Morocco, and eventually took a ship to England, where he immediately joined the beleaguered Royal Air Force. Here he flew in one of the four Czechoslovak squadrons formed within the R.A.F. He again had considerable success with a number of kills, but in June 1942 his luck ran out when flying a Lancaster bomber on a sortie over Germany. His stricken plane was hit by tracer bullets and was losing fuel heavily. Knowing that he wouldn't make it back to England he headed East towards Poland, eventually bailing out with his crew just inside the Polish border.

There then ensued a frantic race to reach them, between the Germans from the West, who had seen the plane crash into the Polish countryside and Jakub's Polish Home Army unit from the East, who had seen the crew parachute in to the centre of a small village on the German border. The Poles won the race, but were unfortunate enough to run in to the German unit when making their getaway out of the village. After a fierce gunfight, they eventually disabled the German unit, but at quite a price. Only Aleksy survived out of the Lancaster's crew and Jakub lost three of his own men. Once they had escaped to safety, Jakub offered to help Aleksy get back to England, but he refused, saying that he didn't want to risk the lives of any more of the unit on account of himself. Instead, he offered to repay them for saving his life by joining their unit and fighting with them. Jakub was always pleased to recruit new blood and so readily accepted Aleksy's offer. Although he found it difficult to settle with them at first, partially due to the language difficulties, he eventually became a valuable member of the unit and even taught them English.

With their mutual military background, Aleksy found he had a lot in common with Jakub and they formed a very good friendship. Aleksy often joked that, technically, he should be in charge of the unit since an R.A.F pilot out-ranked all polish soldiers, even Generals! Jakub considered Aleksy a very good fighter, but most of all a very good friend. At one stage, the pair of them had contested for the affections of the beautiful Kaska, but even that could not come between them. They both realised that defeating the Nazis was far more important than getting involved in the distraction of romance. Besides, Kaska always joked that she could never choose between two such handsome men and that perhaps it would be better all round, if they all just stayed as friends.

******

As they finally reached their destination, a large cottage on the outskirts of a small village, Jakub was now very concerned about his friends' welfare. Pulling up in the court yard in front of the cottage, they were met by an old gentleman and his wife. The old man, seeing that Aleksy was in a bad way and barely conscious, instructed them to get him inside as quickly as possible. Once inside the cottage, they took Aleksy to a small bedroom and laid him on the bed.

"Right, everyone out," instructed the old lady. "I will take care of him now," she said, starting to rip some bed linen to make a dressing.

"Please make sure you look after him well," pleaded Jakub.

"Don't worry he's in safe hands" reassured the old lady, who was called Greta. Tony and the rest of the men returned to the main living area where they were greeted by the old man.

"Hello Ludwik, Jakub, Damek..." he said as he acknowledge each of the men in turn. As he looked over at Tony he just nodded and gave him a half-hearted smile. "Where are the others?" he asked, probably already knowing the answer.

"Dead I'm afraid," Ludwik told him abruptly.

"Ryszard and Henryk were killed two weeks ago when we were blowing up the fuel dump at Gross-Rosen and Olek and Kaska were killed this morning by a German patrol."

"Not Kaska?" he sighed dejectedly, with tears quickly welling up inside his eyes. "I always told her that she took too many risks, but she wouldn't listen," he said despondently. "It's a sad, sad world we live in," he muttered to himself. "Still, life goes on. Would anyone like anything to eat? You all look starved," he asked, reiterating the fact that life must go on for the rest of them.

"Starving is not the word" Jakub answered eagerly. Tony nodded in agreement.

"Let's see, I'm sure I have some sausages here," said the old man, as he proceeded to detach a string of dried sausages from a cord tied to the rafters above his head. "And wine, we must have some wine," he said, as he disappeared down the stairs to his cellar, quickly re-appearing with a bottle of red wine in his hand. Dust filled the air as he blew the bottle. "I've been saving this one for a special occasion," he said, as he opened the bottle. "Please excuse the best crystal - times are hard," he said apologetically, as he passed each of the men an assortment of mugs which he proceeded to fill. As he came to fill Tony's mug he momentarily stopped. "So who are you young man and what's your story?" he asked before continuing to fill his mug with the wine.

"My name is Tony Smith, but I'm not sure that you will believe my story even if I tell you," he answered.

"No, tell him your story" Jakub urged.

"Ok I will, but I do not expect you to believe me," Tony responded.

"If you tell the truth I have no reason not to believe you, but first let me finish the food. I find stories to be far more enjoyable on a full stomach so you can tell me over supper." They all nodded eagerly in agreement. "By the way, I'm Jack," he said, shaking Tony's hand warmly. Very shortly Tony was telling Jack his unlikely tale over a meal of homemade bread and sausages. Jack was intrigued with Tony's depiction of the future and for an old man had a very open and perceptive mind, almost talking as though time travel was an everyday event.

"So this 'paradox' thing, if that's the way you get back to the future, why haven't you vanished in a puff of smoke back to 1995? Since Kaska wasn't meant to die this morning and she will not now kill Herman Swartz. Isn't that one of these paradox things?" he asked intelligently.

"I've already given that some thought" Tony responded, although he still wasn't quite sure of the answer.

"It's obvious," said Jakub interrupting.

"Herman Swartz will still die. I'll make sure of that!" he told them defiantly. "Kaska was hunted down and killed because she was our leader, it doesn't mean that she was necessarily the one that fired the shot that killed him," he added.

"But what about Kaska being shot? According to Tony she wasn't meant to die," questioned Jack.

"Not just yet…but if she was going to die in a few weeks anyway, maybe her dying this morning hasn't actually changed anything," said Jakub.

"Well, nothing to create a major paradox," Tony added, starting to now make sense as to why he was still in 1945.

"Or maybe Olek was right after all. Tony Smith is still here because it's all bullshit," said Damek, still not quite believing a word of Tony's story.

"Well, I'm convinced," said Jack, giving Tony a broad smile.

"I'm still not so sure," said Jakub, "but at the moment you're still the best hope we have of getting to Hermann Swartz."
"Hold on a minute," responded Tony, "I told Kaska that I couldn't help. If I do anything to stop the Germans winning the war, my

past would be little more than a figment of my imagination," he reiterated to them.

"No. You hold on. I heard you promise Kaska on her deathbed, that you would help us," said Jakub accusingly.

"But that was before she died," Tony argued feebly.

"Does her death not mean anything to you?" responded Jakub angrily. "Have you no honour?" he questioned. "It was all down to Kaska, that you were not shot yesterday morning. She convinced us to spare your life - now I'm not so sure we should have listened."

"Traitor!" snarled Damek spitting on the floor in front of Tony.

"Look, even if I wanted to help, how can I?" Tony argued.

"Think back to your history books, when and where was Herman Swartz killed?" urged Jakub.

"I can't remember that sort of detail. It was years ago that I studied history." Tony argued apologetically.

"Think man. Think! You must remember," urged Jakub, despite Tony's protests. Ludwik got out a map and laid it across the table. "We know where he was last seen and we know where he is heading, which would mean he must take either one of these two roads. But which one?" said Ludwik tracing his finger along the roads on the map.

"Yes but, even if we know which road, we don't know how far he's already travelled, so where the hell do we set our ambush?" said Jakub getting more and more frustrated. "It's hopeless, without any co-ordinates or a time, it's impossible."

"What, co-ordinates like W2543 N1356?" Tony asked.

"Yea, something like that," said Ludwik tracing Tony's numbers along his map. "Jesus, that would be perfect," he said looking at Tony in disbelief. "That's right here, on the road between Slupsk and Koszalin," said Ludwik with a puzzled expression growing on his face.

"Where did these co-ordinates come from?" asked Jakub.

"You're not going to believe this, but they came from Klaus Zimmerman, back in 1995," Tony said excitedly. "He wouldn't tell me why, but he told me to remember W2543 N1356 25445 – he said it could be very important and was very insistent that I memorised it," Tony recalled.

"What about the 25445?" queried Jakub.

"That's the date….25th April 1945, three days from now," said Damek grinning. "He will be at these co-ordinates in three days time."

"I thought you didn't believe a word of this Damek?" quizzed Jakub.

"I don't, it's all bullshit! But what the heck, we haven't got anything better to go on," he said with a broad smile on his face. It was the first time that Tony had seen Damek with anything but a scowl on his face and it seemed to brighten the entire atmosphere of the room.

"I don't want to put a dampener on it, but how would Klaus Zimmerman know these co-ordinates?" questioned Jack.

"Ah, good question" said Tony. "Well….err, at some point in the near future we will meet Klaus and we will give him the co-ordinates. He then has to remember them and then tell me in fifty years time," said Tony smugly.

"But how do we know the co-ordinates to give him," questioned Jack bemused.

"I've just told you them haven't I?" Tony replied.

"I know, but how could Klaus, give them to you if he doesn't know them in the first place?" quizzed Jack even more puzzled.

"I've got it!" said Jakub."We don't have to give the actual co-ordinates to Klaus, but we tell him we need them. So then in the future, after Herman is dead and buried he has all the time in the world to find out where and when he was killed. And then he makes you remember them in 1995."

"He could do that…but now we know the co-ordinates why don't we just tell them to him?" stated Damek. They all looked at each other and then burst in to fits of laughter.

"Hang on," said Jack pulling himself together, "Isn't this assuming that Herman Swartz is killed in the first place? If we didn't have the co-ordinates how did we kill him?"

"We do have the co-ordinates, so we can kill him! So what's the worry?" said Jakub. Tony tried to explain to the rest of them that this was a chicken and egg scenario and part of the mind boggling complexities of time travel.

"What's a chicken and egg scenario?" asked Damek.

"You know, what comes first, the chicken or the egg?" helped Jakub.

"I don't understand," said Damek, "What did come first, the chicken or the egg?"

"Eggsactly," said Jack. They all looked at Jack and then fell about laughing again. Even Damek joined in, although they were not too sure he knew what he was actually laughing at. They were starting to get quite jovial, with Jack insisting on opening another bottle of wine.
"I'm sure I've got another one here for a special occasion," he laughed, as he once again disappeared down to his cellar. This time he reappeared with his arms full of six more bottles of wine.

Once the laughing had died down Jakub said in a serious voice, "Look, if all this is true, we now have the co-ordinates and the date, so all we have to do is be there. Only this time I will personally see to it that the documents go up in smoke along with Mr Swartz."

Although Tony's intention was not to help them, it appeared that by blurting out of the grid reference he had quite possibly signed Herman Swartz's death warrant. He decided that he could live with that, since Herman was meant to die anyway, however what did concern him very much was the prospect that this time they may actually succeed in destroying the blueprints.

Many thoughts started to fill Tony's mind.

'What would become of his future?'
'Would he still marry Hannah?'
'What of his son - Karl?'
'Will Karl still be born?'

In fact, Tony even wondered whether he'd still be born? The thought foremost on his mind was that if they actually manage to destroy those papers then surely it would be the mother of all paradoxes. Previously when Tony had endured many a sleepless night worrying about the potential consequences of creating a paradox, even then he had not envisaged one that could be quite as momentous as this. Tony concluded that whether he liked it or not, the entire world's history now lay in his hands. Saving Hitler's life was one thing, but now he faced the prospect of being responsible for changing the future of the entire human race. Tony felt that he was not prepared to take on that responsibility and knew that somehow he had to maintain the original timeline. He knew that he had to ensure the atomic bomb blueprint still got to the SS - but how?

He contemplated sneaking out in the middle of the night and to try and get to Herman Swartz before the men - but with his track record he knew that he would undoubtedly get himself well and truly lost. Besides, he questioned how he would get the keys to the truck, since they were well and truly attached to Ludwik's belt. He also conceded that the motorbike was also no good to him, since he didn't have a clue how to ride one. He fleetingly even thought about killing them all in their sleep. But being a mere scientist, he hardly fancied his chances against such hardened fighters. Besides, he had actually started to like them and so even if he was able, Tony knew that he wouldn't have it in him to kill them in cold blood. For now, he knew that the only thing he could do was bide his time. See how things developed and if and when the chance to preserve the timeline arose, he had to make sure that he was in a position to take it.

"Koszalin is just one day from here, so I suggest we lay low tomorrow and take it easy," said Jakub, breaking Tony's line of thought. "In the meantime it might be a good idea to try and contact Klaus and tell him we have a job for him." he said, looking at Ludwik to get on the radio.

"Yeah, else all this may not have just happened," added Damek thoughtfully. They all gave him a confused look - none of them wanting to start another 'what if' conversation.

"The last we knew of him, was that he was helping the SS with their 'enquiries', so at least we know he lived through that. Get on the radio Ludwik and see if you can get him up here. We could do with the extra help. Besides, Klaus should be able to get Aleksy to somewhere safer until he's recovered," suggested Jakub.

As though she had been waiting in the wings for her cue to enter, Greta walked in from the bedroom with a solemn look on her face. "I'm sorry boys, he'd lost too much blood - there was nothing I could do," she said, and started to cry.

"It's been a bad day," said Jakub also choking back tears.

"Just let me get hold of them German bastards," said Damek angrily.

"We will Damek, don't worry my friend, we will," said Jakub. "And with a bit of luck and thanks to Tony Smith here, we can actually stop the bastards winning the war!" he added raising his mug towards Tony.

They all looked Tony's way.

"To Tony Smith," toasted Ludwik, also raising his mug. "Tony Smith," they all repeated. Tony acknowledged them with a nervous smile.

"To Kaska," said Jack as he quickly refilled the mugs. "Kaska." they all chorused. "May God bless her soul," added Jakub.

"To Aleksy," suggested Damek raising his mug. "Aleksy," they once again toasted.

For the next hour they continued to toast just about everyone they knew. From Klaus Zimmerman to Winston Churchill. Even Herman Swartz got a mention. Needless to say by the end of the evening they were extremely drunk. These men had known unimaginable hardship and seen things that would make your blood curdle, yet beneath it all they were still very ordinary people.

In different circumstances they would just be builders, or bakers, even bank clerks, but war had made them ruthless killers, who knew that it was either kill or be killed. During their evening of drunken conversation Tony felt a closeness that he had never felt before. Like a comrade or a 'Brother in Arms,' but he knew that in three day's time he must somehow betray them.

Chapter 13 - The horror of Auschwitz.

The stillness of the morning, discounting the sound of Damek's snoring, was broken by the sound of a motor vehicle approaching the cottage. The men woke abruptly and in an instant had assumed a combat position with their weapons trained on the door.

"Jack, are you expecting anyone?" Jakub asked him quietly.

"No," replied Jack as he moved nervously towards the door.

All went quiet outside, as the engine of what sounded like a motorbike was turned off. You could have heard a pin drop as the sound of footsteps filled the room, with each step getting louder as they approached the door. Sweat started to drip from Tony's brow as he anxiously awaited a knock on the door. The others however all looked extremely calm, given the circumstances, and remained fully focused on the door. The footsteps stopped.

Knock - Tap - Knock - Knock - Tap.

The tension was suddenly gone as Jack laughed as he stepped towards the door. "I know that knock anywhere," he said, opening the door to reveal a short man, dressed in a dirty leather jacket. On his head was a leather helmet with goggles pulled down over his eyes.

"I got the message and decided it would be safer to travel up overnight. Where is he?" asked the little man with a German accent.

"I'm afraid you're too late Klaus, Aleksy passed away in the night."

"Oh Jesus, when will this ever end?" said Klaus cursing as he took off his helmet. His face was covered in mud, except for two white rings around his eyes, which he revealed as he removed his goggles. His left eye was badly bruised and even through the mud you could see that his left cheek was also swollen. "Olek, Kaska and now Aleksy! To think I was going to moan about the last few days that I've just had," said Klaus with a heavy sigh.

"Yes, we know about your visit to SS headquarters," said Jakub.

"Some lunatic, who was snooping round the Bernau Government building, reckoned he knew me," said Klaus angrily. "It's a good job the SS took him away to shoot, because if I'd got my hands on him I would have ripped his balls off," he said alarmingly.

"So how did you persuade them to let you go?" asked Ludwik.

"I told them that I'd never seen him before in my life and that he had obviously just seen my name on my office door. Luckily, the moron made up some fanciful story about being beamed here from the future and since they knew that clearly wasn't true, they assumed the rest was bullshit as well. So they eventually let me go, but not before giving me the usual treatment," he added disdainfully. "I was also lucky that one of the officers knew of me and thought it hilarious that they thought I could be a spy, especially with my affiliation with the Nazi party. He laughed and said that they'd be keeping a close eye on me from now on."

"I hope you haven't been followed," said a concerned Jack.

"Don't be stupid. He was joking! Besides, you're talking Klaus Zimmerman here, master of disguise. Anyway, they're hardly going to be watching me whilst they think I'm in bed," he said indignantly. "What I don't understand is how he did know my name, since I haven't actually got my name on my office door.

And why would he claim to know me when I've never set eyes on him before in my entire life?" he continued.

"Why don't you ask him yourself?" said Jakub coughing, in a clear your throat sort of way, and looking over towards Tony. Up until now, Tony had stayed back in the shadows, not volunteering to introduce himself. Klaus, not quite understanding what Jakub had meant, reached into his top pocket and pulled out a pair of small round spectacles. He squinted as he put them on and looked over towards where Tony was standing. It took a few moments for it to register who he was looking at.

"Why you bastard...I'll rip ya throat out," he screamed, lunging towards Tony in a rage. Jakub, Ludwik and even Damek all quickly jumped up and held him back.
"Who are you?" he snarled. "And since when have you known me?" he added angrily.

"Calm down and listen to this - it will blow your socks off!" insisted Jakub

.

"Will I fuck calm down! This idiot could have gotten me killed," cursed Klaus as he struggled to free himself from the others.

"Trust me. This is one story you want to hear. Now be calm and listen to what the man has to say," said Jakub sternly. It took a few moments for Klaus to eventually calm down, but as soon as he was settled Tony was beckoned to tell his story once again. Klaus listened intently to every word before dismissing Tony as insane.

"And you lot believe all this crap?" he said accusingly to the others. "I have never heard such a load of nonsense in my entire life."

"You haven't been with him the last few days - if it's bullshit then it's very convincing bullshit," said Ludwik in Tony's defence.

"Your name is Klaus Zimmerman, you were born on the 2nd March 1925. Your first pet was a dog called "Kaiser" and your mother used to call you "Rolly" when you were young," Tony told him remembering their conversations back in 1995.

"My God - I've never told anyone about being called Rolly," he said remembering his childhood fondly.

"You wouldn't, would you?" laughed Jakub.

"So now do you believe him - Rolly?" questioned Ludwik laughing as he said it.

"I'm not sure what I believe," he said bewildered. "So tell me, if I live to be an old man, am I still good looking?"

"Erm, yes?" replied Tony somewhat hesitantly. "Actually you haven't changed one bit, you're still…" but before Tony could finish his sentence Klaus burst out laughing.

"Look, I know I'm hardly an oil painting now, but if I'm alive and well in 1995 that'll do for me. I'm still not saying I believe you, but if as you say, the war is going to end soon, then we had better make sure that this time it's not the Germans who win it!" he stated defiantly.

"But aren't you German?" Tony asked him somewhat puzzled.

"I'm Austrian, actually, although my father was a Serb. I've never been a great fan of the Third Reich, especially with what they are doing to the Jews," he answered. "In fact, that reminds me, rumour has it that there are another ten train loads being shipped into Auschwitz tomorrow - we need this war to end soon for their sake," he said solemnly.

"Kaska mentioned this Auschwitz, what is it?" Tony asked

"It's a concentration camp or to be more accurate, a Nazi death camp," he replied coldly.

"Death camp? What on earth is a death camp?" Tony asked, hardly daring to hear the answer.

"It's a huge prison where the Jews have been sent in their millions - only it's a prison that they never come out of. For the past two years the Germans have systematically massacred them in their droves," replied Klaus.

"I can't believe that. Has anyone actually seen this camp or is it just hearsay and speculation?" Tony asked sceptically.

"It exists alright - the security is tight, but I have heard it from good friends, people that I'd trust with my life, that it is a place of unimaginable horror. A place that once you had seen you could never forget."

"Kaska told me on her deathbed that I must see it for myself, but I didn't realise what she was on about," Tony said recounting her dying words.

"Listen, if Kaska said you must see it, then you must. If it helps you realise what bastards these Germans are, then it will focus your mind on helping us," said Jakub.

"But, where is it?" Tony asked

"It's about a three hour ride from here, I will take you on the back of my motorbike," offered Klaus.

Despite Tony's protests they all agreed that it would be good for him to see for himself and felt that if it was Kaska's dying wish, then it was a matter of honour that he should go.
"But what about the tight security?" Tony questioned, hoping that they would see the folly of sending him there.

"I have papers that can get me places that you would never believe and besides you speak perfect German. As long as we are careful, we should be all right," said Klaus.

"Here!" said Jakub, tossing Tony a revolver. "Just in case."

"I've never fired a gun in my life," Tony protested. "Besides if I kill someone the chances are that I'll be whizzed back to 1995," he added.

"It's easy - just point the thing and pull the trigger," said Klaus, going through the motion with his own gun.

"Besides, if you do go 'back to the future' then you can always use your contraption and come back again - only this time bring some decent weapons," said Jakub.

Tony explained that he had to travel naked and it wouldn't be as simple as that, but their minds were made up - Tony was going to Auschwitz. Tony didn't have a problem with going, but was very concerned that if he didn't make it back that they may actually succeed in stopping the blue-prints changing hands and thus destroying his future. He felt that as far as the men were concerned, that he was of little use to them, especially now that they had the co-ordinates. In fact he surmised that they probably considered his presence here more of a hindrance than a help. If he made it back then that was fine, if not, then that wasn't a problem either. Either way, it would not do any harm them sending him to Auschwitz.

Jack found Tony a pair of old goggles and a worn-out leather jacket. So once Klaus had cleaned up and rested a little, Tony was soon on the back of his motorbike and heading into the Polish countryside. For such an unassuming small man, Klaus drove like a complete maniac! It didn't matter on the quality of the road surface, he just went full throttle. Tony guessed that for any normal person it should have been a six hour journey but, sure enough, they did it in just over three, with their only delay a short stop at a checkpoint. Klaus was superb, bluffing his way past the German guards, laughing and joking with them, whilst Tony sat on the back of the bike tight lipped and extremely nervous. Tony did try to reassure himself that there was nothing to be scared of, since technically he was still on their side. It even entered his mind to give himself in and tell them of the plot to stop Herman Swartz. However, since his experience of German soldiers had not been good so far, with them not previously believing a word of his story, he presumed that he would find himself in the same predicament and so quickly decided against that idea. Besides, having come all this way, Tony was now intrigued to find out what really did go on at this so called 'death camp' and so remained silent on the back of the bike.

Klaus brought the bike to a halt. "It will be safer if we walk from here," he said, as they pulled up on the edge of some woodland. Pushing the bike in to some overgrown bushes, Klaus instructed Tony to help cover the bike, gesturing for him to pick up any fallen branches that were lying on the ground. Once the bike was hidden from view they set off into the woodland. They walked for about a mile, before coming to a clearing that stretched for about 100 yards.

"This is the tricky bit," Klaus said, motioning for Tony to keep his head down. "We need to get to the top of that ridge," he instructed, pointing to the far edge of the clearing. "From there we will be able to see the whole camp in the valley below, although I suggest we don't hang around too long since there's hardly an abundance of cover. Right, on the count of three, we need to run to that rock, just above the overhang, alright?" But before Tony could even confirm that he was 'alright', Klaus shouted "three!" and took off like a rat from a sinking ship. For a little man Klaus was very fast and it took all of Tony's effort to keep within ten yards of him. Finally, both men dived down to the ground a few feet from the rock. Tony, in particular, was exhausted from their short dash. Klaus edged up onto the large rock, which was balanced precariously on the top of the ridge and beckoned Tony to follow him to the top. As Tony got his breath back he peered out to the valley below.

As his eyes tried to comprehend what they were seeing his breath was quickly taken away again by the sheer scale of the place. The camp stretched as far as the eye could see, with row after row, of what appeared to be, wooden huts.

"Every one full of Jews," Klaus pointed out as he motioned his hand across the view of the landscape.

"I suppose they have to house them somewhere until after the war," said Tony, defending what he was seeing. Klaus pulled a pair of binoculars from inside his jacket and started to survey the view a little closer.

"Look over there at those chimneys," he said passing Tony the binoculars. "That smoke is from burning bodies," he added.

"Come off it," Tony retorted. "That smoke could be from anything - this must be some sort of factory or processing plant," he said as he focused the binoculars on the chimneys.

"It is...it's a processing plant of human misery," Klaus argued back. Suddenly Tony recoiled in horror. Lowering the binoculars, he rubbed his eyes in disbelief before returning the binoculars to focus once again on the landscape.

"Jesus Christ!" Tony exclaimed as the true realisation of what he was seeing registered with his brain. "That can't be what I think it is," he said to Klaus in denial of what he thought he had seen, but couldn't quite comprehend nevertheless.

Klaus confirmed that what he was seeing was a huge mountain of naked dead bodies, skeletal in appearance but unmistakably dead human bodies. Workers, also barely much more than walking skeletons, were loading them into carts and pushing them into the building from where the chimneys were billowing smoke. All of which was being overseen by German soldiers with their guns at the ready. Further down were more "workers" coming out of what looked like shower blocks, with wheelbarrows full of entangled dead bodies, men, women and children, with their emaciated lifeless limbs, hanging over the edge of the barrows. These were then added to the mountain of bodies, as though stocking up on fuel for the fires.

One of the 'workers' stumbled and fell. A woman - she was clearly very weak as she struggled to get back to her feet and fell once again. Although, they were some distance away, Tony could still make out, and will indeed never forget the gaunt haunted look on her face. With her shaven head and sunken eyes she looked pitifully emaciated, as she pleaded for some sort of help or compassion from one of the German guards. But to Tony's horror, instead of help the soldier pushed the woman back to the floor and brought his rifle butt crashing down on the back of her head, smashing her skull. Tony threw up. He could not comprehend how the Germans had let themselves descend to such savagery. Even in 1995, he always knew that they were often abrupt and undoubtedly had the potential to be quite ruthless, but he never could have envisaged them acting in such a brutal way. What he was seeing was genocide on a massive scale and it made him feel sick to the stomach.

As if to emphasise this point, and give some perspective of the size of the camp, Tony's vomiting was interrupted by the sound of a train, as it whistled to announce its arrival at the camp. The heavily guarded gates were opened to let the train pull up alongside the rampa (railway platform). Tony counted at least twenty-five carriages, each nothing more than a cattle truck, packed full of more Jews being brought to be massacred. He could hardly imagine how many poor souls had already been killed in this horrendous place.

******

What Tony didn't know was that Auschwitz was just one of many 'death camps' scattered throughout Poland and Germany. Located 37 miles west of Krakow, Auschwitz was the biggest of them all. In 1940, Heinrich Himmler, the head of the SS and German police, had ordered the establishment of a large new concentration camp near the town of Oswiecim in Polish Eastern province of Silesia. Initially, most of the inmates were Polish political prisoners and by March 1941, the prison population had reached 10,900. This was Auschwitz, and very soon it got a reputation as one of the harshest of the Nazi concentration camps. The Nazi system of torturing prisoners was implemented here in its most cruel form. In one of the camp's buildings, Block 11, a special bunker was erected especially for punishments. In front of that building stood the 'Black Wall' where the regular execution of prisoners took place.

With the concentration camp population forever increasing and the 'problem' of the Jews not disappearing, Himmler ordered the construction of a second, much larger section of the camp, Auschwitz Birkenau. No longer satisfied with the internment of the prisoners, Himmler ordered the mass execution of the inmates, therefore Birkenau was built complete with a killing centre - consisting of five gas chambers and a crematorium. It was this death camp that Tony and Klaus were now surveying from the surrounding hills.

The first gassing using Zyklon B gas, took place in September 1941. The victims were 600 Soviet prisoners of war and 250 other prisoners chosen from among the sick. They were soon followed however, by countless thousands. Each gas chamber had the potential to kill 6,000 people daily. The gas chambers were built to resemble shower rooms. The arriving victims were told that they would be sent to work, but that they first had to undergo disinfection and to shower. As the trains with Jewish transports stopped at the rampa in Birkenau, the people inside were brutally forced to leave the cars in a great hurry. They had to leave behind all their personal belongings and were made to form two lines, men and women separately. These lines had to move quickly to the place where SS officers were conducting the selection, directing the people either to one side (the majority) to die in the gas chambers or to the other, which meant designation for forced labour.

Those who were sent to the gas chambers were killed that same day, and their corpses were burned in the crematoria. The belongings left in the cars by the incoming victims were gathered by a forced-labour detachment called 'Kanada'. Those victims not sent to the gas chambers were sent to a part of the camp called the 'quarantine', where their hair was shorn, men and women alike - and they were given striped prisoners' garb. In the quarantine, a prisoner, if not soon transferred to slave labour, could survive only for a few weeks; while in the forced-labour camps, the average life expectancy was extended to a few months. After that time, many of the prisoners became so emaciated and weak that they could hardly move or react to their surroundings. It was no wonder that every prisoner tried to get out of quarantine as soon as possible.

Above the main gate to the central camp, Auschwitz I, was a large inscription: "Arbeit Macht Frei" (Work makes you free), but in truth nothing led to freedom. Once in Auschwitz you were not coming out. One of the most dreaded institutions in Auschwitz was the roll call, known as the appell. The appell occurred early in the morning and in the late afternoon after the inmates had returned from their places of work, and sometimes also in the middle of the night. The inmates were made to stand at attention, motionless, usually sparsely clad for many hours in the cold, rain, and snow, and whoever stumbled or fell was sent to be gassed or shot there and then. Upon arrival at the camps, prisoners were registered and received numbers, tattooed on their left arm. 405,000 prisoners of different nationalities were registered in this way. Not included in any form of registration were the vast majority of the Auschwitz victims, those men and women who, upon arrival, were led to the gas chambers and killed immediately. Therefore it was impossible to tell exactly how many people died at this death camp, although it was estimated that the number of Jews murdered in the gas chambers of Auschwitz prior to the war ending was over one and a half million people: men, women, and children. Almost one-quarter of the Jews killed during World War II were murdered in Auschwitz.

Some of those that were not gassed were prisoners selected for pseudo-scientific medical experiments. Many of these "experiments" were carried out on young Greek Jewish men and women. They underwent unbelievable suffering and torture. The prison population was constantly growing, despite the mortality rate caused by starvation, hard labour, contagious diseases, and the total exhaustion of the prisoners. Electrically charged barbed-wire fences 4 meters in height were built around both Auschwitz I and Auschwitz II, with SS men, armed with machine guns, permanently manning the many watch towers that surrounded the perimeter. The whole system was guarded by a specially organised regiment of the SS-Totenkopfverbände (Death's-Head Units). The Nazi staff of the camp were aided by a number of privileged prisoners who were offered better food and conditions and more chances to survive, provided they helped to enforce the terror regime on their fellow prisoners.

The special trains containing Jews from the occupied countries in Europe were now arriving in Auschwitz almost daily. Sometimes several trains arrived on the same day. In each of these trains were anything up to seven thousand Jewish victims being forcibly brought in by the Nazis from the liquidated ghettos in Poland and other Eastern European countries, as well as from countries in the West and South. The trains stopped at a special siding track that had been built within the Auschwitz-Birkenau camp. Its platform became the busiest railway station in all of Nazi-occupied Europe, with one particular difference, namely that people only arrived there, and never left again. What Tony did not know, was that the Soviet army had already started an offensive from the East and was heading in the direction of Krakow and Auschwitz. The Nazis were already preparing for a withdrawal. Tens of thousands of prisoners, were to be driven out of the Auschwitz camps and put on death marches. Most of them were killed during these marches. Those too weak to join the march were murdered even before the camps were evacuated, although in their hurry to leave, a few lucky inmates were left behind.

When the Russians eventually liberated Auschwitz, they found little more than a thousand prisoners alive. However despite their liberation by the Russians the prisoners joy was short lived. Thanks to Herman Swartz and the Atomic bomb, the Russian soldiers quickly retreated once their leaders had been forced to surrender after the bombing of Volgograd. And so, once the war was over and without the distraction of fighting, the Nazis quickly re-populated the death camps and upped production of the human misery. Between 1945 and 1957 it was estimated that over 20 million more people were gassed at Auschwitz and the other death camps in Poland. Not only Jews, but also homosexuals, Asians, gypsies, prisoners of war and political prisoners from all over Europe.

The Soviets were executed in their millions and even 'German' disabled people were not safe from the 'Purge of the Un-pure.' Anyone who did not conform to the Nazis ideals of a human race, were rounded up and despatched to the various death camps. Usually, they were led to believe that they were being repatriated, or under the pretence that they were being re-deployed for employment and a 'better life'. Although it involved huge numbers of people, the rest of the population, such as Tony and his son Karl, were very much shielded from these acts of genocide and were oblivious of this darker side to their Nazi rulers. The Americans had their suspicions of what was going on in Europe, but with very few prisoners (if any) living to tell the tale - little information ever got back to America.

As part of the 'Cold War' treaty towards the end of the 1950's the Americans offered to take any 'unwanted' nationals from the Germans. So in 1958 a number of dissidents were shipped across the Atlantic to the US, although this was little more than a token gesture. In truth, the Nazis had now all but ran out of people to execute, and therefore the Death Camps were eventually closed down. Himmler's instruction to annihilate the Jewish race with his 'final solution' was all but complete.

******

Tony had seen enough. He asked Klaus to get them out of there. Tony knew that Kaska was right, the Germans were evil and had to be stopped at all costs, even if it meant sacrificing his own future. Tony knew that he had to make sure those blue-prints never ended up in the hands of these murdering German bastards.

"Right, on the count of three," Klaus said once again. But before he managed to say 'three' Tony was off across the clearing, quickly followed by the little Austrian. As they got close to the edge of the woodland Tony heard shouts of "Actung, Actung, halt or I will shoot!" Glancing behind he could see two German guards approaching.

"Shit…" he heard Klaus mutter. "I'm not convinced bullshit will work this time," Klaus panted. "When you hit the woodland keep close to me and run like you've never run before," instructed Klaus alarmingly. As they entered the edge of the woodland they continued to run, in total disregard of the German soldier's instructions. Inevitably the guards opened fire. Tony and Klaus ran for their lives as bullets rattled into the trees, bringing branches crashing down around them.

"Run faster!" shouted Klaus - not that Tony needed much encouragement.

Not being the fittest of men, Tony soon started to lag behind Klaus. "It's no good I can't go on," he said breathlessly, after a pitiful few hundred yards.

"Keep running" Klaus urged, conscious of the fact that the Germans would soon be upon them.

"I can't," Tony pleaded. "You go on and get the hell out of here. I'll be OK," Tony insisted reluctantly.

"We came together, we leave together," Klaus responded, rather heroically.

"Look, don't worry about me, if they shoot me I'll see you back in

1995. Just make sure that the others destroy the blue-prints," Tony continued to argue.

Tony contemplated that if he was in Klaus's position you wouldn't have seen him for dust, but Klaus refused to go. Getting his gun out, he beckoned that Tony did the same. He was either very brave or very stupid Tony thought to himself. He also considered that the truth might more likely be that Klaus was worried that if Tony got captured he would spill the beans and jeopardise the plan to stop Herman Swartz. Then again, maybe Klaus was just as knackered himself and therefore unable to continue.

To be honest, whatever his reasons were, Tony was glad that Klaus was going to stay with him. The theory of being catapulted back to the future if he died in the past was still one that Tony was not particularly eager to put to the test. As they finally came to a halt, Klaus instructed Tony to get down behind a fallen tree trunk. As Tony crouched down he remembered the gun that had been given to him earlier and felt inside his jacket pocket for it. He was breathless and shaking like a leaf, as he fumbled for the gun, which he eventually pulled from his pocket and held out in front of him. Klaus gave a whispered "shush," as he listened intently for any sign of the approaching German guards.

All Tony could hear was his own heavy breathing and his heart pounding loudly inside his chest. Klaus continued to listen and homed in on the sound of twigs snapping as the guards neared their position. Klaus spotted one of the guards through the bushes and before Tony could even blink he had fired off a shot that went straight through the hapless soldier's chest. His comrade, taken by surprise and not knowing where the shot had come from, started firing wildly in Tony and Klaus's direction. Tony started to panic and returned fire back in the general direction of the soldier. Not only giving away their position, but in doing so, he also managed to send himself tumbling backwards into the bracken. Tony fell flat on his backside with his gun going off indiscriminately in all directions. As he hit the ground a further shot rang out, but this time from Klaus's gun as he despatched another bullet with ruthless efficiency straight through the chest of the second German soldier. Then Klaus dropped to the ground himself.

"Phew, that was close," Tony said as he picked himself up off the floor. But Klaus didn't answer, other than to give a bit of a groan. As Tony walked over to see Klaus, it was apparent that he had been badly hit in his arm. Though clearly in pain he still managed to mutter, "You arsehole," through gritted teeth.

Tony then realised what must have happened. As he was tumbling backwards he had managed to hit Klaus just above the elbow from point blank range with one of his stray bullets. As Klaus rolled back what was left of his leather jacket to examine his wound, it was apparent that there was no way on earth that his arm could be saved. Tony felt like puking again, as he saw that Klaus's lower left arm was barely attached to the rest of his body. It was hanging there covered in blood and attached by nothing more than a small strip of skin and a few tendons. Klaus took one look at it and cursed, knowing that his arm was lost.

Tony then couldn't believe his eyes as Klaus pulled a knife out from inside his boot and cut through the remaining tethering of his arm. Tossing it to one side once it was detached, as though it was a rotten piece of meat. Klaus then talked Tony through putting a tourniquet around his upper arm to stop the flow of blood. Luckily the heat from the impact had cauterised much of the wound and given the fact that there was little more than a stump where his arm used to be the amount of bleeding was minimal. To look at Klaus, at little more than five foot tall, with his bald head and small round glasses, it gave you no clue as to the man of steel inside. In all Tony's life he had never seen anyone quite so tough as Klaus!

"I am so sorry" Tony started to apologise. "I really didn't mean to shoot you....I....I...really don't know what to say"

"Never mind apologies, we must get back to the bike," instructed Klaus rather stoically. "Half the German army will be down upon us if we don't get out of here now," he said, staggering to his feet.

Tony helped him as quickly as he could to get back to where they had hidden the bike and sat Klaus down, as he uncovered it. However it still left them with one slight problem.

Klaus was clearly in no fit state to drive and Tony had never ridden a bike in his life. As Tony stood there staring at the motorbike, Klaus must have read his thoughts.

"Don't worry, it's easy," he told Tony. "You just point it in the direction you want to go and pull back the throttle" he said trying to reassure Tony. Tony mused that he had said a similar thing about firing a gun and look where that had got them!

"You concentrate on accelerating and steering the thing, whilst I'll look after the gears from the back" Klaus suggested, adding that it would be a piece of cake. Tony wasn't so sure, but what choice did they have? So Tony started the bike under Klaus's instruction and sat at the front with the petrol tank between his legs. Klaus held on to Tony with his remaining arm and placed his left foot on the gear lever.

"Right, turn the throttle towards you gently, and slowly let out the clutch," he instructed, pointing to what was apparently the clutch. Tony did as instructed but the bike suddenly lurched forward and stalled, nearly throwing both of them to the ground.
"Right, try again, only this time slower," said Klaus patiently. Tony did, but once again the bike lurched forward, cutting out once more. "Ok don't worry - you can do this." said Klaus reassuringly.

But 'don't worry' was easier said than done, since from inside the woodland they could now hear whistles blowing and dogs barking.

"No doubt for us," Klaus said calmly. "Now try again."

With all his concentration and with one hundred percent effort Tony attempted it one more time. Only this time they moved. About six feet before he stalled it once again.

"Shit, shit, shit," said Tony, very much annoyed with his own incompetence. By now the noise from the woods was nearly upon them. "Right, I can do this," Tony said out loud, as he pulled back the throttle and let out the clutch gently. They started to move forward slowly.

As they started to gain pace Klaus shouted, "More throttle, more throttle!" as he crashed it through the gears. Although appreciated, Klaus's encouragement to go faster was not actually necessary, since the Germans who had now appeared out from the trees were doing their best to shoot Tony and Klaus. With shots ringing around their ears, this was as much encouragement as Tony possibly needed to go faster.

As the ping of a bullet ricocheted off the back of the motorbike he threw caution to the wind and opened up the throttle as much as he dared. Tony thought the bike was going to lift off as he accelerated away from the German guards and out of range of their bullets. He considered that he was going recklessly fast, although Klaus kept shouting, "Faster, faster," from behind his ear.

"If you don't get moving, once they get transport they will soon catch us," he shouted, willing Tony to go faster. Tony already felt that he was going like the wind, but Klaus was adamant that it was not quick enough. He concluded that at this speed their only hope of avoiding being caught was to take a few detours. "Left here," Klaus shouted as Tony just about managed to follow his instructions.

"Now right, now right," he instructed again, tugging at Tony's jacket just in case he had forgotten which way was right. Tony turned again, but as he did, the bike skidded on the gravel and they were sent tumbling in a cloud of dust. Klaus winced in pain as the flesh from the remains of his severed arms dragged along the gravel.

"Jesus Christ!" he yelped. "Are you trying to kill us?" he said indignantly.

"I'm sorry, I'm sorry," Tony repeated, as he helped him to his feet.

As he steadied himself Klaus took a deep breath which he exhaled long and hard as he composed himself. "Listen, it's not your fault.

You were riding brilliantly up until then. For a first timer that is,"
he added quickly. "Just remember that you can't steer these things
like a bloody car, you have to lean into a bend to turn. OK?" Tony
nodded, as he picked up the bike. "No damage done...well not to
the bike in any case," said Klaus, grimacing, as he looked down at
the now gravel and dust covered stump that was once his arm.

"I'm sorry," Tony said, feebly trying to apologise once again.

"I'll live," stated Klaus defiantly. "Now let's get going again,
we're not out of the woods yet - If you'd excuse the pun," he
added, trying to raise a smile. Tony smiled back, as he helped
Klaus to get back on to the motorbike. He opened the throttle again
and slowly let out the clutch. Low and behold, this time they
managed to pull off without stalling.
"Well done," said Klaus, patting Tony on the back. "Now turn left
here," he directed once again, although this time adding "slowly,
slowly" as Tony tried to lean into the corner. Tony breathed a sigh
of relief as they successfully negotiated the corner, and very soon
they were off zigzagging through the Polish countryside once
again. After about an hour, Klaus finally concluded that it was now
unlikely that the Germans were still on their trail. He was also
starting to feel the worse for ware and conceded that they would
not make it back to the cottage tonight. They needed to find a barn
or somewhere suitably comfortable to sleep until morning and so
Klaus told Tony to keep an eye open for somewhere appropriate to
crash for the night.

Chapter 14 - A Grey Mare called Chrzan

With darkness approaching Tony spotted what looked like a barn across the fields to his left. Having turned up a small pathway he slowly approached the barn. As they got closer, it became evident that the sound of the motorbike had alerted the occupants of the small farm house next to the barn of their presence. A light came on, quickly followed by the considerable noise of a number of dogs barking. Tony decided to look elsewhere to stop for the night and so endeavoured to turn the bike around on the narrow pathway. He had just about succeeded in getting the bike facing in the right direction when the clutch lever slipped from the grip of his hand and they were catapulted forward straight into a ditch. As the bike hit the base of a large tree with a thud, Klaus winced in pain as he was thrown to the floor.

"When I asked you to find somewhere to crash for the night, I didn't mean you to take it so literally," Klaus groaned. Tony started to apologise as he tried to help him to his feet, however it was clear that the little Austrian was now barely conscious. During the ride Tony hadn't noticed just how much Klaus's condition had deteriorated. He was cold and clammy and Tony guessed that he was going into shock from his wound. Leaning Klaus against the tree, Tony attempted in vain to pull the motorbike from the ditch.

"Who's there?" shouted a voice from the near darkness. "Go away, or I'll set the dogs on you!"

Tony could now make out two snarling German shepherd dogs, being held by a length of rope by who he assumed was the owner of the land.

"I will go once I get my motorbike out of this ditch," Tony told him apologetically. But with that, Klaus collapsed to the floor.

"Your friend is injured? He looks in a bad way," said the farmer, realising the state that Klaus was in. Tony nodded.

"Quickly, get him to his feet. We must get him into the farmhouse," the man instructed. "But I'm warning you any funny business and I'll have the dogs on you," he added as they both struggled to get Klaus on to his feet and into the house. Inside, they were met by the farmer's wife and their two young children, a boy and a girl.

"My name is Thomas Iwanowski and this is my wife Petra," the farmer told Tony, as between them they managed to move Klaus on to a bed. Since they were clearly a Polish family Tony hoped that they would help him and Klaus, once they knew that they were not Germans. Although, since he only spoke German or English, Tony guessed that he might have some difficulty convincing them that he was not the enemy.

"This is a dreadful wound," said the wife as she looked at what was left of Klaus's arm. "Has this just happened with your motorcycle crash?" she asked, concerned that he may have sustained other injuries.

"No, he wasn't injured in the crash, I'm afraid he was shot by German guards earlier today," explained Tony with a little white lie. Although, he had only just met the family, he still didn't feel obliged to admit to the fact that it was his own incompetence that had caused such a mess to Klaus's arm.

"So you are not German?" asked Thomas somewhat surprised.

"No, this is Klaus, who is Austrian and my name is Tony and I'm English," he confirmed.

"English?" exclaimed Thomas. "You are a long way from home young man."

"Further than you think," agreed Tony without elaborating further.

"We have been to Auschwitz today and that is why the Germans had been chasing us and shot Klaus," Tony told Thomas.

"Chasing you?" said Thomas alarmed, "I hope you weren't followed here," he added with concern.

"Don't worry, we lost them some time ago," Tony reassured him, "but I think we also managed to get ourselves lost in the process."

151

"Well, as long as you weren't followed you will be safe here for the night, and we will get you back on your way tomorrow morning," Thomas told him encouragingly. Tony smiled appreciatively. "You mentioned Auschwitz. What were you doing there?" asked Thomas. Tony decided not to burden him with the truth behind his reasons for being there, but explained that he was on a fact finder mission for British intelligence.

"I have heard some pretty appalling rumours about this camp, but I don't know what to believe," Thomas told him.

"Believe me, whatever you have heard is true, only ten times worse," Tony confirmed.

"I guessed as much," stated Thomas. "These Germans have a lot to answer for and will surely get their comeuppance once the war is won," he added. "I'm not surprised they shot your friend, they clearly want to keep it their sordid little secret." Tony nodded in agreement. "It is a good distance from Auschwitz to here, I bet you're starving aren't you?" asked Thomas. Tony again nodded. This time far more enthusiastically, as he was indeed very hungry.

"Petra was just about to give the children their supper. I will serve it up while she tends to your friend. Will you join us?" he asked, indicating that Tony should join the two children who were already sat around a large wooden table in the middle of the kitchen.

"Yes, thank you. That would be wonderful," replied Tony with a smile.

Over some very welcome hot mutton stew Tony elaborated on what they had seen at Auschwitz to Thomas, although he refrained from giving too much detail because of the presence of the children. Thomas said that he was not at all surprised, but was still shocked by Tony's description of the sheer scale of the place. The conversation soon turned to the Iwanowski family as Tony got to know his hosts a little better. They had lived on the farm since Thomas's father had died some ten years ago and had the twins, Halina and Marek two years later. During their meal, Petra occasionally joined them at the table, but kept on disappearing to the adjacent room to tend to Klaus. She was concerned that if she did not get him to a doctor that he would die. Tony assured her that Klaus was a fighter, but he knew that she was right.

Thomas told Tony that there was a doctor in the village, but was concerned that he was known to be a German collaborator and that if they involved him it might be dangerous for all of them. Tony knew if Klaus was to die, then this time it would undoubtedly create the paradox to send him back to 1995, since it would have been him that had killed Klaus. Having seen the atrocities being committed at Auschwitz, Tony was desperate not to let that happen since now, more than ever, he wanted to ensure that the Germans never got their hands on the atomic bomb. Besides, he had grown to like Klaus and did not want to be responsible for taking the life of such a brave man. After all, Klaus had saved his life and all Tony had done to repay him was to shoot him from point blank range! The last thing Tony wanted on his conscience was the fact that he had deprived Klaus's children and indeed his grandchildren of their very existence. Tony knew he could not let that happen and therefore knew that he must succeed.

"Look, I need to get to Koszalin by Wednesday. Is it far from here?" Tony asked.

"No, about an hour drive," replied Petra.

"Good, if I may stay the night I'll set off first thing in the morning on my motorbike," stated Tony, hopeful that somehow he would be able to ride the motorbike on his own.

"I don't think that will be possible," stated Thomas. "I don't know whether you noticed, but the front wheel of your motorbike was very badly buckled," he added.

"I hadn't noticed. I was more concerned about the welfare of Klaus," Tony told him.

"There is a blacksmith in the village, perhaps he could fix it? Mind you, with the limited resources available I'm guessing it would take more than a couple of days before it was up and running again," he added.

"That's it then, it's over. Germany will win the war!" Tony stated despondently.

"You can't say that. No one knows how this bloody war will end," said Thomas defiantly.

"Trust me. I do. If I'm not in Koszalin by the day after tomorrow then the Germans will be victorious and the plight of many more Jews will be in peril," Tony informed him solemnly.

"In that case, you must take the horse," suggested Thomas. Tony had never ridden a horse in his life and the thought of it filled him with dread, but then again, nor had he ridden a motorbike and he was proud of the fact that he had managed to escape from Auschwitz, albeit with a bit of help from Klaus.

"Your horse? But won't you need it to work your farm?" questioned Tony.

"Of course, but if it is as important as you say, then what is my farm compared to the outcome of the war? If there is any truth in what you are saying then you must take it and get yourself to Koszalin." Tony appreciated the gesture and thanked Thomas with all his heart. Tony confirmed that he would set off on horseback first thing in the morning.

"You must get my friend Klaus, to the doctor as soon as I have left," Tony requested. "Don't worry about the doctor being a collaborator, because if I'm successful in my mission then this war will be over very soon. I'm sure that Klaus would then be safe. Just tell the Doctor that Klaus crashed his bike on your driveway, which is nearly the truth after all. Besides, there is nothing to implicate you in any wrong doing. Klaus is a pretty good liar and will corroborate your story," laughed Tony as he instructed Thomas. Tony enjoyed their hospitality for the rest of the evening. Thomas and Petra were poor folk, who enjoyed the simple things in life. Although they had little to their name, what they had they were happy to share. The fact that they were prepared to let Tony ride off in the morning with their one and only horse was testament to their generosity, although it was also down to their hatred of the Germans. They loathed what had happened under the German occupation to their beautiful country.

"If your mission brings an end to this tyranny then losing a horse or even this farm, is a small price to pay," Thomas told Tony. After

Petra had put the children to bed, Tony spent the rest the evening listening to stories of the hardship and suffering that the Germans had inflicted on the Polish people. This strengthened Tony's resolve even further to ensure that the Germans did not win the war. On the assumption that he survived the trip to Koszalin, Tony promised that he would make every effort to return the horse to the Iwanowski family. They joked that they would keep Klaus hostage until he did, but Tony sensed that they had the feeling that they might not see either of them again.

They talked about many things, although Tony refrained from telling them the truth as to where he had come from. His story was always a difficult one to comprehend and the last thing he wanted was for them to doubt his integrity. Instead he told them what a brave man Klaus was, and how he had met and lost the most incredible woman in the world in the last few days. Tony told them that as long as he lived he would always remember Kaska.

That evening was the best night's rest he had since arriving back in 1945 and he fell into a deep sleep as soon as his head hit the pillow. All too soon Tony was woken, but nevertheless refreshed, by the sound of a cockerel. As he wandered into the kitchen, Thomas was already preparing breakfast.

"Good morning, ready for some horse riding lessons young man?" he asked. Tony nodded and greeted him good morning back.

"You're lucky we still have a horse," Thomas stated. "During the winter, times were very harsh and we thought we were going to have to eat her. But we made do and now I'm glad we did," he said with pride. "Please make sure you look after her."

"Don't worry I will," Tony assured him. "I just hope she looks after me," he added, smiling at Thomas. They were soon joined by Petra and the children for breakfast.

"I will take Klaus's breakfast in shortly," said Petra. "He had a fever in the night, but is sleeping now, so we'll let him rest," she suggested. Tony hadn't realised but Petra had stayed up all night, tending to Klaus, keeping his dressing clean and mopping the sweat from his brow as his fever worsened. Tony was most grateful and thanked Petra for her efforts.

"Klaus is a strong man and I'm sure he will live, but we do need to get him to a doctor as soon as possible. I'm worried that otherwise his arm will become gangrenous," she warned. Tony agreed and told her that he would leave as soon as he had finished eating his rather delicious porridge. Once he had finished, Tony thanked Thomas and Petra and went to check on Klaus and say goodbye. Klaus was still sleeping as Tony stood next to his bed. Tony felt quite emotional and despite the fact he was asleep he wished him all the luck in the world and apologised for the mess he had managed to get him into.

"I suspect the next time we will meet will be in 1995 and I promise to buy you the biggest beer you have ever seen in your life," Tony informed the sleeping Klaus. He whispered his final goodbyes and turned quietly to leave the room. However, just as he was about to close the door behind him he heard Klaus's voice.

"I hope you're not thinking of leaving without shaking my hand," said Klaus faintly.

"Errr… of course not, sorry, err, I thought you were fast asleep," Tony replied as he returned to the room, surprised at the fact he was awake after all.

"Well, you will find it attached to a bit of my arm in some woodland near Auschwitz," he said sternly, but at the same time struggling to keep a straight face. Klaus finally broke out into a full blown smile.

"Very funny! At least I didn't manage to dampen your sense of humour," Tony told him, relieved that he seemed to be taking the loss of his arm so well and had clearly gotten over the worst of the fever from the previous night.

"If you don't have a sense of humour, this war would drive you insane," Klaus said, grimacing with pain as he tried to move himself further up the bed. "I hope my supervisor, back in Bernau, also has a good sense of humour when I try to explain why he now has a one armed midget working for him," he said pointing to where his arm should have been. "I have spent years convincing them that I was a humble clerk, not capable of killing a spider, never raising any suspicions. Now look at me!" he moaned.

"I'm so sorry. I really didn't mean to shoot you," Tony said apologetically. "Needless to say, if I fail this mission I will never mention a word of this when I get back to 1995," he added rather pathetically.

"What do you mean, if you fail? You must promise me that you will not fail. You saw Auschwitz didn't you?" Klaus said crossly. "I remember a good Germany before the Nazis. Even if they lose, the German people will rebuild their lives but, if they win I fear for the future of the entire world. Please do not let that happen," he pleaded.

"Look, I have already let you down very badly and I do not intend to do so again. Besides I owe it to Kaska," Tony reassured him.

"Good, now get my bag," he said, weakly pointing to the bag that he permanently wore over his shoulder. Tony picked up the bag, which had been hung over the corner of a chair next to the bed.

"You may find something in there to help you," said Klaus, motioning for Tony to look inside. Tony unbuckled the bag and was amazed to find an alarming arsenal of goodies inside. A gun, two knives, wire cutters, three sticks of dynamite, various fuses and detonators, a compass and, the thing that really caught his eye, a hand grenade.

"My God, you're a one man army," Tony laughed.

"Tools of the trade," he grimaced back, wincing in pain as he tried to move his stump in to a more comfortable position. "Like the look of the grenade then?" asked Klaus, noticing that Tony's eyes had lit up when he saw it. "Pull the pin and throw it, it's a piece of cake," he instructed, encouraging Tony to take it. According to Klaus everything was a piece of cake, but Tony had to admit that he did fancy having a grenade at his disposal. He knew he hadn't had much luck with the gun, but Tony was confident that even he could use a grenade. Tony had always had a good throwing arm and knowing the way these things exploded, he guessed that he didn't even need to be that accurate.

"Just remember that once you pull that pin, you have just ten seconds to get it as far away from you as possible," Klaus advised him. So Tony thanked Klaus and took the hand grenade, the compass, and also a knife, more for its practical value, rather than his desire to get involved in hand to hand combat.

"I must be going shortly," Tony informed him, and once he had finished arming himself with Klaus's 'goodies,' Tony thanked Klaus again and told him that everything would turn out fine.

"I'm sure it will – I have every faith in Jakub, Ludwik and Damek," he laughed, reminding Tony that he wasn't the only one trying to stop the blue-prints changing hands. Tony laughed in agreement with him.

"Let's just say, I'm the last chance saloon, if all else fails," Tony suggested.

"You can say that again. Just make sure you don't blow Jakub and the others to smithereens with that grenade of mine."

"That's not funny, you know I didn't mean..." Tony started to argue.

"I was joking, I was joking!" Klaus responded stopping Tony in mid flight. "I was just having a bit of 'armless' fun," he said, smiling at his own bad joke. "Look, I know you didn't shoot me on purpose. Guns are dangerous things in the wrong hands and I should have been more careful. At the end of the day, it's wartime and in wars people get hurt. Please don't worry about it, OK?" he asked. Tony nodded in agreement.

"If you want to make amends just make sure that you and the men finish the job properly this time," he added. Tony assured Klaus that they would. They talked for a while longer, before Tony told him that he now needed to go and change the future.

"If all goes well, I will see you back in 1995. Until then, be lucky," Tony told him as he turned to leave.

"I was lucky. Until I met you!" he added, raising a smile again. Tony smiled back and left the room. Outside, Thomas had saddled up the horse; a beautiful grey mare called Chrzan, and brought it out into the yard.

"My God, she's huge," said Tony, as he saw the size of his predicament.

"Yep, we'd have certainly eaten well last winter had we killed her," Thomas laughed.

"Don't worry though, she is a very placid animal and very easy to ride," he added. Tony thought that Thomas was being a bit optimistic, given his total lack of horsemanship. In fact the only thing he'd ever ridden before was a donkey on the beach at Blackpool, when he was eight. Even that had scared the living daylights out of him!

"Right, Tony, climb aboard," Thomas instructed.

Oh well, here goes, Tony thought to himself as he took a run and jump at the horse. Up. On…and straight off the other side much to the amusement of Thomas, Petra and the children. Three attempts later and Tony was finally sat astride Chrzan and receiving a round of applause from his spectators.

"That's the easy bit," laughed Thomas, "now all we need to do is get her to move."

How hard could getting a horse to move be? Tony wondered to himself. And so, trying to show a bit of initiative, he jerked the reins and shouted 'Gee up'. Chrzan just stood there defiantly. Move it, Giddy Up, Yahoo, Yee Haw and even a few German words also all failed to have an impact on the stupid horse, but amused the watching Iwanowski family.

"You must remember this is a Polish horse and therefore she only speaks Polish," laughed Thomas. "Try the word 'Wio!' and you might have a bit more luck," he added. So with another jerk of the reins Tony shouted 'Wio!' and lo and behold, the horse started to move around the courtyard. Thomas gave Tony a few more useful Polish words that he assured him Chrzan would understand and before long Tony was confidently trotting around the farm. Tony did manage to fall off once, when he got a bit too ambitious by trying to jump a small gate, but by the time he was finished Tony was confident of making it to Koszalin. With time being critical, Tony decided that he should make haste and leave. He gathered his belongings, including his newly acquired hand grenade. Petra handed him some freshly baked bread and a container of water, which Tony duly thanked her for. He also thanked them all for their hospitality and promised once again to look after Chrzan.

The family wished him luck and waved enthusiastically until he trotted out of their sight. Tony knew that if he was to reach Koszalin by nightfall that he would pretty much have to ride all day. The aim would be to find somewhere near to the co-ordinates to sleep and then search out the others first thing in the morning. As he rode, Tony had plenty of time to contemplate the enormity of what he was trying to do. Since the future of Europe, if not the world, was in his hands he was determined to succeed in his task. Tony knew that tomorrow he must be stronger and more resolved than he'd ever been in his life. The future of millions of people depended on what was going to happen tomorrow and the last thing Tony wanted on his conscience was the fact that he had failed mankind.

Chapter 15 - Paradoxical Ripples.

Karl Smith was born in Leeds in 1981. Although only fourteen years old, he was already nearly six foot tall, with a lean muscular physique. With his blonde hair and blue eyes, he was already growing into a handsome young man. Not only was Karl good looking, but he also had the brains to go with it. He was now in the fourth form of the Heinrich Himmler Mittelschule in Leeds and was already being fast tracked to go to one of the top Universities. He hoped that one day he would be a scientist just like his father. Given Karl's academic prowess, there was no reason not to believe that one day he would even surpass his fathers' achievements.

In fact you could say he was the perfect pupil. He was popular with his classmates and found friends easy to come by. The teachers also found him a pleasure to teach, rarely did his grades deviate from straight A's. Karl had everything going for him. A nice house, lots of friends and a school he loved going to.

Heinrich Himmler Mittelschule was renowned for being one of the best schools in the country. They excelled in both academic results and in sports. The German government ensured that their top employees were well looked after, and since Karl's father was one of their top scientists he certainly came under this category. Most schools were good, but this school was exceptional and both Karl and his father considered it a privilege that Karl was able to go there. Karl now found himself following the school prefect, and heading at great haste to the headmasters office. As he walked, Karl pondered what he could have done wrong. It was very unusual indeed for anyone to interrupt lessons and it was even rarer for Karl to be in any sort of trouble. Once he got to the office, he knocked on the door.

"Come," shouted the headmaster from inside the room. Karl marched ceremoniously into the office and stood to attention.

"Thank you for coming so quickly Karl," said the head. "Please take a seat," he added.

"Yes, Sir. Thank you, mein Lehrer," Karl responded in his customary military manner.

"At ease, please Karl," instructed the headmaster.

"Yes, Sir. Thank you, Sir," said Karl, still rather formally.

"Karl, I haven't a clue why, but there is a military jet waiting at Leeds airport to take you to the Eastern Provinces. I have instructions to get you to the airport without delay," the headmaster told him.

"The Eastern Provinces?" exclaimed Karl, "that's miles away! What about the parade, this Saturday?" he asked, alarmed that he might not be back in time.

"Unfortunately, whatever they want you for is apparently far more important than the celebration parade. It's a matter of national security," he added, without pausing for breath.

"What can be more important than representing Yorkstein in the victory parade in London?" Karl questioned, now getting agitated that he was going miss out on one of the proudest moments in his life.

"All I know is that the instructions have come from the highest level," said the headmaster, pausing to look out of his window. "Take a look at this," he said, beckoning Karl to come forward. Karl approached the window, and they both looked out in amazement, as a huge convoy of police bikes and cars, all with their blue lights flashing and sirens wailing, came up the long driveway to the school.

"Bloody hell, Karl. Whatever they want you for is big. Very big!" said the headmaster nervously. "Remember you are representing Heinrich Himmler Mittelschule, so make sure you are on your best behaviour," he added.

"Of course, mein Lehrer" said Karl, now somewhat daunted by that fact that all this fuss appeared to be for him.

In Bernau town hall, the paradoxical ripples of Tony's actions back in 1945 had caused a great deal of debate amongst those monitoring his progress. It was evident that Tony's primary mission to save Adolf Hitler had failed, since the history books still recorded his suicide in a bunker near Berlin. Furthermore, there was no mention of anyone materialising in front of the Führer during his visit to Bernau. It was therefore apparent to all those gathered in 1995 that something had gone wrong. The question was what? The 'spotters' had been busy continually comparing the documents in the stasis chamber with those in the plain glass cabinet. They laboriously scrutinised page after page to spot even the minutest of changes in the time-line, hoping that whatever they found would give them a clue as to what had happened to Tony Smith back in 1945.

They even considered the fact that Tony could be dead, vaporised into a million particles by his own time-machine. But as they debated this prospect a monumental change took place. Whilst they had been scanning the small print, it was the headlines that were suddenly different!

"Oh my God!" shouted one of the 'spotters,' as he beckoned everyone around him to witness what he had found. "Look at this," he exclaimed as he pointed to the cover of one of the many history books in the Stasis chamber. The cover of the book in the chamber showed a picture of an emaciated woman chained to the metal gate of Berlin, whist the book outside the stasis field, was showing a picture reminiscent of Hans Baur's spectacular view of the first atomic explosion over Cyprus.

The name of Kaska Galinski had completely disappeared from the history books. Herman Swartz had still been killed getting the blue-prints to the SS, but history did not record who had killed him, just stating that a number of unknown Polish terrorists had been killed in the fierce battle that had taken place just outside Koszalin. It caused a great deal of debate amongst the powers that be. Why had Tony Smith deviated from the original plan? Since he had obviously failed to save Hitler, had he taken it upon himself to try and save Herman Swartz? Who was this Kaska Galinski, and why did she no longer kill Herman Swartz? Had Tony Smith killed her? If Tony Smith had killed Kaska Galinski, why hadn't he reappeared in 1995? They had no answers to these questions and were therefore very uneasy with the situation.

They were sure that Tony's intentions would be good, whatever he might be doing. However, it still unnerved them that they had no way of knowing what he was doing or, more alarmingly, planning to do next. The last thing they wanted was a loose-cannon, running amuck back in 1945. Especially seeing as he had now already proved, quite dramatically, that he could change history. Although they were confident that they could trust Tony Smith, they also knew that his actions in the past could inadvertently affect their lives now. Even threatening their very existence. Needless to say, this made them somewhat agitated. As the debate continued there was suddenly a commotion from another one of the 'spotters'.

Whilst scanning the photograph, taken just before Tony had disappeared back to 1945, he had noticed something very peculiar. He had summoned his supervisor, who in turn had requested the presence of his manager. The three of them were scratching their heads at what they were seeing, but there was no mistake. One of the people in the photograph had inexplicably lost an arm. In the first picture the man was standing next to Tony Smith with his hand clearly visible by his side, whereas in the second his shirt was neatly folded and pinned just above the elbow. More people gathered around the two glass chambers, until one of them recognised the little bald man with the round glasses, it was Klaus Zimmerman!

This set even bigger alarm bells ringing amongst the hierarchy. Their fears had now been realised, a paradox created by Tony Smith back in 1945 had now affected someone involved in the experiment back in 1995. Klaus was immediately fetched from his home and asked to explain how his appearance had somehow managed to change so drastically in the two photographs. At first Klaus pleaded ignorance, saying he couldn't remember since it happened fifty years ago! However, the officials were not impressed with his memory, since losing an arm is not something you forget in a hurry, however long ago it was. They therefore threatened Klaus, that if he wasn't more forthcoming with his answers, they would have no alternative but to involve the SS. Klaus, although now in his seventies, was not about to let on what happened all those years ago.

"You can get whoever you want, but I have nothing to tell them," he said stubbornly.

"Why won't you tell us?" they asked.

"Tony Smith has already done something in the past which has cost you your arm. There's no knowing what other damage he could do!" argued one of the Government officials. "You're not in trouble, we just need to know what Tony Smith is doing back in 1945."

"Before he does something that destroys us all!" added a second official.

"Look, whatever happened or is about to happen, is going to happen anyway," argued Klaus, bewildering the gathered officials. "You cannot stop Tony Smith doing whatever he is destined to do back in 1945. If he succeeds then you will know about it sooner or later, if not, then it serves no purpose me telling you more than you need to know."

With that Klaus reached into his pocket and pulled out a small white capsule. Before anyone realised what Klaus was doing he had already swallowed the cyanide. Very quickly his body went into convulsions and in no time at all he was dead. Klaus had always known that this was a possibility and so had decided to take precautions. What he also knew was that his body was riddled with cancer and had little time left anyway. In typical Klaus fashion he had not wished to trouble anyone else with this fact. He knew if he ever got questioned about Tony Smith then it would implicate himself as to being a traitor all those years ago. This would not only cause great embarrassment, but possibly endanger his entire family. He also wanted to spare them from his suffering as the cancer took over his body and couldn't stand the thought of being a burden. Either way, he had planned to take his life if the situation arose.

The officials were now mortified that Tony Smith was going to do something to destroy the world as they knew it. They still had no idea what he might be planning to do, but felt that it most likely revolved around Herman Swartz. They already knew about Kaska, from the changing history books and now, having checked Klaus's medical records, they found that he had spent two months in a Polish Hospital just south of Koszalin at the end of the war. This all pointed to Herman Swartz.

Since his death, or more specifically, his getting the blue-prints to the SS, was the pivotal moment in the Germans winning the war, they knew that they could not afford to ignore the fact that Tony Smith might just be planning something to jeopardise this historic event taking place. They had to do something and do it quickly. It was lucky therefore that they had a contingency plan. Hence they had sent for Karl.

Chapter 16 - Karl's Mission.

Karl Smith was somewhat bewildered. He didn't have a clue why, but he suddenly found himself in a military jet flying across the German Channel to the Eastern Provinces.

The man who had met him at Leeds Airport had insisted that he couldn't tell him what it was all about, but stated that he did know it was of national significance. He had told Karl, that he would be briefed as soon as he got to the airfield at Koszalin in the Eastern Provinces.

It had dawned on Karl that it may have something to do with his father, since he worked for the Government and he had told him that something historic could happen by this weekend, but what his father could have done to warrant them sending for him in such a dramatic fashion totally bemused Karl.

Since he was clueless as to why he now found himself in this situation, Karl decided that he might as well sit back and enjoy it. One hour ago he was sitting in class studying Economics and now, here he was, sitting in a Stukajet fighter plane, flying at the speed of sound to Europe. It was certainly exciting, although Karl felt that he would enjoy the experience a little more if he knew what all this was about.

As the plane approached the runway, out of his window Karl could once again see a line of police vehicles, all with their blue lights flashing, parked at the side of the airport building. He concluded that they were no doubt waiting to forward him on to his destination.

Indeed, no sooner had the plane engines been shut down that Karl was being rushed in convoy at breakneck speed to the Police HQ in Koszalin.

As the procession of vehicles screeched to a halt outside the impressive steps of the police building, Karl was greeted by

Wolfgang Kustaft, the commandant of the German Police force in the Eastern Provinces.

"Karl, I thank you very much for coming so quickly" he started.

"I didn't really have much choice" Karl complained.

"Arr, yes, I'm sorry about all the secrecy. I guess you are wondering what all this fuss is about, aren't you?."

"You can say that again," exclaimed Karl.

"Come inside to my office and I will explain, but please do not worry, you are not in any sort of trouble. In fact, far from it" confirmed the commandant reassuringly.

"Thank goodness for that, I thought maybe someone had spotted me smoking behind the bike shed," said Karl, in a half hearted attempt at a joke.

"Smoking behind the bike shed?" said the commandant slightly bemused. "Arrr yes, I see now - very funny" he said acknowledging Karl's attempt at humour, but at the same time hardly cracking a smile. "No, the reason you are here is to ensure the future of the German Republic" he said very seriously.

"Oh, is that all!" said Karl, again, trying to make light of the situation. "I thought it was going to be something important," he added, in order to reiterate his joke.

"But it is important......oh I see, yes very funny – I have heard about you Englanders and your sense of humour" he said, this time almost, but still not quite, smiling.

"No more jokes please, Karl. You see, we do not have much time and you have a very important mission," he said, removing the hint of a smile, which had never actually managed to materialise on his face.

"As I said, please come inside to my office and I will explain further" instructed the commandant.

Karl followed Wolfgang Kustaft up the steps and in to the impressive building which was Koszalin Police HQ.

Once in his office the commandant began....

"Your father – Tony Smith..."

"I knew this would have something to do with him" exclaimed Karl.

"Yes, your father – Tony Smith needs your help"

"Why what's happened to him? Where is he?" he questioned, now alarmed that his father could be in danger.

"Karl, it's not so much a matter of where your father is – it is when that is important."

"Sorry, I don't understand" Karl apologised.

"You see Karl, your father has invented a Temporal Energy Separation System."

"A temporal what?" questioned Karl.

"A Temporal Energy Separation System, or to the likes of me and you, a time machine."

"A time machine!?" repeated Karl loudly, not quite believing what he was hearing. "But that's impossible" he added.

"Apparently not!" replied Wolfgang Kustaft. "As we speak, your father is somewhere close to here, but back in 1945!"

"1945? That was when the war ended. Is this some sort of joke?!" Karl questioned, but given his lack of a sense of humour and the dour look on his face he guessed that Wolfgang Kustaft was incapable of telling a joke.

"No, not a joke" confirmed Kustaft.

"You're telling me that my father has invented a time machine?" he questioned once more.

"Yes, that is the truth" said the commandant.

"Wow, how cool's that. He will be famous. Very famous in fact" said Karl, smiling broadly.

"Yes he will be, Karl, and so will you."

"Why, what have I done?" Karl asked, starting to worry.

"Your fathers mission in 1945 was to save Adolf Hitler from committing suicide" said the commandant.

"Wow, cool mission" said Karl, starting to think just how famous (and rich) something like that would make his father.

"The problem is Karl, something has gone wrong! Tony has not managed to save Hitler, but he has affected our time-line" the commandant continued.

Karl suddenly didn't like the sound of this.

"According to the history books before your father went back in time, a lady called Kaska Galinski, was blamed for killing Herman Swartz, and subsequently paid with her life as punishment. But now her name has disappeared without trace from the records" he informed Karl.

"But I've never heard of Kaska Galinski and I know everything there is to know about Herman Swartz. I'm doing a project all about him at school" Karl told the commandant.

"You see in our time-line she did not kill him, but before Tony went back she did. So Tony must have done something to stop her killing him."

"So my father's trying to save Herman Swartz's life then?" Karl questioned excitedly.

"At first, that's what we thought, but a gentleman called Klaus Zimmerman, has put a certain amount of doubt in our minds. We fear that your father might be trying to kill Herman Swartz or stop him succeeding in getting the blue-prints of the Atomic bomb to the SS."

"Never! My father would not do such a thing. Herman Swartz was a hero, why would my father wish to kill him?" Karl shouted angrily.

"I can understand you not wishing to believe this, Karl, but we believe that the Polish resistance may have got to your father somehow and maybe have even tortured him in to helping them" the commandant answered.

"But my father wouldn't help them! He'd never betray the German Republic" argued Karl, in the defence of his father.

"This might be the case Karl. But we don't know for sure what he is going to do; he might even be still trying to save Herman Swartz's life. The fact is, we don't know. And we simply cannot take the risk of doing nothing. Do you know what it would mean if Herman Swartz did not succeed in getting those documents to the SS, as history tells us he did?" he asked.

"Germany would not have the World's first atomic bomb?" answered Karl.

"Indeed. And if Germany does not have the first Atomic bomb?"

"They would not win the war?" answered Karl, stating the obvious.

"Very good" said the commandant. "And if Germany does not win the war?" he added.

"I would be speaking with a slightly different accent" said Karl, trying to think of a witty answer.

"Maybe, maybe not" said the commandant. "Let me ask you this Karl - where did your father meet your mother?"

"How would I know - I wasn't born" Karl answered indignantly.

"Let me tell you Karl – Your father met your mother at the Goring Research Centre in London, whilst they were both working for the Government."

"So?" said Karl, not following the purpose of his question or his answer.

"Do you think they would have been working for the German Government in London if the Germans had not have won the war?"

"No, I suppose not, but what's that got to do with me?" Karl again asked, not quite sure what the commandant was getting at.

"I assume you do know the facts of life, Karl? You know…, the birds and the bees and all that stuff?" Wolfgang Kustaft, rather sarcastically.

"Of course, I am 14 you know." said Karl, losing patience with his questioning.

"So Karl, you obviously realise that if your mother and father don't meet – then 'whoosh' you no longer exist. In fact you will have never existed!"

"Oh…I see" said Karl, somewhat embarrassed about his previous failure to grasp the situation.

"So speaking with a slightly different accent Karl would be the least of your troubles. The chances are that there would not be a Karl Smith at all!" he told him bluntly.

My mother and father met as part of the de-contamination unit working in Crete. Do you think they would have been in Crete if Germany had not dropped the first Atomic bomb there?" the commandant asked rather sternly.

"No, I suppose not" said Karl, realising what he was getting at.

"So whoosh – then I also no longer exist!" exclaimed the commandant. "You see Karl, many millions of people will not have existed or be living as they are today if Herman Swartz does not deliver those documents! Millions of lives will change and it will not be for the better, I can guarantee that. And for many, like us Karl, it will be a disaster!"

"I understand all this now, but what has it got to do with me? I can't help anyone." Karl said apologetically.

"Arr, but you can Karl, you most definitely can." said Wolfgang Kustaft, smiling for the first time.

"Sorry, but I don't understand" said Karl, apologising once again. Completely mystified as to why the commandant thought he could possibly help.

"You see, Karl, we found a program under your name on your father's computer. It was identical, other than some slight differences in the DNA profile, to the one that Tony used to send himself back to 1945. We also found his diary notes and it would appear from them that he had originally planned to make you the first person to ever travel back in time. However, at the last minute he changed his mind because he thought it was too risky. Instead he wrote a second program to send himself back, hence he is now in 1945 and you are still here."

Not wishing to seem too stupid Karl just nodded, but he was still unsure how he could now help. "I see, but what has that got to do with me now?" he asked, still managing to appear stupid after all!

"As it happens, we have run the program with your name on it and we are convinced it will work."

"What, you mean to send me back in time as well?" asked Karl, as the penny finally dropped.

"Ten out of ten, Karl!" said Wolfgang Kustaft.

"We have transported the time-machine from Bernau to here in Koszalin. In fact it is right here in this building. All we need now is our time traveller."

"And that's me." replied Karl, stating the obvious.

"Absolutely." confirmed Wolfgang Kustaft.

"But what about the Celebrations in London this weekend? I'm meant to be leading my school in the victory march." complained Karl, still failing to grasp the severity of the situation.

"Karl, if you are not successful, then there will be no victory parade, in fact there won't even be a Heinrich Himmler Mittelschule! Do you understand, Karl?"

Karl nodded.

"But what good will I be back in 1945? How can I help save Herman Swartz?" asked Karl, not exactly feeling confident that he was up to the task.

"Did you or did you not win the Yorkstein Hitler Youth Cup for marksmanship?"

Karl again nodded.

"Have you or have you not, spent the last three years in the Hitler Youth Army Cadets?

"I have," Karl confirmed.

"So Karl, it seems to me that you are just the man for the job" affirmed Wolfgang Kustaft, trying to instil Karl with confidence.

"You see Karl, not only are you the right man for the job – you're the only man. Your father spent years encoding your DNA into the program and since we do not have the luxury of time on our hands, we cannot program it to send one of our agents back. There are only two people in the world that can travel in time. One is already in 1945 and the other…"

"Is me!" said Karl completing the commandant's sentence.

"Exactly" confirmed Wolfgang Kustaft. "I know you're only a boy, but I've heard very good reports about you. I have every confidence that you will succeed in your mission." he told Karl encouragingly.

"Which is what?" asked Karl, who was now resigned to the fact that he was about to become the world's second ever time traveller, whether he wanted to or not.

"Karl, your mission is to ensure that the exchange of the blue-prints takes place. As simple as that."

"And how am I meant to do that?" Karl asked impertinently.

"Just put to use everything you have learnt at your military school training. We know you can do it. To help, we have already sent a little something back to 1945. You see, your father is not the only clever person. Since your father has been gone, we have had a team of scientists writing code to send a couple of items back in time. We are confident that once you arrive in 1945 you will find a set of clothes and more importantly a gun! Now, admittedly it's pretty basic in design, since we had to cut down on the component parts for ease of programming. But take it from me, it is still far more advanced than anything they had in 1945. It is laser guided to help with your accuracy. In fact, once you see the red dot on your target then it's pretty difficult to miss" he assured him. "However, remember you will only have about a dozen bullets, so do not go shooting people indiscriminately."

"Now listen carefully. Everything you do in 1945 will have a consequence in the present. If you do something whilst in the past that radically changes the future - it is called a paradox. If you kill someone in the past, then you also effectively kill their children, their children's children and so on. The paradoxical effects could be far reaching, so use your bullets wisely. Having said that, the success of your mission is paramount so if anyone does try to stop you, then do not be afraid to use your gun and kill them if necessary. We can worry about the consequences afterwards. And by anyone - I mean anyone. And that includes your father!" instructed Wolfgang Kustaft.

"What? You expect me to kill my own father?" asked Karl, somewhat taken aback by the very suggestion that he could shoot his own dad.

"Look, it is possible that the resistance may have got to your father, even brainwashed him. If so, you must not let him destroy those documents. Remember both our lives and countless others depend on it."

"My father is very clever - he would know that if he destroyed those papers then I would not exist. He's hardly going to do that to his own son is he?" asked Karl.

"Look we do not know the state of mind that your father is in. All we are saying is that you must be prepared for any eventuality. You must do whatever is necessary to succeed!"

"Be strong, even if your father tries to convince you otherwise. It is your father's theory that if you create such a paradox, that you will find yourself back here in 1995. So even if he does die in 1945, the paradox that it would create should send him alive and well, back to 1995. Once here then we can help him."

"Has anyone ever done that before?" questioned Karl, already knowing that the answer was an obvious NO.

"Of course not" replied Wolfgang, "but it was a theory your father was convinced about – and as you have said, he is a very clever man."

"What about me? What happens if I get hurt or even killed? Do I come zapping back?" asked Karl.

"Yes, in theory you do. But if you fail and the documents are destroyed, then the only place you will zap to is absolute nothingness. We all will! You do understand the importance of your mission, don't you?"

"Yes sir, absolutely sir" said Karl, standing to attention.

"Good, then it's time for you to go. Follow me young man," instructed the commandant as he led Karl out of his office.

As they walked, Wolfgang Kustaft gave Karl a bit of a briefing. He explained that the town of Koszalin had somewhat grown since 1945 and that where they were now, would have been nothing but open fields in 1945.

"We should be some three miles due west from where Herman Swartz was killed" he explained to Karl.

"I'm afraid that the only way that it is possible to time travel is naked, but remember when you get back to 1945 there should be a pile of clothes already there waiting for you" he told him reassuringly. "You should arrive in the morning of the day on which Herman Swartz died and will therefore have approximately six hours to complete your mission" the commandant advised him.

"Save Herman Swartz if you can, but more importantly make sure those documents survive" he reiterated to Karl.

"Right we are here" advised the Commandant, as they arrived at one of the stations conference rooms.

In the room there were a number of technicians each dressed in the customary white coat, as well as plenty of military personnel and a few important Government officials. Karl was even introduced to the Lord Mayor of Koszalin.

The men in uniforms were wishing him luck, whilst the technicians were frantically rushing around, making sure the equipment was all working.

Karl was ordered to strip off, which he found rather embarrassing, although Wolfgang Kustaft encouraged him, saying that what he was doing was for the whole of the German Republic and that he would go down in history as a great hero.

Karl was asked to sit on a chair and then had an assortment of wires and electrodes attached to various parts of his body.

The machine whirled into action and Karl sat there nervously, not knowing what to expect. He heard Wolfgang Kustaft wish him luck and then suddenly he was blinded by a flash of light.

Karl felt himself fall backwards, landing on what felt like wet grass. He was utterly disorientated, with his head spinning and feeling extremely nauseous. As he lay there on the grass he brought his knees up to his chest and curled into a little ball like a sleeping baby. He hoped that wherever he now found himself that he was alone, since he would have been acutely embarrassed if there was anyone else there to witness such a pathetic display. He tried to open his eyes, but each time he did, it felt like he was about to throw up. It must have been nearly five minutes before the feeling of sickness disappeared and he could actually keep his eyes open.

Karl knew one thing for sure, that he was no longer in Koszalin Police HQ. As his senses returned he saw that he was in the middle of a field, and as promised by Wolfgang Kustaft, next to a pile of clothes and a gun already sent back from 1995.

Karl was indeed relieved to find that he was alone and that the only things there to witness his 'embarrassing reaction' were a couple of startled horses. To spare his blushes further, and so not to embarrass the horses, he quickly got dressed into the clothes. They were not like any clothes he had seen before. The design was very plain and they had been made from just one fabric, which was black and slightly elasticised. There were no zips, buttons, belts, or any other distinguishing features. He assumed this was to keep the time spent programming down to a minimum. Although the result was not very pleasing to the eye – he was at least relieved that he wouldn't have to roam around the countryside naked.

Karl saw that the gun was also very simple and was made entirely of stainless steel. Despite not exactly being stylish, he assumed that it would be functional. He picked it up and toyed with it for a while. Taking aim at one of the horses, Karl could see the red dot of the laser sight, flickering directly between its eyes. Rather mischievously Karl shouted the word 'Bang' as loud as he could. The startled horse, reared up on its hind legs, before running off at great speed in the opposite direction, much to Karl's amusement.

Karl liked the idea of having a gun, although deep down, he hoped he could complete his mission without having to use it, especially on his father!

Wolfgang Kustaft had told him that he needed to head east, so taking his bearing from the position of the sun in the sky (he always knew his attendance at the military academy would come in handy one day), Karl set off to find his father and save the German Empire!

Chapter 17 – Herman's Ambush.

Having spent the previous day travelling by horseback, Tony Smith had been pretty exhausted by the time he found a haystack to bury himself in for the night. His plan had been to get as close as possible to Koszalin before stopping, but having lost his bearings half way through the day, he now awoke to the realisation that he had no idea where he was or how far he had travelled. He had the destiny of the entire world resting on his shoulders and he was utterly lost. He knew he had been heading north from Klaus's compass, but how far north was anyone's guess. To make matters worse, he was not only lost, but his body felt like it had gone fifteen rounds with Max Schmeling, the German Republic heavy weight champion. Every muscle in his body ached from spending the whole of yesterday riding a horse. Talking of Chrzan, Tony wondered where the hell the horse was now? When they had arrived the night before, Tony had thought that Chrzan was as exhausted as he was. He had therefore assumed that she wouldn't venture far and would still be around come the morning. But clearly Chrzan had other ideas and now the morning had arrived there was no sign of her. Tony was concerned that without Chrzan, his chances of reaching Koszalin were somewhat diminished, although given the way his body ached, he was also relieved that he wouldn't have to ride her again today. In fact, if he never saw another horse again in his life, it wouldn't be too soon.

After washing in a nearby stream, Tony set off on foot. With Herman Swartz due to hand over the blueprints some time later today, he knew that if he was to have any chance of stopping him then it would be more by luck than judgement. Given his current predicament, he just hoped that Jakub, Ludwik and Damek were more reliable than he was and would complete the task in hand, with or without him. Having walked for about an hour, Tony stopped to rest. In the distance he could hear a vehicle. He knew that walking was hopeless and sooner or later he would need transport, so he decided to flag it down and get a lift or, at the very least, find out where he was. If they were German, he hoped that some of Klaus's bluffing skills might have rubbed off on him and that, if questioned, he would be able to convince them that he was a reporter on the way to the front. As the sound of the vehicle got louder, Tony got more nervous. He had never been a good liar. As the vehicle drew near Tony realised that the noise of the engine actually sounded familiar. As he listened intently, a sudden loud bang once again had him jumping out of his skin. He now remembered this sound so well, it was the truck that Kaska was driving when he was first liberated from the Germans. Tony jumped up and started waving his arms frantically. The truck screeched to a halt in front of him.

"It's OK, it's Ok!" shouted Jakub, instructing Ludwik and Damek to put their machine guns down, as they appeared from under the canvas at the back of the truck."It's our friend Tony Smith. Are you trying to get yourself killed, Tony? Where's Klaus?" he also asked, before Tony had chance to answer the first question. Tony explained that he had left Klaus at a farmhouse and told them about his arm, although he refrained from telling them that it was him that shot Klaus! He told them what he had seen at Auschwitz and how it had made him determined to make sure the Germans did not win the war.

"Well, if there is any truth in your story, then you do realise that today is the day," stated Ludwik as he stepped out of the back of the truck.

"I know, that's why I am here," Tony reassured him.

"You have done well to get here," said Damek, as he also joined them from the back of the truck.

"If I'm honest I'm not even sure where I am," Tony said, reluctantly admitting that he was lost.

Ludwik laughed as he informed Tony that they were no more than half a mile away from the co-ordinates that Tony had given them a couple of days ago. Tony told them about his horse ride the previous day and how the dumb animal had abandoned him in the night. They laughed, and Ludwik informed Tony that they had passed a grey mare heading in the opposite direction some hours ago.

"Obviously didn't think much of your company," he laughed again.

Jakub pulled out the map and proceeded to show Tony where they were.

"We're here," he said pointing to the map. "Just up here is where this road joins the one coming from Slupsk," he said, at the same time demonstrating by moving his finger along the page. "As you can see, this is also where it crosses the stream and my guess is that there will be a bridge here," he said, tapping his finger on the map.

"Yes, and a bridge is as good a place as any to set an ambush," added Ludwik, smiling and waving a stick of dynamite at Tony.

"Besides the grid reference for the bridge is W2543 N1358, which is pretty much where you said he'd be; so we don't want to upset the future historians by making their books all wrong, do we?" said Jakub smiling at Tony. With that he turned to Ludwik and Damek and told them that here was also as good as any place to hide the truck and that they would travel the rest of the way on foot. As usual Jakub's orders were carried out quickly and efficiently. Pretty soon all the men were walking along the road, carrying an assortment of weapons and explosives.

"Since you are here, you might as well make yourself useful," instructed Jakub pointing to a box of ammunition for Tony to carry. With his aching limbs he was struggling to carry himself, let alone a box of heavy bullets. However, Tony didn't argue, since he did not wish to appear to be a burden to the men. He still felt that he had something to prove to them, especially Damek, and therefore struggled on, despite his discomfort. Since he had started to lag behind a little, by the time Tony got to their destination Jakub and the others had already started to set explosives to each side of the bridge.

"This is perfect," said Damek enthusiastically, at the same time finding a place to position his machine gun. Jakub agreed, and very soon the trap was laid.

"Since we're not sure how he will be travelling we must be prepared for every eventuality," said Ludwik. "If he's in a truck, or a car we blow the bridge. If he's on a motorbike we bring him down with the wire" he said, demonstrating with a tug on the wire that had been laid across the road.

"If he's on foot, then we just blow his brains out," he said, this time gesturing with his machine gun.

"What happens if he's in a tank?" said Jakub.

"Shit, I hadn't thought of that," said Ludwik with a worried look on his face.

"I'm joking you idiot! Where the hell do you think he's going to get a tank from?"

"There is a war going on, so you never know what he might find lying around." said Ludwik defending his original answer.

Jakub then looked over to Tony.

"He didn't have a tank, did he Tony?" he asked in all seriousness.

"Not that I can remember. But the history books did say that he managed to give the blue-prints to the SS after he had been shot, so I guess that Herman Swartz will not be the only one we have to worry about," he warned them.

"If Herman Swartz dies here, then the SS must already be on their way here from Kosalin to meet him," said Jakub.

"Or maybe he is already being escorted by them," added Ludwik.

"Either way, we must be ready for them," commanded Jakub.

"Tony, you may need this," he said tossing him a hand gun.

"Erm…I'd rather not, if you don't mind," Tony said apologetically. The last thing he wanted to do was to shoot one of his own men again. "I've got this instead," he said, taking the hand grenade out of his jacket and displaying it, like a school boy showing off his prize conker.

"Impressive!" said Jakub. "One of Klaus's by any chance?" he added. Tony nodded.

"I hope you know what you are doing, since I've seen what one of them things can do to a man. And if it's one of Klaus's you can guarantee that he's tinkered with it to make it ten times more powerful."

"Don't you worry about me," Tony responded with a certain amount of bravado, although in reality he was now a little concerned that he had just spent the whole of the previous day, bouncing up and down on a horse, with a 'home-made' bomb about an inch away from his chest!

"I suggest we get in position," Jakub commanded. And as if by magic, the men quickly merged into their surroundings.

"What about me? What do you want me to do?" Tony asked.

"Here, take this" Jakub tossed Tony a silver cigarette lighter.

"Whatever happens to us, you must get hold of those blue- prints and make sure they go up in smoke. OK?" Again, Tony nodded in agreement.

"Good, now make yourself invisible and wait for all hell to break loose."

Tony quickly hid himself in the ditch alongside the road, pulling whatever grass and foliage he could over himself for camouflage. Given their original scepticism, the men were now lying in wait to ambush Hermann Swartz. If they still doubted the validity of Tony's story they were certainly not showing it. Tony got the impression that each and every one of them genuinely believed that the appearance of Hermann Swartz was as sure as night follows day. Tony just hoped that he had remembered Klaus' co-ordinates correctly. So they waited and waited. Tony was starting to get impatient hanging around doing absolutely nothing.

It was only midday, but already the time was beginning to drag. He only wished that we knew what time Herman Swartz was destined to arrive. His mind was beginning to wander, thinking of Kaska and also wondering what was happening back in 1995, when he realised that he could hear vehicles in the distance.

"Right, everyone alert!" shouted Jakub.

The noise quickly turned from a distant drone, to a thunderous rumble, as what appeared to be a German convoy approached them. Jakub signalled with his hands for them all to stay hidden as truck after truck of German troops roared over the bridge.

As the last one passed and the dust started to clear Ludwik spoke. "Well that's it then. Herman Swartz was probably in the middle of that lot. We've failed in our mission."

"No, I don't believe so," Tony reassured him.

"The history books say that he dies here, and since we have done nothing to change his time-line, then I've no reason to believe that it won't happen. We just have to be patient, that's all."

"I think we could have taken them anyway," said Damek jokingly. Well, they assumed he was joking since he didn't crack a smile.

"Damek, there must have been a thousand men in that convoy!" said Jakub dismissing his optimism.

"I know, but we had the element of surprise," replied Damek finally breaking out in to a smile. They all laughed that Jakub could have taken him seriously and for a short while the tension that they had felt all morning was broken. Then they heard the sound of another vehicle.

"Positions again," ordered Jakub. Very quickly the men were back hidden in their surroundings. This time there was a single jeep. As it approached they could see that inside was a driver, two German soldiers dressed in the black uniform of the SS and what looked like a civilian.

"This is it. That has to be Herman Swartz," whispered Jakub.

As the jeep got closer Jakub started a countdown with his fingers.

Five, four, three, two, one....Ludwik detonated the dynamite at the precise moment that the jeep hit the bridge. The impact of the explosion caught the driver full on and he was killed instantly. Unfortunately, the dynamite on the right hand side of the bridge had failed to go off, which meant the force of the explosion rolled the car over into the stream, rather than blowing it to bits. With the jeep rolling over, the two SS officers were both thrown clear and were able to get cover behind the upturned jeep before anyone could get a clear shot at them. A fierce gunfight followed with the SS officers exchanging bullets with Jakub and the others. The first officer went down with a bullet to the chest and finally the other, shot in his face by Damek, but this was not before they had mortally wounded Ludwik with a bullet in his stomach. As the air became still again, Jakub ran to comfort Ludwik, who was clutching his stomach with his blood drenched hands.

"We did it old man, we've stopped the Germans winning the war!"

Ludwik started a smile, but before it was finished the life ebbed away from his body and his eyes stared blankly towards the sky.

The death of Ludwik incensed Jakub and so he turned to vent his anger on the dead German SS officers. He walked over to where they were and started to kick them as they lay motionless on the ground.

"You bastards!" he repeated as he kicked them over and over again, stopping occasionally to hit them with the butt of his rifle. He suddenly stopped dead in his tracks.

"Ssssshh" he said, bringing his finger to his mouth, which was rather pointless, since it was only him that was making any noise.

"It's Herman Swartz, he's still alive!" he shouted as he realised what he could hear was coming from under the upturned Jeep. Damek quickly positioned himself, with his machine gun aiming at where the noise was coming from. Jakub waved for Tony to come out of cover and approach the vehicle.

"What can you see?" Jakub asked, motioning for Tony to look under the Jeep, whilst he covered him with his rifle. Tony crouched down and looked. It was Herman Swartz and he was still alive, although he looked to be in a bad way. His leg was crushed under the jeep and it looked like he had taken a couple of bullets to the arm and shoulder during the shoot out.

"I don't think he's in any shape to be a threat," Tony told them as he stood back up.

"Good, help me roll the Jeep back over" instructed Jakub, as both Damek and Tony obliged. As they rolled the jeep back onto its wheels, Herman Swartz let out a yelp as it rolled on to his crushed leg. Once the jeep was up-right, it left Herman Swartz laying there, a sad and pathetic figure. His leg badly mangled and his upper body soaked in blood from his bullet wounds. Jakub stepped over to where Herman Swartz was lying, cocked his rifle, and put it to his head.

"I think it's time to complete this arsehole's destiny," he said as he started to squeeze the trigger.

"No, wait a minute!" Tony shouted.

"We must make sure that this is Herman Swartz," he said, as he approached closer to him.

"We must find the blue-prints," Tony told Jakub, as he started to frisk his body.

"We know who you are and we know what you are carrying; now where are they?" demanded Jakub as he kicked Herman's broken leg. Herman let out a shriek and ranted something in German.

"He claims that he hasn't a clue what you are on about and that we have the wrong person," translated Tony.

"Bullshit," barked Jakub. "Never mind, I will search his dead body once I have blown his brains out."

Jakub positioned his rifle against Herman's head and starting to squeeze on the trigger.

"No, please wait!" implored Herman, this time in English. "I'm not carrying anything, you have the wrong person." But as he spoke Tony noticed that Herman gave a momentary involuntary glance towards his mangled leg.

"Hold your fire," Tony instructed Jakub, as he knelt down by Herman's leg and started to feel his boot and around his ankle. Herman tried to struggle but it just caused him more pain. As Tony explored his blood soaked sock he felt something solid. He rolled the sock down to discover a small pocket sewn on the inside. Anxiously he ripped the pocket apart and was overjoyed to reveal a small metal container. It was still intact, despite what had happened to Herman's leg.

Tony unscrewed the lid and smiled broadly as he slowly pulled out the contents. Inside was a roll of microfilm, which Tony triumphantly held it up to the light.
"This is it. This is the future of mankind!" he told the others.

All these years Tony had always pictured the blue-prints to be large sheets of slightly blue paper, but here they were no more than two inches wide and three feet long.

The Nazis had always been good at painting a heroic picture of events that mattered in their history. Propaganda was one thing they excelled at. They had made Herman Swartz out to be some sort of superhero, with the statues of him throughout the German Republic, depicting him as a larger than life character. But here he was, a small and insignificant, pathetic little man. And now without his precious blue-prints he was about to be denied his place in history. Tony took out the lighter from his pocket and lit the flame. Stretching out the roll of microfilm he held it in front of Herman so he could watch it burn, along with the hopes of the German Empire.

As Tony moved the flame towards the microfilm he suddenly noticed a red light flickering on the lighter. Intrigued Tony turned the lighter towards himself, but before he could examine it further it he heard the crack of a gunshot, and in an instant the lighter was blasted out of his hand by the impact of a speeding bullet. Jakub, realising what had happened, dived behind the jeep for cover, but before Damek could react he was shot down in cold blood, with a bullet whistling straight through his chest. His lifeless body slumped to the floor. Hardly realising what was happening Tony stood there frozen, until Jakub cried at him to get down. Tony eventually dived to the floor, although the only thing giving him any cover was the hapless Herman Swartz. Jakub was frantically looking around trying to find where the shots were coming from. Tony looked at him in bewilderment.

"What the hell is going on? Where are they coming from?" he shouted at him.

"I don't know, but you must destroy the blue-prints, else all this will have been in vain," said Jakub desperately. Tony tried to tear them but they were too strong.

"It's no good, they won't tear" he shouted, showing Jakub as he tried.

As Tony was looking at Jakub for guidance as to what to do next he noticed a red flickering light on his forehead.

"Get down!" Tony screamed at him, but before he could move, a bullet ripped through the top of his head, spraying his brains out the back of his skull, as the bullet exited. He too slumped to the floor. Tony was now numb with fear.

"Not looking so good now," laughed Herman Swartz as he lay next to him. Tony kicked his broken leg out of spite, at which Herman let out a yelp as he winced in pain. But he was right. It had once again all gone horribly wrong. Tony was now all alone and realised that he had little chance against this anonymous sniper. He assumed that he was a German soldier and knew that once he got hold of the blue-prints then the original time-line would continue, with only a few minor alterations.

Germany would win the war and millions of innocent people would be massacred. Tony had failed and it appeared that there was absolutely nothing he could do about it. Then he spotted a person walking towards him. Tony frantically started to scramble towards where Jakub was lying, in a desperate attempt to get his gun. But before he got close, he heard a voice.

"Dad?" the voice questioned. Tony continued to clamber to the gun, not quite catching the voice.

"Dad!" the voice repeated.

"My God, it's you Karl!" exclaimed Tony. "Get down son, before the sniper gets you," he pleaded with him anxiously.

"You don't understand Dad, it was me. I'm the sniper."

"Don't be stupid, you're not a sniper," Tony found himself saying to his son. Then it dawned on Tony that there was no one else here and therefore Karl had to be the one that had shot Jakub and Damek.

"I don't understand. You don't belong here! How did you get here? Why did you shoot these men?" Tony blurted out all at once. Tony had a thousand and one questions he wanted to ask his son, but he was totally confused and bewildered by the whole situation. Tony's mind had been blown apart by Karl's sudden appearance.

"Dad, they were concerned that you would do something stupid, and by the look of it they were right. They sent me back using your time machine to preserve the original time-line and to make sure the blue-prints still get delivered to the German High Command."

"But I'm the only one who can use T.E.S.S," Tony argued, rather pathetically, since the proof that he wasn't, was standing right there in front of him.

"No Dad you are wrong. They found a second program with my name on it and as they say, the rest is history," he said smirking to himself.

"Of course! I had always intended to destroy the original program once I had travelled in time myself, but with all that was going on I had obviously neglected to do so," uttered Tony, as the situation started to make sense.

"Dad, I just can't believe what you are trying to do! Why do you want to destroy the blue-prints and why would anyone in their right mind want to kill Herman Swartz? He's an absolute hero!"

Herman Swartz, who by this time was barely still alive, still managed to laugh again and thanked Karl for his kind words.

"You don't understand Karl. The Germans are evil people! If they win the war, millions and millions of people will die. There used to be a race of people called Jews. The Germans have exterminated them in their thousands, even millions. I've seen it with my own eyes."

"Dad, even if that was true, it happened during a war. Wars make people do bad things. You were happy in 1995. They looked after you well didn't they? Why destroy all of that?"

"Karl, you haven't seen the things I have seen!"

"That all happened 50 years ago. Forget it! We can go back to a good life in 1995. If we're not too late to save the life of Herman Swartz, then we could even go back as heroes. Besides, when you go back you will be so famous! You've invented a time machine for God's sake! Just imagine how rich we will be and how much fun we will have travelling in time together."

"I don't think they will let me use my time machine again. Not after this."

"Think about it Dad, they don't know any of this has happened. We just tell them that you were trying to stop the 'resistance' from killing Herman Swartz and you will be a hero."

Tony had to admit that what Karl was saying was starting to make sense and he started to feel tempted. But, he then thought of Kaska, and Klaus, and Jakub, in fact all of them. But most of all, he thought of what he had seen at Auschwitz. Tony knew that if he went back to 1995, as Karl suggested, then he would be condemning millions more of them to death and knew that he could not have that on his conscience.

"I can't son, it's not right."

"No, I'll tell you what's not right! You're not stupid Dad, you must know that if Germany does not win this war, then the chances are that I will not even exist! Are you prepared to kill me for the sake of a few of these 'Jews'?" ranted Karl.

"Son, I..." but before he had time to respond, Karl continued.

"Besides, you are hardly in a position to argue. You have already shown that you can't destroy the microfilm and if you haven't noticed, I am the one with the gun. So Dad, be sensible and give me the microfilm now. I will make sure it gets into the hands of those that need it. Germany will win the war and we can then create one of those paradox things so we will be back in 1995 being heroes. Come on Dad you know it makes sense."

"It won't work Karl. Causing a paradox doesn't send us back. You have already killed two men. Don't you think that is a paradox? We are stuck here in this time-line for the rest of our lives."

Tony didn't actually believe a word of what he had just said. He assumed that Karl hadn't gone back since, according to their original time-line, the men who killed Herman Swartz were killed anyway. Karl hadn't actually changed anything, so no paradox had been created. But Tony knew that Karl wasn't likely to know that.

"In that case I'll have to be a hero in this time-line," he said stubbornly.

"If I'm the one that saves Herman Swartz's life or even the one that gets the blue-prints to the SS, then I'll be a hero. Besides, I will know when things are going to happen. I'll be able to come up with ideas to invent things, long before they were ever thought of. I might even beat you to invent the time-machine," he said laughing and giving the impression that he might actually enjoy being trapped in this time-line. That didn't quite work out how Tony had hoped, he concluded to himself.

Karl had a point. How could Tony stop him taking the blue- prints, since he had the gun. Tony doubted very much that he would actually kill his own father, although having seen the way he had killed Jakub and Damek in cold blood, he wasn't so sure. Tony realised that with all the time he had spent working on T.E.S.S that he now hardly knew his own son!

"Please Dad, don't make me hurt you. Give me the microfilm."

"Come off it Karl, you wouldn't shoot your own Dad. Just look at what kind of person you have become, Karl, living under German rule. You have killed two men and you are now even contemplating harming your own father? Give me the gun."

Karl's reply was just as stern.

"No! It is you that is in the wrong. It is you that would even contemplate wiping out your own son's very existence - so what sort of person are you?" he argued back, starting to get agitated. His concentration was briefly interrupted as Herman Swartz gasped his last breath of air. He coughed up some blood and then shuddered a few times before his head flopped to the side, evidently bereft of life. This incensed Karl.

"They said you might try and talk me out of this. They said you might have been brainwashed, but I didn't want to believe them. But look at you. You are a traitor! You have killed the one man I looked up to. Herman Swartz was a hero and you and your cronies have killed him. You are no father of mine! Now give me the microfilm or I will be forced to shoot you. Believe me, I will do it." Karl stated menacingly. With that he pointed his gun at his father, emphasised by the fact that Tony could now see the red beam from his laser sight flickering on his chest. Instinctively Tony touched his chest, where the light was pointing, as though to brush it off and, as he did, he felt something hard under his jacket - it was his hand grenade! There was a sudden realisation of what he must do. As he felt the grenade through the material of his jacket Tony could now feel the pin sticking out from its top, and without a second thought, he gently squeezed it out.

"Here," Tony said to Karl, holding out the microfilm towards his son. Karl went to grab it, but as he did Tony pulled it back to his chest. As Karl instinctively came closer Tony grabbed his hand.

"Karl, you do know I love you. Don't you?" Tony asked. Karl looked at his father with disdain, trying to pull his hand away, but before he had a chance to answer the question, a blinding flash of light and heat ripped through them both. In an instant Tony found himself sat alone, naked in a strange room and feeling rather sick. Where or when he was, he did not know, but of more concern to him was that there was no sign of Karl.

Chapter 18 - Back to the Future.

As Tony slowly regained his senses from the unpleasantness of time travel, he realised that he was in a sparsely furnished office. It reminded him of an interrogation room at a police station. Not that Tony had ever been in an interrogation room at a police station, but this was how he imagined what it would look like. Judging from the style of the telephone on the table, it was apparent that he was no longer in 1945. Tony assumed that he was back in 1995, but it was evident from his surroundings that he was not where he expected to be; the Government building in Bernau. In his previous experiments, wherever he was at the time he had created a paradox, Tony had always returned to the present, in the same space co-ordinates from where he left, with the electrodes from T.E.S.S still attached to his body. This time he certainly wasn't in the room where he had started his journey back to 1945 and, furthermore, there was no sign of T.E.S.S. The only assumption Tony could make was that T.E.S.S had been moved. Since Karl had been sent back to 'rescue' him, Tony guessed that, in all probability, they had moved it somewhere closer to Koszalin. But why was it not here and, furthermore, where was Karl?

Although Tony didn't have much time to think about it at the time, he honestly believed that when he pulled the pin on that grenade, Karl would be safe and zap back to 1995 with him. Thinking about it now though, Tony wasn't so sure. He could only assume that in 1945, both he and Karl had been blown to pieces. Thankfully, since Tony was still alive, it appears that his theory of being killed in the past and creating a paradox was correct and that he was now back in 1995. But why no Karl? Tony surmised that surely the same forces that had got him back here, safe and sound, would have protected Karl. Unless, of course, what Karl had said was true and that by affecting the time-line, Tony had managed to eradicate his son's very existence. The thought of this suddenly made Tony feel sick.

Why hadn't he listened to Karl? Perhaps his son was was right and he should have thought about his own family first,' Tony contemplated remorsefully, as the enormity of what he had just done started to dawn on him.

If Tony was in 1995, then the question was, what sort of 1995 had he created? The explosion must have destroyed the blue-prints, so had he now come back to a Europe no longer ruled by the German Republic? This set Tony's mind running.

'If the Germans didn't win the war, then I wouldn't have worked for the German Government. If I didn't work for the German Government then the chances are that I would have never met Hannah. If I'd never met Hannah then Karl would never have been born!

What's more, if I didn't work for the Government then I also doubt that I would have ever been working on the time-machine in the first place.

In which case I couldn't have invented it, and this would therefore be a pretty good explanation as to why I was now sitting in an empty room.'

It now dawned on Tony that he would be the only person in the world that knew how the war was meant to end. There would be no evidence from the past to suggest that he had saved them from the fate of German rule. What's more, if he now went around telling them so, they'd probably think he was some sort of maniac. Whereas everyone else in the world would only recollect the new history that Tony had created for them, Tony himself only had memories of the original time-line. Everything he had ever done, everywhere he'd ever been and everyone he had ever met, would now be little more than figments of his imagination, that not another person in the entire world could substantiate. As far as this time-line was concerned, Tony didn't exist. He would have no friends, no family, no money, nothing. In fact there would be no record of him ever having lived. Tony suddenly felt very frightened and very alone. He hoped he was wrong, but the more he thought about it, the more it seemed to make sense. Tony realised that he had been racking his brain so much for an explanation, as to how he had found himself here and all alone, that he had almost forgotten the fact that he was sitting there stark naked.

He knew he had to find out the truth and see what sort of world he had created, but didn't much fancy going straight to the authorities. It would make more sense for him to get out and see for himself and then, if appropriate, choose who and when to tell his story to. However, given the fact that he was sitting naked in some sort of official building, quite possibly the local police station, he knew that if he wasn't careful he would have some rather difficult explaining to do. Tony knew he had to get out of the building and as quickly as possible. He tried the door, which was thankfully open. He could hear voices and movement from some of the adjacent offices, but could not actually see anyone. This was the first indication that something was different. The voices he could hear were certainly not German. Tony considered that if he was in Kosalin in his 1995, then this was part of the German Eastern Province. Poland and indeed the Polish language no-longer existed. Throughout the whole of the German Empire the spoken language was naturally German. If any traditional languages were spoken then it would have only been in private and behind closed doors. What Tony was hearing were conversations being conducted in public, in a language completely foreign to him. Tony could only guess that it was indeed Polish that he was hearing and therefore indeed an indication of something being different.

Given what the Germans had done to them in the War, Tony started to wonder what sort of welcome he would now receive if they thought he was German. He therefore decided that, if and when, he had to speak, it might be prudent to talk only in English. However, whatever Tony was going to do, it was evident that he could no longer hang around naked in this room and so his more immanent problem was to find some form of clothing. Tony cautiously peered out of the door and along the corridor. As he did so, Tony got a strange feeling of deja vu. He just hoped that this time he didn't have the misfortune to bump in to a fat chef with a frying pan again. There were a number of rooms coming off the passageway and so he decided to zig-zag across the corridor trying each door in turn. Hopefully he would find some clothes before someone else found him. Most of the noise he could hear was coming from the front of the building and so he decided to head away from it and towards the back.

'Here goes,' Tony thought to himself, as he ran to the opposite side of the corridor and straight in to a door recess. Pressing his ear to the door he could not hear anything and so tried the handle. It was open, so he cautiously entered the room. For once he could not believe his luck. Tony was in a locker room. Around the walls were a number of pegs and a fair number of them were adorned with cloths. Tony's assumption had been correct since every so often, as well as civilian clothes, were odd assortments of Police uniform. Tony felt a bit uneasy about stealing from the police but, given his predicament, he considered that he had little choice. He opted against taking any of the uniform, since in his 1995, impersonating a policeman was a very serious crime. He therefore got dressed in a rather ill fitting and odd mixture of civilian clothing.

Once clothed, he felt far more confident. For obvious reasons walking around naked made Tony feel very vulnerable and defenceless. So now being dressed was a blessed relief. The locker room had a number of frosted windows above the benches and pegs, so Tony decided to survey his surroundings. He stood on one of the benches and unlatched one of the small windows. He was pleasantly surprised to see that below was an open courtyard with nothing more than a small gate keeping him from the outside world. Tony was suddenly aware of noises from outside the locker room and froze as the door opened slightly. He remained perfectly still, hardly daring to breathe, as he could hear two people talking at the door. To his relief they stood at the entrance to the locker room continuing their conversation, rather than entering through the door. Tony realised that it was now or never, so he pulled himself up to the level of the windows and, although a tight squeeze, managed to get through it and drop to the ground below. Then, as quickly as his legs could carry him, he ran across the courtyard and clambered over the gate. Tony ran down a short high walled alleyway and was relieved to find himself out in the town square, of what he could only assume was Kosalin.

Chapter 19 - Halina the Librarian.

The town square was flanked with tall buildings, mostly four or five storeys tall. In front of the buildings were wide pavements, lined with trees, spaced at regular intervals. These trees, which were starting to show the first signs of spring, enclosed the town square. In amongst the trees were lots of stalls, so it was Tony's guess that he had arrived on market day. There were lots of people going about their business, buying everything from fruit and vegetables to leather jackets. Tony tried to blend in with the hustle and bustle of the market, but still felt very conspicuous. He felt in a daze as he walked around, not quite sure where to go or what to do. Since he was dressed in 'borrowed' clothes from the police station he felt like an escaped convict and, although not necessarily true, he was convinced that people were staring at him. His whereabouts were quickly confirmed when he came across a large sign proclaiming 'All are welcome in the Library of Kosalin.'

A library - what a good place to catch up on fifty years of history, Tony thought to himself. This should prove, one way or another, if he had altered the time-line. Although having seen what he had so far, Tony had already surmised that this was a foregone conclusion. He went in to the library building, and entered a surprisingly spacious room with a very high ceiling. The whole room was dimly lit with shelf upon shelf of books filling every rafter, although most of them looked like they hadn't been touched in a hundred years. The whole place looked like something out of a Charles Dickens novel. Compared to the 'state of the art' libraries Tony was used to in England, this was dated to say the least. Looking around there were just two other people in the library; an old man sitting on a bench reading a newspaper and a young girl behind a desk, who Tony guessed was the librarian. He plucked up enough courage to go to the desk and was greeted by the young lady. As she looked up over a small pair of glasses, she asked, in what Tony assumed was Polish, if he needed any help. Tony gestured that he didn't understand and muttered a few words of English. At this the librarian became quite excited.

"Oh, you are English?" she said enthusiastically. "We don't get too many tourist gentlemen in Kosalin. I have learnt English at University. Am I good, no?" she said, hardly pausing for breath and smiling broadly.

"Yes, you are very good," Tony commended her, relieved to find someone he could speak to in English.

"How can I be assisting you?"

"I would like to look at some history books, please," requested Tony.

"In English, I am assuming?"

"Yes, that would be very good, thank you."

She led Tony to the far corner of the library, where she pointed out a number of shelves. He thanked her and began looking through an assortment of books. Most of them were old and referred to 18th century Polish history, but then one caught his eye; 'The Chronicles of the Twentieth Century.' It seemed totally out of place compared to all the other books. It was much bigger and was brightly illustrated with lots of coloured pictures. Picking it up and opening it eagerly, like a young child with a present on Christmas Day, Tony began to turn the pages. Although excited, he was also fearful of what he might find. He read the first page, and then the next. As he read page after page, he stood in a total state of shock. To say that he had created a paradoxical change was an understatement! Much of it wasn't sinking in, but it was clear that the world was unrecognisable from how he had left it. Tony shook his head in disbelief. The world's entire history had been re-written from that one event back in 1945. He continued to read, absorbing every bit of information but, at the same time, struggling to take in what he was reading. There had still been atomic bombs, only this time just in Japan and not Europe. He read how Germany, in fact Europe, had been split in two after the war - The East and the West. Not only had Germany been split in two, but even Berlin now had a great wall dividing the city.

There had still been a cold war, with both sides having a huge arsenal of atomic weapons, only this time it was between

Russia and America. Many things had happened which were similar, for instance man had still walked on the moon, but it was someone called Neil Armstrong and not Sepp Muller who made those historic first steps. Tony read all about the ending of the war and the Nuremberg trials. People like Hermann Goering, Heinrich Himmler and Rudolf Hess (who had ruled the German Republic for many years after the war) and were immortalised in his 1995, had now been tried and executed as war criminals.

One person he didn't read about, however, was Hermann Swartz. He concluded that Klaus's hand grenade had blown him in to very small pieces, along with the blue-prints. Since he had now failed to deliver the secret of the atomic bomb to his compatriots, as he was originally meant to, his part in the war was now insignificant. So from having a statue of himself in just about every city in Europe, he was now just a forgotten casualty of war, whom in this time-line no-one would have even heard of. By destroying those blue-prints Tony had changed the world's history beyond recognition. Despite the fact that his actions had clearly been the pivotal moment in the war, Tony felt rather indignant that there was not a single mention of this in the history books. Tony Smith should have been a great hero for them, yet in this time-line they were oblivious to his very existence. His bravery and selflessness back in 1945 had probably been the most important moment in Twentieth Century history, yet here and now in this time-line, they were blissfully unaware that it ever happened. Tony had become so engrossed by the book that he nearly jumped out of his skin when the Librarian interrupted him.

"I'm very sorry, I not wish to disturb you, but I should have closed the Library forty minutes ago. You have been reading that book for hours."

"I'm so sorry, I didn't realise the time," he said apologising. "I will come back tomorrow."

"Thank you. Where are you staying? In the Astoria Hotel?" she asked.

"Astoria? Er... no, I'm not actually staying anywhere."

"The Astoria is very good. It is where most of the tourists stay."

"To be honest I have no money. I had an accident and bumped my head. Now I can't remember where I was staying, or even who I am," he lied, rather unconvincingly, although, for once, he was at least trying to think on his feet. "In fact, that is why I was looking at that history book, since I cannot remember any of the events mentioned in it. I hoped that this book might help jog my memory and remind me a little," he told her. At least that wasn't a lie, since everything that Tony had just read about had not previously happened. Not in his time-line in any case.

"And did it help remind you?" questioned the Librarian.

"Not really, I'm afraid."

"That must have been a big bump on your head you poor soul, we must get you to a hospital quickly."

"No, I'm sure I'll be alright, that is…once my memory returns," Tony reassured her.

"Listen, I have to lock up, but there is a small bar just across the square where they serve some nice food. Perhaps a nice hot meal will help you regain your memory. If not, then maybe later we could go to all the hotels in the town, not that there are that many in Kosalin, to see if anyone recognises you," she said very helpfully.

"This is too much to ask of you, besides I have no money to pay for food," Tony apologised.

"Do not worry about the money, I'm sure I can spare the cost of a bowl of 'Bigos and Kopytka' and perhaps even a few vodka's. Besides, as I said we don't get many English people in Kosalin, so perhaps you can help me with my English and tell me all about that wonderful country of yours, well the bits you can remember at least. Hopefully we may even figure out how you have magically appeared here in Kosalin. My name is Halina," she said, offering her hand to Tony.

"Well, it's a pleasure to meet you Halina," responded Tony shaking her hand warmly. "I'm sorry, but I haven't a clue what Bigos and Kopy-what-you-call-it is, but I'm sure it will be wonderful. You are a very kind young lady."

"Bigos and Kopytka is delicious, it is a kind of stew with, I think you call them dumplings in England. Perhaps I can teach you a bit of Polish as you help me with my English yes?"

"Yes, that would be very good indeed and my name is Tony Smith by the way."

"Well, Tony Smith, it seems that your memory is getting better already, see you have remembered your name!"

"So I have!" he laughed rather sheepishly back. "So I have."

She smiled. "If you don't mind, Tony Smith, I have to lock up. Once I have done so, then the bar is just across the square. I hope you are hungry." With everything that had happened, Tony hadn't even considered eating, but now she had mentioned it, he realised that he was famished.

"Yes, very," he said eagerly.

"Good, then follow me," she instructed as she headed back to her desk and grabbed a large bunch of keys. She asked him to wait whilst she went off on her rounds, locking doors and turning off lights. When she returned, she smiled at Tony and beckoned for him to follow her out of the library and back on to the main square. As they stepped out of the building Halina turned to lock the main doors, whilst Tony stood at the top of the large flight of steps which led up to the library to survey his surroundings. It was now dark and the square was lit by a number of old fashioned street lights which were positioned every so often between the trees. The market had all but been cleared away, with just a few remaining traders packing away their wares.

"Right, Mr Smith, if you would like to follow me the bar is just over there," said Halina pointing to the far corner of the square. As she spoke Halina unclipped her previously tied back hair and shook it free. Now that Tony wasn't so busy burying his head in a book he noticed that Halina was quite a pretty young lady. She was around five feet tall, slim, with mousey shoulder length hair and dark brown eyes. As she turned she caught Tony's eye and he gave her a big smile. She responded by returning the smile and then grabbed him by his hand.

"This way," she said, as she led him enthusiastically down the flight of steps and across the square towards the bar.

As they approached Tony was surprised just how rundown and dilapidated the bar looked from the outside. A single red door with much of its paint bubbled and peeling fronted the five storey building out onto the pavement. A white sign with the single word 'BAR' painted in fading black hung at an angle above the doorway. The white paint on the stone sills of the single window on each of the five storeys was also discoloured and peeling badly. Whilst the windows themselves looked like they hadn't been cleaned in decades and were partially obscured by rusty metal bars, which protruded from the surrounding walls. From the outside it looked far from welcoming. Halina noticed the concern in Tony's expression and began to apologise.

"I'm sorry, too many years of neglect under Soviet rule I'm afraid. I'm sure this is not what you are used to in England, but I can promise you that the food here is warm and tasty and the people friendly. And as for the vodka, well that's the same as everywhere in Poland - we only have the one type," she laughed.

"I'm sorry, this is fine. I was just thinking to myself that it has been a long time since I was last in a bar," said Tony, not wishing to appear ungrateful of Halina's hospitality. "I'm sure there are places just as run down as this in England," he added, although in reality Tony actually doubted that to be true. Under German rule virtually all of the old spit and sawdust pubs in England were demolished in the modernisation of the cities. They were replaced by larger, 'ultra-modern' bier halls or café style bars and were always maintained to a high standard and kept spotlessly clean.

"Run down? What are you trying to say Tony ? This is the most salubrious bar we have in all of Kosalin," teased Halina.

"I'm sorry, I didn't mean…" but before he finished the sentence he saw the smile on her face and realised that she was joking. Halina ushered Tony into the bar and as he walked through the door, the half a dozen or so people already in the bar abruptly stopped what they were doing and the bar momentarily fell silent as all heads were turned towards Tony.

"Good Evening Halina," greeted the owner in Polish from across the bar as she also came in to view. Knowing this stranger was with someone familiar was the cue for the room to spring back into life and as if by magic the noise level returned to normal just as abruptly as it had fallen silent. As the pair of them made the short walk across the room to the facing bar, Halina was greeted by all of the other drinkers.

"I take it that this is your first time in this bar also?" Tony joked.

"No, not at all. I come in here most evenings after work for an hour to read my book or have a bowl of Bigos," she said straight faced.

"I'm was joking - it is obvious you come in here often," said Tony trying to explain his sarcasm.

"So was I Tony," she responded, with her face cracking a smile as she chuckled to herself. "Just because I am a librarian does not mean I am not allowed a sense of humour you know. As I have told you, I have studied English at university and my favourite subject was English sarcasm."

"My God, they teach English sarcasm as a separate subject?" questioned a bemused Tony.

"Of course they don't you fool, now it is my turn to joke with you." She told him, laughing profusely. As they stood at the bar, the pair of them had fits of giggles as they struggled to compose themselves. Tony had only know Halina for a very short time but had already warmed to her immensely. She was bright, funny and overtly friendly. Given the way she had been greeted in the bar, she was clearly also very popular. Tony considered he could not have been befriended by a better person than Halina. As she finally composed herself she started a conversation in Polish with the owner, who had been stood patiently behind the bar waiting to serve her and once finished she turned to Tony.

"He just wanted to know if it had been a good day in the library and asked why I was slightly later than usual. He wanted to know what was so funny and also wondered where on Earth did I find you from."

"And you replied?"

"I told him, that it was very boring as usual in my Library, until you came in that is. I also told him that I am late because I did not have the heart to throw you out sooner. And I told him that you are from England and do not quite understand the Polish sense of humour and that you are also a pretty unconvincing klamca."

"A klamca?" Tony asked somewhat puzzled.

"Klamca - er…you know, how do you say, a fibber?"

"Oh…so you do not believe my story about my bump on the head then?" he asked, not at all surprised by her assertion.

"Come on Mr Smith, do I look like I am a person that is so gullible. I wasn't born tomorrow you know."

Tony smiled to himself, opting not to correct her English.

"I'm sorry, you are right, there was no bump on my head. However, I was not lying about losing my memory. It is completely true that I have no recollection of any event that has taken place in the last 50 years."

"How can that be?" she asked somewhat puzzled.

"I would tell you, but the problem I have, is that if I did, you would think that I am two sandwiches short of a picnic and not believe a word I say."

Halina giggled at Tony's phrase.

"Listen, as long as you tell me the truth I will believe you, but remember I will soon know if you are a fibber - I must tell you, I am a very good reader of people. Now, I suggest I order some food and a drink and then you can tell me your 'unbelievable' story over a vodka or two. When you have told me your story, then it will be up to me to decide whether or not you are, shall we say, 'two bricks short of a Berlin wall' or not," she said, once again chuckling to herself.

"Very funny - you might think I'm a few more than just two bricks short once you have heard my story," he laughed. "I am immensely grateful for the food and drink and also your company, but do not understand why you are being so kind to me, especially when you have already rightly supposed me to be a liar. Why are you helping me?" he asked bewildered by the benevolence being shown to him by Halina.

"Listen Tony, I have worked in that library for three years and you are the first English person who has ever walked in there. I have already told you that I have learn English at university so I am hoping you will help my improving, but most of all I am intrigued as to how an Englishman who claims to have no memory, with no identification or money and wearing clothes, that by the look of them, he has borrowed from a 'Wloczega' ends up in my library. I could not let you go without solving this mystery first you see?"

"Yes, I guess I am a bit of a mystery," he smiled, "but excuse me, how did you describe my clothes? They look like they were borrowed from a what?" he laughed. "What is wrong with them?"

"From a Wloczega! You know, how you say, a bum, a hobo...a tramp, that's it, a tramp."

"Oh I see, I didn't think they were that bad!" he laughed again. "I guess that's why everyone in this bar keeps staring at me."

"They do not mean to stare, but we are not used to strangers in here, especially foreigners and yes I suppose they are wondering what the hell you are wearing," she laughed. "Now excuse me, I must order this food and drink. Is vodka ok?"

Tony hesitated as vodka wasn't his usual drink, not that he particularly had a usual drink. His work had meant that that he rarely got out of his flat, let alone visited bars.

"Er, yes vodka would be fine - thank you."

"Good, because we don't have much choice. Since glasnost and the fall of the Soviet Union, we are free people. However, after so many years of communism it is going to take a long time yet before our economy recovers. Sadly, we are still a very poor country and a long way off being a free market. Here it is vodka or nothing I'm afraid."

"No seriously vodka will be great, thank you, but what the hell is Glasnost?"

"You really have lost your memory. How can you be in Poland and not have heard of Glasnost? It is a Russian word which means openness, and was a complete change in way we were governed by the Soviets, perhaps I will explain more once we have eaten."

As Halina ordered the food and drink at the bar, Tony sat at one of the empty tables and looked around the room.

The décor inside was just as bleak and desolate as the outside had suggested it would be. The room was pretty much rectangular in shape with the bar at the opposite end to the entrance. The single window next to the entrance consisted of a dozen smaller panes, two of which had been broken and therefore boarded up, whist the rest were desperately in need of a clean. The other two walls were flanked with bench seating which ran the length of the room, in front of which were an assortment of long wooden tables each with an equally odd assortment of hard wooden chairs positioned haphazardly around the other sides of each table. What was once called a carpet was completely threadbare and in places was so worn and ingrained with dirt that it was shinny. The wallpaper was barely hanging on to the wall and in places was covered in mould, whilst every single thing in the room was a dirty smoke stained yellow colour.

Tony wondered what Halina saw in such a place and why she chose here to come each night. He also wondered whether he was indeed back in 1995, as the décor was more reminiscent of the bars a long time demolished in England. Halina joined Tony at the table and placed a couple of small glasses and a bottle of vodka in front of them.

Tony thanked her, as she told him that the food was also on its way.

"So Halina, please tell me more about Poland?" Tony requested.

"Well, I will give you a brief lesson of history, Tony, but as you promised, you must tell me the truth about yourself afterwards." Tony agreed, although he still wasn't quite sure whether to tell her the entire truth or make up something a little more plausible.

"Anyway, Vodka first," she insisted. She poured two glasses and toasted 'Na zdrowie! Cheers' as she downed hers in one. Tony followed suit, but nearly spat it straight back out as it hit the back of his throat.

"Wow!" exclaimed Tony, coughing and spluttering from his first taste of Polish vodka.

"Yes, it does take a bit of getting used to," laughed Halina, as she poured another two glasses.

As Tony sat there with his eyes watering and throat still burning from his first taste of Polska vodka the owner of the bar, brought their food over and placed it on their table.

"Eat," instructed Halina.

Tony didn't need a second invitation and quickly tucked in to his Bigos and Kopytka. After a few mouthfuls Tony soon realised why Halina chose this bar.

"This is wonderful," he told her as he relished every morsel. Halina nodded knowingly.

"So Halina, tell me, how did the Soviet Union fall?"

"Well, the communists could no longer contain the will of the people for greater freedom and once Mikhail Gorbachev introduced the policy of perestroika, which meant an end to central planning, there was a complete reconstruction of the Russian political and economic system and a new openness. This gave many of the Soviet satellite states a will for self governance and so eventually lead to the collapse of the USSR in 1991 and the creation of 15 individual republics," she told him, hardly pausing for breath.

"Wow," said Tony, surprised at her text book answer.

"You forget, I went to university," she laughed "If I was to put it more simply, that maybe an Englishman with memory problems could understand, the Soviets were totally fucked!" she said laughing wholeheartedly.

"Tell me more..."

So Halina continued to tell Tony how life had been very tough under Soviet rule and being part of the 'Eastern Bloc'. She told him how they had lived in fear of nuclear attack by the Americans fed by Soviet propaganda. And of how the shelves in the shops had been empty with the economic reality and harshness of living through the cold war, where the Russians were more concerned about the arms race than feeding their people, and that the Polish government were mere puppets to the Soviet regime. However, she told him how glasnost eventually led to a 'revolution' in Poland and the rise of the Solidarity movement and mass strikes led by a Trade Union activist called Lech Walesa, who was now unbelievably the Polish president.

Although her English wasn't perfect, Tony found Halina's brief history of Eastern Europe fascinating and easy to understand. However, what he found somewhat harder to comprehend was how the Russians had won the war and liberated Poland from the German's, yet still oppressed the Polish people. In fact it was clear from what Halina was saying that Russia had even mistreated its own people and kept them in abject poverty for the last fifty years.

"So Tony, I have told you all about Poland, now it's your turn to tell me the truth about yourself. And remember I will know if you are lying."

Tony had never drunk vodka before and it soon made him very talkative and rather jovial. His initial apprehension about telling the truth had completely disappeared and so in the spirit of glasnost decided to tell Halina the true account of how he now found himself drinking vodka in this bar.

"Where do I start? You see, the truth is that there is no me. I don't exist. Well, not here. Not in this time-line," he told her.

"I think you've had too much vodka, Tony, you're not making any sense."

"Listen, there is no sense - nothing makes sense anymore."

"Look, start at the beginning. Where were you born Tony?" Halina questioned.

So Tony started from the beginning. In fact, he told her his entire life's story. From his earliest memories, living in England under German rule, to meeting her in the library today. At times he rambled on a bit, probably due to the vodka, but Halina listened to every word, occasionally asking questions and making comments. He told her of his time travel experiments and the plan to save Hitler. He told her about the brave Polish resistance fighters and how he had fallen for Kaska. He told what he had seen at Auschwitz and therefore why he had decided to change history. He also told her about the killing of Herman Swartz and the destruction of the blue-prints, and also about the fight with Karl and how he now feared that he had killed his own son. And finally he told her about ending up naked in Kosalin Police station and therefore why he was now dressed like a 'Wloczega.'

"So you see, if it wasn't for me, you'd now be living under Nazi rule, in the German Eastern Provinces. Or for all I know, you might not have even existed. Just like I don't exist now," slurred Tony.

"My God Tony, that is the most unbelievable story!"

"See, I told you that you wouldn't believe me," he sighed. "I probably wouldn't believe it either if someone told it to me, but honestly it is the truth."

"But I do believe you Tony. I really do believe you. As I said previously, I know when people are not being truthful, but I honestly do not think you are lying. But oh my God Tony, it is such an inconceivable story. In fact it is the most incredible story I have ever heard in my entire life," she said excitedly. "My Grandparents were in such a concentration camp and only just survived. If the Germans had won the war, they would have undoubtedly perished along with many millions more and therefore, I guess, Tony Smith, that if what you are saying is the truth, then I owe my life to you! In which case I thank with all my heart. Na zdrowie!" toasted Halina, as she downed another shot of vodka.

Tony smiled at the thought that perhaps Karl had been sacrificed to save Halina and many more like her. It seemed to give it some meaning, and in a small way made the burden of killing his son a little easier for Tony to bear. However, since the conversation had now turned to the plight of his son, Tony began to get a little emotional and very remorseful. He eventually found himself crying uncontrollably. It seemed that all the emotions and traumatic experiences of the last few days came flooding out all at once.

"I've killed him. I've killed my own son," Tony kept repeating to himself as he downed more vodka.

As he continued to sob, Halina tried to reassured him that perhaps Karl was alive and well back in England, but Tony was adamant that it was impossible and that he had been wiped out of existence. In the end Halina accepted what he was saying and just tried to console him as best she could.

"It's the vodka, you know. It has this effect on some people," she told him, encouraging him to 'let his emotions out'. As she thought of a way to move the conversation away from Karl to spare Tony anymore anguish, Halina suddenly had a moment of inspiration.

"Tony listen," she exclaimed. "I have thought of a way that you can prove to everyone that you are telling the truth."

"What, some sort of lie detector test?" Tony asked.

"No, easier than that," she said excitedly.

"Come on then, tell me how?"

"Klaus Zimmerman!" she answered elatedly. "Klaus Zimmerman the man whose arm you shot off, was the only person you came into contact with back in 1945 who wasn't killed or was young enough to still be alive today. Since you have already told me that he was still alive in 'your' 1995, why wouldn't he still be alive in mine?"

"Klaus Zimmerman. Of course Klaus Zimmerman. My God, you're right. My friend Klaus should still be alive and well in Bernau. He will remember me, I'm sure!" said Tony jubilantly.

"It might have been a couple of days ago for you, Tony, but if what you are saying is true, then Klaus hasn't seen you for fifty years.

What makes you think he'd remember you after all this time?" questioned Halina.

"Would you forget the face of the idiot who blew your arm off?" Tony asked her, laughing to himself. "Besides, as far as he's concerned I won't have aged one bit, well a couple of day's maybe, and therefore my appearance to Klaus will be just as it was fifty years ago. You're a genius Halina, thank you. Thank you so much. This is fantastic! We must go and see him now," Tony demanded, standing ready to leave this instant.

She had given Tony hope and now a reason to live.

"If I was to meet Klaus and he verified my story, then people would believe me. I might even become some sort of celebrity. I could travel the world, telling people my story and of how things could have been so different for them, if it wasn't for me," Tony said, starting to ramble again.

"Tony please sit back down. You should not get too carried away. Firstly, you are in no fit state to go anywhere tonight. And secondly, we might be liberated, but travel throughout Europe is still restricted. You need passports, visas, and things like that to travel outside Poland. Bernau is about one hundred kilometres from here, but without paperwork it might as well be one thousand. Germany is still coming to terms with unification and since Poland still has high unemployment and economic problems, the last thing the Germans want is thousands of Poles coming into their country looking for work and making matters worse. The borders are very strictly controlled and it will not be easy to get in. Especially for someone who does not exist," she said, bringing Tony back down to earth with a bump.

"I will walk there if necessary and climb whatever fences are put in my way," stated Tony defiantly and somewhat drunkenly.

"Look, don't worry, I have some good friends and I'm sure we will think of a way in the morning," she told him reassuringly. Tony was very grateful to Halina for looking after him and now giving him hope. In his drunkenness he told her what a wonderful person she was.

"Halina, you are a wonderful person. No, I really mean it, you are a wonderful, wonderful person. I've never met anyone so wonderful," he told her over and over again.

"And I've never met anyone quite so drunk," she told him back.

"No, seriously I'm not drunk, you are a wonderful, wonderful person."

"I think you need to go home, Mr Smith - whilst you can still walk," she added, as she helped Tony to his feet.

"I have no home remember," slurred Tony "I don't even exist."

"You can sleep at mine tonight. I will sleep on the couch," she told him, as she helped him to his feet.

Tony protested that he should be the one sleeping on the couch, but he was in no fit state to argue as the bar owner and one of the locals helped carry him to Halina's apartment, which fortunately was not too far away from the square.

The next thing Tony was aware of, was that he was waking up in the morning with a head that felt like it was clamped in a vice.

"Oh, you are finally awake," remarked Halina, as she entered the bedroom noticing that Tony was beginning to stir.

"Where am I?" groaned Tony.

"You are at my apartment. It took three of us to carry you back here last night,"

"I am so sorry, you should have left me there," Tony said apologetically.

"I would have, but I felt guilty since it was me who got you drunk in the first place. I should have known that Polska vodka would have been a bit strong for you. You're here now so there is nothing you can do about it. Anyway, Good afternoon Mr Smith" she told in an annoyingly bright and cheerful voice as she stood the bottom of the bed.

"It's not afternoon already is it?" groaned Tony.

"Nearly," she replied, still far too cheerily.

Tony let out another groan as he struggled to fully open his eyes. As the room came into focus, he could see that Halina was not alone and that a man was standing next to her.

"This is my boyfriend, Stefan," she said introducing Tony to the stranger.

"Your boyfriend!" declared a somewhat confused Tony. "I'm sorry, I er...you didn't mention a boyfriend last night" Tony said apologetically as he struggled to get his words out, realising what this must look like to Stefan.

"Well, you didn't ask," said Halina smiling.

"But don't worry, Stefan knows what I am like and you were so drunk last night I did not wish you to come to any harm."

"Please apologise to him for me," requested Tony.

"You can apologise yourself, as I have been teaching him English."

"I'm very sorry about last night, but I honestly cannot even remember coming back here. It's nice to meet you Stefan, my name is Tony Smith," he told him, rather sheepishly.

"I know, Halina has been telling me all about you," Stefan responded with a half hearted smile.

"You have a wonderful girlfriend," Tony added, still slightly bemused by the situation he now found himself in.

"I know she is wonderful. I'm always telling her so myself. Apparently, you also happened to tell her once or twice last night," he laughed.

"Yes, I suppose I did," Tony admitted reluctantly. "I think I might have been slightly drunk."

"So I hear," replied Stefan. "Poor old Ivan, the bar owner, had to carry you over his shoulder to get you upstairs and in to the bedroom."

"Oh no, I am a complete embarrassment!"

"Don't worry about it. Vodka has a habit of doing that to you. Besides, you're not the first and won't be the last drunk that Ivan has had to help carry out of his bar," Stefan replied. "Halina has also told me about your fantastic story of time travel and alternative time-lines, and I've told Halina that she's the most gullible person in all of Poland," he laughed.

"But it is the truth!" Tony heard himself protesting.

"Look, if you expect me to believe that you are some sort of time traveller from a 'different dimension' then you've got more chance of convincing me that Poland will win the next World Cup!" exclaimed Stefan. "But Halina here, believes everything anyone tells her and she has made me promise to help you. So reluctantly, help you I will."

"Thank you," Tony said gratefully.

"Don't thank me, thank Halina." said Stefan. "Besides, although I don't believe a word of your ridiculous story, I'm still intrigued as to whether this one armed bald chap in Bernau will actually exist," he said laughing loudly. "Listen, I have a friend who drives lorry's for a living. He's always going in and out of Germany. I am sure that for a few Zloty he will hide you in the back of his cab."

"That would be great except for the fact I don't have any 'Zloty'. I have nothing to offer him," responded Tony, assuming that Zloty was the Polish currency.

"Then, I do not know what to suggest," Stefan said apologetically.

"Look, take this," said Halina reaching into her purse and handing Tony a wad of notes.

"I can't take your money," Tony protested weakly, "you have already been far too generous to me."

"Oh, yes you can," Halina insisted. "I will only spend it on Vodka if I keep it," she said pressing the money in to Tony's hand.

Stefan shook his head and said something to her in Polish.

"Look, it's my money. I told Tony I would help, so just mind your own business," she told him dismissively.

Stefan shrugged his shoulders and said a few more words to her in Polish, before leaving her apartment.

"Don't worry about him," Halina apologised to Tony, "he is always grumpy in the morning."

"I thought you said it was afternoon?" questioned Tony.

"Not quite," she laughed. "I thought you would prefer these, rather than the one's you stole from a tramp," she giggled, as she handed Tony a pile of clean clothes. "They are some of Stefan's that he left here some time ago. He hasn't worn them in ages, so he won't miss them," she assured Tony. He protested that he couldn't, but in reality he was very grateful that he didn't have to put the clothes back on, which he had 'acquired' from the police station. And so after a little persuasion got dressed into Stefans clothes and joined Halina in the lounge. After a short while there was a knock at the door, which Halina opened and was pleased to see that was Stefan again. He hurried in and spoke to Tony.

"Listen, my friend Jerzy, is just leaving for Berlin, if you are very quick he has said that he will give you a lift."

"He will be here in…" but before he finished his sentence Stefan stopped in his tracks as he noticed that Tony was wearing his clothes. Without saying anything he looked Tony up and down and then turned his contemptuous gaze towards Halina. Halina just smiled at the bemused Stefan. Again without saying anything he turned his eyes up to the ceiling in despair and let out a large sigh before continuing his sentence.

"My friend Jerzy will be here in just five minutes, so you must go now."

Tony nodded in approval and thanked Stefan for all his help. He was grateful to Stefan for organising this for him and not making a fuss over the clothes, but words could not express his gratitude towards Halina.

She had been his saviour. Not only with her acts of kindness and looking after him in the first place. But, for giving him hope, and believing in him. Although, Tony had known her less than twenty-four hours, he still found saying good bye to Halina to be very emotional. Once again he told her that she was a wonderful person and that one day he would repay her for her kindness.

As Jerzy pulled up in his lorry, Halina gave Tony a kiss on the cheek and wished him good luck.

"If all this is your doing," said Halina as she gestured by opening her arms to the surroundings, "then I hope you can enjoy what you have created. Live for the future, Tony, not the past," she told him.

"I will, don't worry. But for me to have any future, I need people to believe in my past and my only hope of that is finding Klaus Zimmerman," he told her as he boarded the lorry.

Tony introduced himself to Jerzy, as he climbed into the cabin and quickly wound down the window so that he could continue his goodbyes to Halina.

"Thank you…for everything," he told her, as the lorry pulled slowly away.

"Good luck with finding Klaus!" he heard Halina shout as they drove off.

If everyone was going to be as nice as Halina in this 1995, then Tony concluded that what he had done in 1945 might have been for the best after all.

If only this had been the case.

Chapter 20 - Mission to find Klaus.

Jerzy, seemed a nice enough chap, but spoke no English and only a little German, therefore their conversation was very limited.

When they started to get close to the German border Jerzy pulled his lorry over to the side of the road. Pulling forward his seat he revealed a dirty brown curtain. This he pulled back, to show a sleeping compartment, around 6 feet long and 3 feet by 3 feet square. Inside was a grubby sleeping bag, which looked like it had been well used and dozens of empty cigarette packets. Pointing, he gestured for Tony to get in.

Tony reluctantly clambered over his seat and in to the cubby-hole. Tony's reluctance was down to the fact that he wasn't feeling too good. He'd never been a particularly good traveller, and with the after effects of last night's vodka still in his body, he felt decidedly ill. Tony didn't fancy this claustrophobic coffin at all and hoped that they would pass through the border check-point pretty quickly.

They hadn't travelled much further when Tony felt Jerzy's lorry come to a halt. Tony guessed in reality that he had only been in there about 15 minutes, but already it seemed like a lifetime. He'd never actually considered himself to be claustrophobic, but the smell of stale tobacco and his own delicate disposition, were combining to make him feel decidedly unwell.

Through the window of his cab Jerzy was talking to one of the border guards. Tony could hear the ruffle of papers as Jerzy showed him his manifest and personal documentation.

'Hurry up, hurry up, hurry up', Tony muttered under his breath, as he felt himself going in to a cold sweat.

Outside the guard was finally in the process of thanking Jerzy and wishing him on his way, however, inside this 'black hole of Calcutta' Tony could stand it no longer. He could do absolutely nothing to stop himself from being violently sick.

Hearing the commotion coming from inside the cab, the guard immediately ordered the barrier to remain down and instructed that poor Jerzy got back out of his lorry. The guard pulled back the seat, followed by the grubby brown curtain, to reveal Tony, lying there, somewhat green and covered in sick.

He ordered Tony to get out, which Tony considered to be blessed relief.

"You know you could lose your exporter's licence, not to mention receiving a large fine" Tony heard the guard tell Jerzy as he led him away. Jerzy looked over to Tony and snarled something inaudible under his breath, before disappearing into the control room.

Tony tried to apologise but, very quickly, he too was also being led away by another of the guards. The guard took Tony past the red and white barrier, which was still blocking the road, and into a small 'interview' room in the gatehouse. Here Tony was ordered to sit down.

"When will you Poles realise that the work situation is no better here in Germany than in your own country" stated the guard.

"But, I'm not Polish or looking for work" Tony explained to him in German.

The guard was quite taken back by Tony's revelation.

"Then why are you trying to sneak in to Germany?" he asked.

Tony told him that he had been mugged in Poland, whilst on route to Bernau to visit a friend who he had not seen for many years. "Since they took my passport and other documentation, I felt I had no choice but to sneak in to Germany" he added.

Tony was starting to get quite used to this making up stories.

"If you are German, why did you not report the mugging to the authorities? You should have gone to the embassy or German consulate" he questioned.

"I'm not German, I'm English. I would have reported it in Poland, but you know how slow the authorities are there. My friend is very ill and I was worried that any delay, might have made me get there too late to see him before he passed on. I was going to report to the English embassy in Berlin, once I had seen my friend" Tony promised him.

Tony obviously didn't have a clue about the Polish authorities, but he knew all bureaucracy was slow and so guessed that the Poles would be no different. Even Tony was relatively impressed with how convincing he been, making his story sound genuine.

"You can say that again about the Polish authorities" said the guard, confirming Tony's hunch, "but you should have still reported it there. You cannot just go smuggling yourself across borders." he said sternly.

Tony apologised, saying that he would not do so again.

"Do you have anyone who can vouch for your story?" asked the guard.

"Yes, my friend in Bernau. If you take me to him he will vouch for me" Tony assured him.

"I'm sorry, we cannot take you anywhere, but if you give me your friend's name and address we will contact him. In the meantime I'm afraid that you will have to remain in our custody.

"I do not have his address, I just know that he lives in Bernau" Tony told him apologetically.

"Right, let us take some details from you, and then we will do our best to find your friend" said the German guard.

"Your details first" he questioned. "Name?"

"Tony Smith"

"Date of Birth?"

"15/3/60"

"Address?"

At this point Tony hesitated. It occurred to him that his address would no longer exist or at least would be very different to what it was in his original time-line. In Tony's 1995 nearly all streets were named after Germans. Even many of the towns and city's now had German names. So Tony gave him the closest interpretation of his address in English, but he knew, that even if they could trace it, there would be no record of him living there.

Tony could also not answer many of the remaining questions and had to make up his answers.

Even those that he did know, like the name of his wife and children, were unlikely to verify his existence, even if they did exist in this time-line. Tony just hoped that they would find Klaus and therefore wouldn't need to contact the English authorities. If they did, then Tony knew that he would then have some explaining to do.

"Right, Mr Smith, what is the name of your friend?"

"Klaus Zimmerman" Tony answered.

"Bernau isn't a particularly big place, but there may be more than the one Klaus Zimmerman. Do you have any further details which will help us locate him?" asked the German guard.

"Yes, I guess he would now be about 75 years old, very short, bald head, small round glasses and errrrm, oh yes, he's only got one arm!"

"OK, that should narrow it down a little" he said encouragingly.

"A bald headed one armed midget shouldn't be too difficult to find" he laughed as he turned to leave the room.

"Oh, and when you find him, it might be that he doesn't remember me. Tell him that I'm the 1945, Kaska Galinski, Herman Swartz - Tony Smith. He will know what you mean." Tony assured him.

"Ok, we will see what we can do." he said, as he jotted the names down in his notebook.

With that, the border guard turned and continued out of the room and as far as Tony can remember this is where his nightmare began.

He was driven, in the back of a police van, to a detention centre somewhere near Berlin, where he was to be 'temporarily' retained. Even though the guard had thought that Klaus should be easy to find, Tony was frustratingly locked up in the detention centre for over a week. He was kept in a small 'cell' which was little more than 10 foot square. The only furniture was a hard wooden bench, which also doubled up as his bed and a sink with cold running water. Despite his protests, all they would say was that they were still trying to locate Klaus Zimmerman.

Eventually a man in a black suit and carrying a large brief case was escorted in to see Tony.

"Good morning, Mr Smith. My name is Jonathan Denby, I have been assigned by the German court to deal with your case."

"Case? What case? I haven't done anything wrong!" Tony protested.

"Maybe not, but we need to sort a few things out. Firstly, your "friend," Klaus Zimmerman. I am afraid that you have arrived too late. I have to inform you that a Klaus Zimmerman, matching your description and living in Bernau, died just three weeks ago from cancer" said Denby, with a total lack of emotion.

"I am very sorry" he added, again, without any emotion or conviction that he actually meant it.

Tony dropped his head both in sadness at the news, but also in frustration that it meant he could not now verify his story.

Mr Denby continued to speak. "However, they did manage to talk to his widow, Victoria"

"Oh yes?," said Tony excitedly, hoping that Klaus had told her all about himself, and that she would be able to verify who he was.

"She confirmed that her husband had mentioned the names which you gave the officer. But…." he continued, "She also stated that as far as she knew they had all been killed over fifty years ago in the Second World War. However, she also said that for as long as she could remember her husband had always maintained that he had met a 'time traveller' back in 1945, funnily enough, from the year 1995. And get this….., his name was 'Tony Smith.'."

"That's Me. I'm the time traveller!" Tony found himself blurting out excitedly.

"Yes, and I'm Luke Skywalker" replied Mr Denby sarcastically.

Not that Tony had a clue whom Luke Skywalker was, but from the tone of his voice, it was apparent that it was a feeble attempt by him to be funny.

"No honestly, I invented a time machine and changed history!" Tony tried to explain to Denby.

"I'm sorry Mr Smith, or whatever your real name is. I'm afraid I'm into facts not science fiction. Mrs Zimmerman also mentioned that her husband's story was well known around Bernau. He would tell it to anyone who'd listen. She therefore believes that you have heard of her husband's story and have decided to come here pretending to be this 'Tony Smith' in a vain attempt to somehow 'cash in' on the small fortune that Mr Zimmerman, left his wife in his will. I am sorry, but I'm afraid it won't work because she wants nothing to do with you."

"But it's true. I did invent a time machine. I'm not after her money" Tony pleaded.

"And, if I may continue" he said interrupting Tony. "Since you are clearly not this Tony Smith fellow from 1945, we took the liberty of checking out the rest of the information that you gave us. As you already know, this also turned out to be a pack of lies" he said sharply.

"So shall we start again? Do you want to tell me your real name?" he asked.

Tony tried to convince him that he was Tony Smith, but every time he tried to tell him the truth, Denby just laughed and then got angry, accusing Tony of wasting his time.

"Since you refuse to co-operate, you leave us with a dilemma. In normal circumstances, in a situation like this, they would deport you back across the border from whence you came. But we have spoken to the Polish authorities and since you are clearly not Polish, they don't want you back. We could lock you up in Germany, until we get proof of who you really are, but since you claim to be English, the German government do not want you either. They believe it is a matter for the English authorities to clear up.

We have contacted the English embassy in Berlin and, I might add, they weren't particularly keen to have you either, not knowing who you are and you with no identification papers. However, after a certain amount of persuasion, you will be pleased to know that they have reluctantly agreed to take you off our hands. So once we have cleared the deportation papers, you will be on your way back to Blighty" he stated cheerfully.

"Oh, and by the way, I would drop this bullshit about time travel once you get back there, else they are likely to send you off to the funny farm" he added sarcastically.

With that he thanked Tony for his time and wished him a 'Good Day', packing his papers back in his briefcase, before making a hasty exit.

Tony considered that this was becoming a nightmare. No one was going to believe his story now, since they already had him labelled as some sort of con artist or even a nutter. Clearly he couldn't go around claiming to be a time traveller, but what plausible story could he now give them to get him out of this mess? To make matters worse, they kept him in the detention centre for a further three weeks, whilst they 'sorted out' his deportation. Tony hoped that when he was finally deported to England that things would improve, but since he was the man who didn't exist, Tony doubted it very much.

225

Chapter 21 – The irony of winning the War

Ten years have now passed and unfortunately things did not improve for Tony. In fact they got very much worse! He spent the first three months in England in a 'secure' unit in the port of Folkestone, whilst they decided what to do with him. Tony couldn't give them any names, addresses or information, which could verify that he had even been to England before, let alone confirm that he had actually lived there. The places that Tony knew from his 1995, either didn't now exist or were completely different. Tony's frustration grew, as he could offer them nothing that would authenticate who he was, although he did take the advice of Mr Denby and refrained from telling them why they were different. The last thing he wanted to do was give them a reason to keep him locked up any longer than necessary. Having them think he was a mental case, by telling them that he thought he was from an alternative time-line would have been just the excuse they needed.

Tony quickly realised that if he had told them that he was a foreign national seeking asylum, they would have found him accommodation, given him state handouts and no doubt treated him a lot better than they did. But, since Tony continued to insist that he was English and they could not trace him on any of their databases, they assumed he was hiding something from them. And so to satisfy themselves that Tony wasn't some form of security risk, they spent an age checking him against missing person's lists, escaped prisoner details, wanted terrorists and just about every other conceivable data list.

When their searches, including fingerprints and DNA , drew a blank, they eventually decided that had little choice but to reluctantly let him go. They couldn't justify keeping him detained indefinitely, since he hadn't actually committed any crime. But since they were convinced that he was not being honest with them, they refrained from offering him any help and simply released him in to the waiting world. One day Tony was sitting in the rest room, waiting for his next bout of questioning and trying to cope with the tedium of being locked up, when they came in and said 'you can go now'. Just like that!

Tony was cast out on to the streets of Folkestone like a pet, received as a Christmas gift, and now unwanted. The only advice he was given, was that "if he really didn't have anywhere to go then he should consider going to the nearest DHSS offices and maybe they would help him out." Tony had no money, except for a few 'Zloty', which he soon found to be worthless. He also had no possessions, other than the clothes he was standing in.

No family, no friends and nowhere to live. The fact was, he had nothing whatsoever to give him any hope that things would improve.

Tony had had his fill of bureaucracy and decided the last thing he wanted was to go to another Government agency like the DHSS, and therefore concluded that he had no choice but to fend for himself. For a while he lived on the streets and in hostels for the homeless. Firstly in Folkestone, but then he moved up to London. They say that 'money makes money'. Well, the opposite is also true. When you have no money things just seem to go from bad to worse. Tony was in a perpetual poverty trap. With no paperwork, the only work he could find was low paid, cash in hand, manual labour work, which he'd be the first to admit, that he had always been crap at. He had no chance of getting a proper job, since he had no qualifications, well not in this time-line and without money no chance of getting any. Let's face it, even if he did have some documents, what sort of job could he do? Tony had spent virtually his entire working life, theorising about quantum physics and time displacement. Hardly the sort of work they advertise in the local job centre or interview stinking tramps for. Tony contemplated how he had ended up in this state. He, one of the world's greatest scientists, a bloody genius - the man who had invented the sodding time-machine, was now begging for food on the streets of London. It made him feel sick to the stomach just thinking about it.

It wasn't surprising that Tony sank into the depths of depression and soon found that his only solace was in alcohol. Spending most of the time drunk seemed to numb the despair. Every penny he managed to beg, borrow or steal went on cheap wine. Although it made him feel better at the time Tony knew that if he continued to live how he was, then one day they would find him dead and lying in the gutter.

Tony had always considered himself to be quite a private man. Sociable when he needed to be, but generally happier with his own company. But, even for Tony, he found that being a tramp on the streets of London was a very lonely existence. He found that the only people who wanted to befriend him were other drunks and tramps. In essence, the dregs of society. Admittedly Tony was in no position to be snobbish, since he was in the same boat as them. No doubt they all had their own hard luck story to tell as to how they found themselves in this predicament, but Tony still found himself looking down his nose at them. Despite being no better off than his fellow tramps, Tony shunned their company and generally treated them with the same disdain that he was receiving from everyone else.

Being a tramp opens your eyes to the way a society reacts to wealth. London in the 1990's was full of people who were only interested in their own wealth and didn't care about others or the environment around them. Tony considered that some people just about tolerated him, many were aggressive or abusive towards him, but most, didn't even notice that he was there. They were too absorbed in their own materialistic world to be concerned over the greater needs of society or the pitiful existence of a dirty tramp. Tony decided that he hated this new time-line! He had never regretted anything more in his life, than the fact that he pulled that pin out of the hand grenade back in 1945.

He was now acquiescent to the fact that he had destroyed everything he cared about and loved. He realised that if he had of listened to his son, his life would be so much better. If Karl was right, Tony could have now been a hero, rich, famous and well respected, instead of festering away in this shithole. If London was typical of the rest of the country Tony decided that he despised the England that he had now created.

Compared to the London ruled by the Germans, this was a dirty horrible place. Crime was virtually non-existent in Tony's original time-line, yet here he was, regularly spat on, kicked and on two separate occasions he had even been beaten up. In Tony's original time-line it would not have been tolerated. Criminals were dealt with very severely, so as a consequence there were very few criminals. Everyone knew where he or she stood and respected the law and each other. Law and order was paramount. There was little crime. There was no litter. No graffiti. In fact there weren't even any tramps!

What Tony found most ironic was the number of foreigners in the city. Back in 1945 the English had fought so bravely to defend the country from foreign invasion. Yet, having won the war, London now found itself full of foreigners of every race and creed under the sun. Having lost the war in his original time-line it was very different. Except for a number of Germans in eminent positions, England remained very much English. Admittedly, German was now the national language, but other than that, England, and especially London, remained quintessentially very British. The old traditions and indeed even the Royal family were very much encouraged by our German conquerors. With travel in or out of the greater 'German Republic' pretty much impossible, there were very few, if any, non Europeans in England at all! Tony didn't have any personal feelings against any of these foreigners in this new time-line, in fact some of the few acts of kindness that he had encountered since being here, had come from Asian or West Indian people. But having them here was one of the most noticeable differences between the two time-lines. Tony mused that he was 35 and until he came back to this time-line he had never seen a black person in his life! Although this 'multi-racial' population clearly had its benefits and they had obviously integrated well into society, he couldn't help thinking that England had lost a certain amount of its Englishness, which given the circumstances he found pretty ironic indeed.

The irony of what had become of the world as a whole in this time-line, was also not lost on Tony. Since the end of the Second World War in his original timeline the World had been ostensibly at peace. Admittedly, it was an uneasy peace at times, especially when the cold war between the German Republic and America was at its height, but nevertheless not a single bomb had been dropped in anger between nations, since 1945. Yet here, in this timeline, wars had continued to rage at regular intervals. Conflicts had taken place in Korea, Vietnam, Afghanistan, Iraq and even the Falkland islands, to name but a few.

When wars weren't being fought, death and destruction was still a daily occurrence throughout the world. Perpetual civil wars were ongoing in many countries, whilst in others there had been the mass genocide of entire ethnic minorities and sections of the population.

In Russia, despite leading his country to victory against the Nazis, Joseph Stalin had inexplicably proceeded to massacre millions of his own people over the next two decades.

Was this really the vision of the future that mankind had for the world, after they had rid the planet of the scourge of the Third Reich? Did they really envisage a world where the constant threat of global terrorism was an ever increasing reality?

In the world where the 'evil' Nazis had won the war, the irony was, that world peace was now tangible. Tony had grown up in a world where individuals felt safe and secure in their own environment, and mankind in general, was able to live in peaceful co-existence. The irony brought a bitter smile to Tony's face.

Chapter 22 – Tony's demise.

One thing Tony had kept to himself during all the time he was locked up in Folkestone was the fact that he was married. He had already concluded that if he told them about Hannah, even if they traced her, she would no doubt deny all knowledge of him.

Then what? They would have accused Tony of lying and wasting their time. And then, no doubt, they would have made life even more difficult for him.

Even after he was released, as painful as it was, Tony promised himself that he would not try to find out if Hannah existed in this time-line or, even if he knew she did, he swore that he would not try to contact her.

Tony knew deep down, that if a complete stranger confronted her; claiming to be her ex-husband from an alternative world, it would freak her out. He didn't think it would do him any favours either. Seeing Hannah would only remind Tony of what he had lost and what he had done to his son, Karl. Inventing the time-machine had been the biggest mistake of his life and seeing her now, would have been too much for Tony to bear.

So he made a promise to himself that come what may, he would stay as far away from Hannah as possible.

All I can say is that Tony wishes he had kept that promise!

In his original time-line he had spent a lot of his working life in London and had felt very much at home there. However, now under these rather different circumstances Tony detested the place. As time went by, he decided that he could stand it no longer and made the decision to head to Leeds. Leeds was where he had grown up and since it was his home town, Tony hoped that he would be happier there. If nothing else he hoped that the people would be friendlier than those in London. Tony knew he had vowed to keep away from Hannah, but he couldn't stand London any longer and Leeds seemed to be the logical place to go. Tony convinced himself that he would be able to resist the temptation of trying to find her once he got to Leeds, and to be honest he considered the likelihood of her even existing to be pretty slim.

At first things went well for Tony. He found a small bed-sit through a shelter charity and they also convinced him that contacting the DHSS would not be such a bad thing. Tony told the DHSS that he had no recollection of who he was, due to years of alcohol abuse. Given how he looked (and probably smelt) they didn't take too much convincing and so he was able to secure a regular income through the social security system and they proceeded to create a new identity for him. Now Tony was on 'the system' he felt this was a new start for him and decided to clean himself up and, although it proved difficult, pack in the bottle.

He still struggled to find any meaningful work – well, work to satisfy the mind of a brilliant scientist, but he did manage to do some voluntary work for the shelter charity. It wasn't particularly brain-taxing work but at least it kept him off the street and gave his life some purpose.

Then one day it happened. Tony bumped into Hannah! She was coming out of a suite of offices in the town centre, when he literally walked into her. Her hair was in a different style, but there was no mistaking that it was Hannah. Tony was so taken aback that he couldn't even get the words out of his mouth to apologise and just stood there gawping frozen to the spot. Hannah, assuming that was still her name, just said a courteous "Sorry," and walked on. But for Tony, seeing her again sent a shudder down his spine.

Tony knew that they had split up in his 'real' time-line, but that didn't mean that he did not still love her. Seeing her now, reminded him of all the passionate times they had spent together and what a mess he had managed to make of his life. Although totally misguided, having now seen her, Tony felt that he could re-kindle her love for him. He knew that he would be starting from scratch, but she had fallen for him once, so why not again? Tony was now a man with a mission. Unfortunately, a futile and somewhat obsessive mission. He started by confirming that she worked in the building from which she had just come out of. She did, and Tony soon found out that her name was still Hannah.

At first he watched her from a distance each day as she left the building for her lunch, but soon he found himself following her around. Initially she didn't notice Tony, but after a while, she would occasionally give him a nervous smile. Tony took this as encouragement, since she had now acknowledged his existence. On a couple of occasions, Tony even managed to initiate a conversation. He felt that was starting to form a relationship and decided the time was right to take it to the next stage and ask her out on a date.

One day, when she had visited one of her usual snack bars for lunch, Tony plucked up the courage to sit opposite her. However, before he could start a conversation she started ranting and raving, accusing him of stalking her and saying that if Tony didn't leave her alone that she'd call the police. Tony pleaded with her to give him a chance to explain himself, not that he was too sure what he would have told her, but she stormed off, shouting at him as she went.

Unfortunately, instead of acting as a warning and putting Tony off, it made him more determined to win her affections. Tony didn't want the woman who he once loved and indeed who loved him, thinking that he was some sort of mad stalker. He knew he had to somehow convince her that he meant her no harm and that his intentions were good.

Tony didn't want another public scene like the one in the snack bar, so he hatched a plan to follow her home. At least if he knew her address, Tony considered that he could write to her and explain his true feelings. Maybe even get her to talk to him again.

Tony had watched her walk to the car park on many occasions and therefore knew what sort of car she drove. So one night he waited at the exit of the car park in a taxi and when she appeared he simply told the taxi driver to 'follow that car'. Hannah eventually pulled in to the drive of a rather pleasant semi-detached house on the outskirts of Leeds.

By the fact that she let herself in to the house, Tony assumed it must be where she lived.

Tony paid the taxi driver and then went closer to the front door to see the house number. Tony had only wanted to find her address, but now he was there, the temptation to try and talk to her was too great.

Looking back, Tony knew he wasn't thinking straight, but he thought that perhaps she would be more prepared to listen to him at her own home. He also decided that he would tell her the truth. He knew she wouldn't believe him but at least if he got it off his chest then, maybe, he could get on with his own life again. Although he also still deluded himself that she might just fall for him once again, if she knew the truth.

Tony slowly walked up her garden path to her front door and taking a deep breath, he rang the bell. He waited nervously for Hannah to answer the door; however Tony was not prepared for what happened next. The door opened, but instead of Hannah answering it, there in front of him stood Karl!

He didn't look completely like the Karl Tony remembered and some of his features were slightly different, for instance darker hair, but it was still Karl no doubt.

"Karl!" Tony said excitedly.

"Errr, Yea, who are you?" replied Karl in bewilderment.

"Karl, my son, it's me your dad!" Tony told him, stepping forward to embrace him.

But instead of greeting Tony, he pushed him away - saying that he didn't know what he was talking about.

Then Karl's mum arrived at the door step and all hell broke loose. Hannah just totally lost it, kicking and punching Tony. She was screaming 'Leave us alone, leave us alone."

Karl pulled her off Tony, but he too was very agitated and also started shouting at Tony to go away and leave them alone.

Just then another car pulled up in the driveway, and seeing the commotion, a man jumped out. He was about six feet tall, with blonde hair – in fact not dissimilar to Tony.

"What the hell's going on here?" said the man, partially as a question but more as a threat towards Tony.

"This is the madman that I told you about. The one who's been stalking me at work" screamed Hannah.

With that the man pushed Tony to the floor and with both hands held around his throat, threatened that if Tony came near his family again he would kill him.

Your family? That's rich Tony thought to himself.

But then it occurred to him that this stranger was Hannah's husband and Karl was his son! Karl had always looked more like his mum than Tony and therefore Tony guessed that, despite having a different father he had kept most of his features. As for his name - Karl, it had been Hannah's idea from the start to call him Karl, so it stood to reason that she would choose the same name again, or for the first time as far as she was concerned.

Resigned to the fact that it would be futile arguing with them, Tony nodded in order that her 'husband' would release his grip on his throat. When Hannah's husband eventually released Tony and stood back, he continued to threaten Tony as he got to his feet. Realising that he had made a big mistake Tony backed away to leave them, but before he got out of their driveway he suddenly found himself being manhandled and forced into the back of a police car.

One of the neighbours, witnessing the commotion, had called the police and therefore before he knew what was happening Tony was down the local police station, with his hands restrained behind his back by a pair of handcuffs.

Hannah's husband made a formal complaint and although Tony escaped with a caution, he had a restraining order put on him, banning him from going within five miles of Hannah or her family.

Despite this, and knowing that he now had no chance of getting back with Hannah, it still burnt Tony up inside that this stranger now had his wife and his son!

From this point onwards, things went from bad to worse.

Tony's depression set in again and with that he returned to the bottle. Tony stopped doing his voluntary work, choosing to spend most of his time drinking himself to oblivion in his grotty bed-sit. Tony felt so worthless, that he now let himself go completely and lived like a pig in its own squalor. Not much caring what he looked like or how he lived.

Tony didn't realise at the time but his depression had made him very unstable. So much so, that he finally decided that he'd had enough, and therefore made the decision to end his life. Tony hated this England he had created, he hated what he considered to be his hellish life, but most of all he now hated the fact that a complete stranger now had his wife and son and was living the life that should have been his.

So with no hope and no future, Tony decided to kill himself. He bought the most expensive bottle of wine he could afford (if you are going to kill yourself, Tony considered that it might as well be with decent wine), and drank it accompanied by a huge overdose of pills. However, the truth was that Tony couldn't even get his own suicide right. Tony hadn't bothered reading the letter informing him of a visit by Social Services that day.

No sooner had he fallen unconscious than they were bashing down his door. Apparently it was touch and go, but thanks to a stomach pumping and three days in hospital, Tony's pitiful life was saved.

Tony was subsequently admitted to the Psychiatric unit of Leeds hospital. In Tony's mind this was a miserable place full of nutters and weirdo's. Although Tony had no right to, he again felt himself looking down his nose at these people and considered that he didn't belong there.

Tony viewed it as ironic that they would send someone with chronic depression, to one of the most depressing places in the world. He dismissed any hope that Leeds Psychiatric hospital would improve his state of mind.

Although under strict supervision, Tony was officially a voluntary patient and so when he eventually decided to discharge himself, they couldn't stop him. Tony concluded that if he was going to be depressed then he would rather be so in his own home, rather than in a 'lunatic asylum'. So Tony went back to his bed-sit.

After that, he had regular visits from social services and Tony managed to convince them that he was alright - or 'surviving' as he put it.' However, deep down, he still felt very, very depressed. Not quite suicidal, but not far off. Again, the only way he found that he could get through each day was to get blind drunk.

This continued for many weeks and then one day when Tony was particularly out of it on cheap wine and anti-depressants his world crashed around him. To this day he can't recollect how or why he was stood outside Hannah's house shouting and bawling like a demented idiot. He can't even remember buying the large kitchen knife. But when Hannah's husband rather foolishly confronted Tony and tried to restrain him, Tony just lost it.

After just a few short frantic minutes of utter chaos, Tony found himself staring down at the grotesque and lifeless body of Hannah's husband. Tony's bright red hands and blood splattered shirt and face gave evidence to the brutal way in which he had repeatedly stabbed his victim over and over again in his chest and abdomen. The poor sod had stood no chance at all.

Tony looked at the knife still clenched tightly in his hand and then back at bloodied corpse lying at his feet. As the blood ran down the blade and dripped on to pavement, Tony relaxed his grip and let the knife fall to the ground. As the realisation of what he had done began to dawn, Tony stood there in silence, staring blankly at the body. Devoid of any emotion he waited patiently for someone to come and take him away.

Tony's downfall was now complete - He had gone from being an eminent scientist with the world at his feet to a deranged murderer. The only saving grace was the Hannah and Karl were not there to witness the brutal killing of their husband and father, having left shortly before Tony arrived to go shopping in Leeds.

Chapter 23 - Why not build a TESS2?

"Right, is there any other business?....Dr Yates?."

"No, I think we've just about covered everything thank you."

"Dr Jones?."

"Yes there is actually, I want to know when we are going to come to our senses and utilise the computer that we are wasting on Dr Rose's 'time traveller'."

"I'm sorry Dr Jones, but this is the finance committee. The use of the computer in the case of Tony Smith is part of his therapy and therefore is a matter for the medical committee to discuss at its next meeting" I argued.

"I'm sorry, Dr Rose, but Dr Jones is right. The purpose of this meeting is to talk about the finances and resources of this institute, and frankly we cannot afford to waste such a valuable piece of equipment on such a futile experiment. We all know he is never going to make a bloody time machine, so why not tell him? For Christ's sake he's had it over a year!" stated Dr Blackmore, the chairman of the finance committee.

"Look I know it's dragging on, but Tony Smith is convinced that it is nearly finished. The purpose of the therapy was to convince him that time travel is impossible. If we take it away from him before he proves this to himself, then we will not have closure and the last two years will have been a complete waste of time." I continued to argue.

"It's been a waste of time anyway. Everyone can see it but you. He's been playing you along and you are too blinkered to see it." stated Dr Jones rather tersely.

Unfortunately Dr Jones was the senior consultant and a very well respected man. It took a brave man to argue with him. He could stop a man's career dead in its tracks if he took a dislike to you. I'd always had a good relationship with him, but the last thing I wanted to do was get on his wrong side.

"Look, Arnold," I said, hoping to appeal to the good side of his nature, "I know it's taken longer than I originally envisaged, but I am concerned that if we remove it now, it will have a considerable detrimental effect on his progress. I really think I've made a significant breakthrough with this patient and all I ask for is one more month" "Besides, it's only a computer" I added rather feebly.

"All you ever ask for is one more month. And you know damn well that it's more than 'just a computer'" replied Dr Jones. "Mr Smith is no more a time traveller than you or me, but there is little doubt that he's a very clever man. I've seen what he's done to that 'computer' and I have to admit that I'm very impressed. How he's done it, I do not know, but we could power half of the institutes systems off it. I am sorry but we cannot afford to waste such a valuable resource!" he said in a tone that left little doubt that he was not prepared to carrying on arguing about the matter. "I suggest we put it to the vote?" he added.

Once Arnold Jones had stated his position, the outcome of any subsequent vote was usually a foregone conclusion. Once he voted to have it removed, "with immediate effect," I knew that none of the others would vote against him. As he went round the table taking votes, other than my own token gesture, the decision was unsurprisingly unanimous.

I'm sorry, perhaps I should introduce myself? My name is David Rose…,Dr David Rose. Unfortunately I've been left with the task of telling Tony Smith, one of my patients that at 9 o'clock in the morning his 'time-machine' is going to be dismantled and its component parts are to be used to power our new finance system. I know it's against normal protocol, but I've become quite friendly with Tony Smith. Even though he is in here for a quite brutal killing, I have to admit I enjoy his company very much. He's very articulate and exceptionally bright. Our conversations are sometimes outstanding. He has an ability to always see things from a different perspective, and if I'm honest he has made me more open minded to other people's view point. In fact I would go as far to say that he has helped make me a better physician.

He is also the most convincing delusionist that I've ever come across. His account of life in his 'alternate' time-line and his stories of the people he had met back in 1945 were so vivid, that at times he's almost had me believing him!

I know that time travel is not possible, but I honestly believe that his recollection of events is very real in his own mind. Even under hypnosis he's not relented in his belief that he is not from this time-line. I had made it a personal goal of mine to get into his mind and find out what has happened in his past to make him create this 'alternative' reality.

I was hoping that once he realised that he couldn't invent a time-machine for real, that he would open up to me, and the tell the truth about the real Tony Smith.

I'm concerned that now I have to abandon my 'experiment' that it will set our progress back years. If that happens then I'm not sure that I'll ever convince Tony of the fact that this whole façade, is nothing more than a figment of his own imagination. It could of course be an elaborate game he's playing with us all. In which case he is very good at it.

The question is, how do I tell him that the hours he has spent building TESS2, as he calls it, have been a complete waste of time. I know that he's not going to take this well. He's spent hour upon hour on that machine, and for us to take it away from him tomorrow morning is going to be devastating for him.

Sorry, perhaps I should explain who Tony Smith is, that's if you haven't already read about him in the papers. Some 10 years ago Tony was committed to my care, here at Brampton DSPD (Dangerous and Severe Personality Disorder Unit) for the brutal killing of Tony Beresford. What made the front pages was the fact that he claimed to be a time-traveller who had come from an alternative world where the Germans had won World War II. When questioned why we were not all speaking German and flying swastikas from every flag pole, he had tried to convince the court that it was because he had travelled back in time, changed history and therefore, he alone was responsible for the Allies winning war. When Tony told the court that he killed a man, who rather uncannily was also called Tony, in a jealous rage because he had stolen his wife from his other time-line, it caused quite a stir. For a few weeks Tony was on the front page of every newspaper. Of course, no one believed his story and it would have been viewed as quite entertaining if it were not such a sad and brutal killing. When he sentenced him, the judge called Tony a dangerous delusionist and suggested that he remained 'indefinitely' at her Majesty's pleasure.

The funny thing was, that despite being in the papers every day, no one came forward claiming to know Tony Smith. No parents, no brothers, sisters, or even old school friends came out of the woodwork to feed the papers with the usual stories of how they always knew that he would turn out to be a killer one day. In fact right up until today, Tony's true past remains a complete mystery.

I had watched his trial with a professional interest and to be honest I did feel quite sorry for him. Obviously he had mental health issues and was clearly guilty of the killing of Mr Beresford, something he never actually denied. But during the trial it was so apparent that Tony Smith believed every word he was saying about his past life. It was clearly very traumatic for him, seeing Hannah, the woman he claimed to be his wife from this alternative time-line and Karl, his apparent son, sat in the court room. Knowing that they hated him beyond comprehension was hard for him to take and his psychological meltdown during his trial was like watching a car crash in slow motion. He got away with the murder on the grounds of diminished responsibility, although given the brutality of the killing he's still not likely to get out of here in a hurry.

When he first arrived at Brampton, he went very much into a self preservation state, refusing to talk to anyone for the best part of a year. It was only through my own perseverance that I finally managed to get him to come out of his shell. I encouraged him to talk openly about his past and hoped that I could trigger a response that would reveal his true history. However, to this very day Tony has maintained the façade of this time-traveller. Although clearly he has a delusional disorder, I have to admit that of all my patients, Tony Smith, is the most fascinating case I have ever dealt with.

Once Tony realised that people weren't out to harm him he has actually settled down to be a model patient. He actually admits that he feels more at home locked up in here, than he has at any other time since he supposedly came back to this time-line. He enjoys the strict timetable and routine that life revolves around in here and in general considered that people had been kind to him.

I have encouraged him to talk openly about his past, "as part of his therapy." I obviously try to convince Tony that what he is claiming is impossible, and have told him many times that the sooner he realises it, the sooner he'd be able to start his true rehabilitation. Tony knows that he won't convince me that he is telling the truth but, as much as I have tried to convince Tony otherwise, he sticks stubbornly to his story. I know I mustn't lose sight of the fact that he is in here for a brutal killing, but over the years we have developed a good friendship. Tony knows that he is just another one of my patients and I am mindful to retain the doctor/patient relationship and sometimes have to point it out to Tony if I think he is crossing the line, but there is no doubt that I am probably fonder of Tony than anyone else in the unit.

I would say that we have a mutual respect. Tony appreciates the fact that I always find the time to talk with him, whilst I can genuinely say that I have never had such intellectual and deep conversations such as ours, in my entire life.

I know that the majority of doctors in here still think he is a bit of an oddball, but they haven't got to know him over the years the same way I have. To some degree I have become quite protective towards him. Because Tony's was such an unique case he always seems to have a queue of 'shrinks' coming from all over the world, happy to listen to his story and to analyze his every word. Over the years Tony had numerous psychiatrists, psychoanalysis's, psychologists, in fact, if their profession began with 'Psycho', Tony has had the lot of them come to see him. He has also had a constant queue of journalists and even 'film' crews hoping to get the latest story or produce a documentary on the 'time travelling murderer'. Tony says that he doesn't mind and that it breaks the monotony of this place, but I've now started to vet every request and say 'no' more often than I allow them access. An American team even brought a couple of 'top' scientists in with them, to add weight to the argument that 'time-travel' was impossible. I had to laugh when this nearly backfired on them. Far from convincing Tony that Time-travel wasn't possible, Tony nearly convinced them that it was!

Tony obviously wasn't going to tell them how he had done it and let them get all the credit of inventing a time-machine of their own. But, he gave them enough 'food for thought'. The scientists told the authorities that, in their opinion, Tony's theories were based on sound scientific principles and were therefore very plausible; adding that they should not discount the possibility that Tony was actually telling the truth. Their opinion was met with such derision that at one stage I thought the pair of them were going to end up locked in Brampton and sharing a cell with Tony! They were eventually laughed out of the building – and went back to the States, never to be seen in here again.

I think that all this constant questioning of his 'theories' and indeed his sanity, by all of these so called 'experts' and journalists, was what actually planted the seed of his idea. Tony decided that he wanted to build a new time machine to prove once and for all that Time Travel was possible. Since he had already built one time-machine - why couldn't he do it again? Why not build a TESS2?

When Tony first hit me with his request to let him build a time-machine – I laughed at him and gave him a point blank no answer. But then it occurred to me that it might not be such a bad idea after all. Not for him to build a time-machine, which is obviously impossible, but for him to fail to build one. Once he realised that it can't be done, he would have to admit that his previous existence was all fantasy and confronted with this, he will hopefully revert to the truth, which would be a major step in his rehabilitation.

So I put it to Tony that if I allowed him to build a time-machine and somehow it failed to work, would he accept that time-travel was impossible?

"So, Tony. Let's just say we do allow you to build TESS2. What if it fails to work – where does that leave us?" I asked him.

"If that were the case then I'd have no choice but to put a stop to all this 'nonsense' about time travel and accept your diagnosis of my mental illness" he assured me.

"You really mean that?"

"Of course" was the expected reply.

"But just remember I have already built one, so I can see no reason why this one should fail. Where would that leave us" he added with a broad grin.

To be honest, this wasn't part of the equation. As far as I was concerned the consequences of it working were irrelevant since in my tiny mind, as Tony would often describe it, I could not comprehend such an outcome and, therefore, I didn't even believe it to be a consequence worth considering.

"Well maybe it would prove that you're not quite as mad as some people think you are," I laughed.

"Good, then we have a deal do we?" he said enthusiastically.

"It isn't entirely up to me, but we will see"

"We will see" I repeated as I left the room.

Excited about this new line of treatment for Tony, I put my weight behind his request to build a time machine and presented the project to the board. They were very sceptical about the idea, especially Arnold Jones and believed it would be a waste of time and effort. However after much debate, I finally managed to convince them to let him try. The authorities therefore granted Tony access to a computer and agreed to get him any additional components that he would need.

When I told Tony - he was elated. He felt he had pulled a master-plan by getting permission to build a new time-machine. He claimed he had used a bit of reverse psychology on me, by making me think that it was my idea to use it as part of his treatment. I reiterated that it was MY idea, but nevertheless I had never seen Tony Smith so happy or passionate about anything since he had been in here.

Well, that was over eighteen months ago and Tony has been building TESS2 ever since.

Although, in theory, he said it should be easier to build the second time around, in practice it was more difficult. Some of the components that Tony had used in his 'original' machine, hadn't even been invented in this time line. He therefore, had to design them from scratch and then ask the institute staff to get them made for him.

At first my colleagues were fine about this and I convinced them to go along with all his requests. If they argued, Tony would just say 'how do you expect a time-machine to work without a hugeamathingy or a thingymabob and they would shrug their shoulders and get it made. But more recently, they have started to question everything Tony has asked for, saying 'look, haven't you given up yet' or 'come on, you know it's a waste of time' and have also been applying pressure to me to bring my 'project' to a conclusion.

I have to admit that even I was now starting to lose patience, and have continually told Tony that I cannot go on supporting this 'project' indefinitely. With resources as they are, I have been under increasing pressure to utilise the equipment elsewhere in the unit.

What I didn't know, was that Tony was very close indeed. In fact TESS2 was already actually working! Tony had already sent an apple back in time by one day and he would have derived great pleasure from showing me that he wasn't mad after all. However, as far as Tony was concerned the point of the exercise had not been to prove the thing could work, but to get himself out of Brampton and to a better life. Tony thought that if he showed me that it could work on an apple, then I would take the machine away from him and stop him using it to escape. He was probably right.

And so Tony has been making continual excuses as to why it isn't yet working. He is under no illusion that if it wasn't for me he would have had the plug pulled on him a long time ago. He knows that I have continuingly stuck my neck out for him, for which he says he is very grateful. However, since recently my judgment has been questioned at the highest level I have made it very clear to Tony that he was now on borrowed time and the fact is, that he is now testing our 'friendship' to the limit. Tony knows that time is against him and, sooner or later, even I will have to bow to the pressure to have it removed. With this in mind, Tony spent every available minute on the laborious task of inputting his entire DNA structure in to the computer once again. He was restricted to how much time he could spend on the machine, but since he'd already done it a couple of times before, the coding this time around, was a little easier.

When he wasn't able to have access to TESS2, Tony started to write everything down. Not just what he was doing at the moment, but what he had done in the past. He supposed that it was sort of his autobiography. If he proved that his machine worked by disappearing into the past, then he wanted everyone to know the whole truth. Tony surmised that if he managed to disappear from such a secure unit as Brampton, then surely the authorities would have no choice but to realise that he had been telling the truth all along. If that was the case then he wanted the world to know of the heroism of people like Kaska, Jakub and Klaus and of how things might have been for them - if he hadn't pulled that pin from the grenade. He also wanted them to know that he wasn't mad and for Hannah to realise why he had done the terrible things that he had done, especially to her husband.

Time had marched on, but finally Tony had just about finished. He had just to dot a few i's and cross a few t's, but essentially it was now complete. For the last couple of days he had been biding his time, while he finished his 'book'. Other than that Tony was confident that he had once again built the world's first time-machine.

Despite having plenty of time to think about it during the last 18 months, Tony was still unsure where to go to next. Although technically, his problem was not where to go to - but when. Since his machine could only travel in time and not space, Tony knew that however far back he went that he would still be on this exact spot. Therefore, unless he went back far enough he would still be in this asylum. He also knew that if he went back within the last ten years, then whenever he went back to, there would be two of him in here!

He mused how he would love to see my face if that happened and considered that I would obviously have no choice but to believe him, with two Tony's arguing the case.

But would it still get him out of here? It might prove that he wasn't mad, but since he had still killed someone, he knows that we are hardly going to be queuing up to set him free. Or set both of them free, since there would now be two Tonys locked up. Besides, Tony doesn't entirely trust the authorities. He trusts me, but knowing some of the 'other bastards' in here, as he calls them, Tony firmly believes that they would take his time-machine off him and claim the credit of its invention for themselves.

Tony realised that he was starting to sound a little paranoid, but let's face it, even if you were sane when you first came in here, after 10 years of being locked up in a lunatic asylum 'twenty-four seven' would be enough to send anyone around the bend eventually. Paranoid Schizophrenia was just one of the many issues Tony had to deal with during his stay at Brampton.

With consideration Tony determined that a more sensible idea would be to go back to before he killed Hannah's husband, and therefore wouldn't yet be locked up in here. He considered that maybe he could even try and stop himself killing him. However, he contemplated that even if he went back before he was locked up in here, he would still be locked up in here, if you understand his meaning. Before he could stop himself committing 'manslaughter' again, he would first of all have to get out of this place. If he was to materialise in this exact spot sometime in the past, unless he went so far back that this place wasn't even built, Tony knew that he would still be in this building, and so how would he explain his presence in here?

If a complete stranger suddenly appeared naked in a loony asylum it might just create a bit of a stir. Tony chuckled to himself when considered that it would be the first time anyone would have been accused of breaking in to this place! Even if he did convince the authorities to let him out of here and he was successful in stopping himself killing Hannah's husband, what would happen then? By saving his life he would have created a major paradox and be zapped back here. However, since Tony would not have now killed him, he would have never have been locked up in here in the first place, and if he had never been locked up, he wouldn't have invented the time-machine for the second time! As far as Tony's memories were concerned he would have still spent the last 10 years locked up in this place. Nothing he could do would change that, so what would he gain?

Tony knew that he would no doubt find himself back in this exact spot. He would then have the problem of having to explain how he has suddenly appeared in Brampton yet again? He would no doubt eventually be set free, since he wouldn't have actually done anything wrong. Other than appear naked out of thin air in a secure mental facility with no plausible story. So when we let him out, what then? He might well be free again, but surely he would just return to his wonderful life, as a penniless, drunken, manic depressive?

'No thank you' he thought.

No, the only sensible thing to do, Tony considered, would be to go back far enough to ensure this place hadn't yet been built. This he found out to be 1980.

Prior to then, this place had been nothing but fields and countryside, therefore as long as he went back before 1980, he would at least be free to go wherever he wanted to.

So how far back should he go? He questioned himself.

The more he thought about it, the more he hated what had become of England. Tony felt that the changing of the time-line had created a brutal England where crime and violence were rife. A dirty England, with graffiti and filth everywhere you looked. An under achieving England with no heart, soul or identity of its own, governed by 'European' bureaucrats. An intolerant England, where materialistic gain was more important than helping fellow human beings. He knew his 'original' England wasn't perfect, but from where he was sat, it was paradise compared to this. How they have managed to screw up such a great nation in this time-line beggared belief for Tony.

Tony knew that there would be consequences, not least for the Jews, but he had made up his mind to teach these bastards a lesson and undo what he had done back in 1945.

Tony convinced himself that this wasn't how it was meant to be! The real time-line was how it was before his interference, so what right did he have to change history for all mankind?

None. The decision was made. He would go back and stop himself from pulling the pin on that hand grenade and therefore stop this shithole of a place from ever existing. 'It wasn't as though I will cause anyone any pain' he contemplated. 'They would just be erased from an existence that they were never meant to have had in the first place. Anyway, who's to say that all those people I erased from the original time-line weren't more deserving of a life. At least they hadn't managed to screw up the world!'

Tony concluded that he would have to go back to before the onset of the Second World War. This would hopefully give him the time he would need to get halfway across Europe, intercept and stop himself from killing Herman Swartz.

So Tony spent every available minute from the last two weeks programming the machine with the time co-ordinates of 1937. Two years before the outbreak of war.

And so finally TESS2 is now ready! The problem is, now that he'd finally finished inputting all the data, he hated to admit it, but he was having second thoughts. The drawback with being locked up, is that you have too much time on your hands to think about things. And the more he thought about it, the more unconvinced he was that he had made the right decision. He hated himself for being so indecisive, but he started to convince himself that his plan was doomed to fail. The more he thought about it, the more the doubts grew in his mind.

He was sure that he would still be able to find the place where it all happened, since Klaus's co-ordinates are still indelibly marked in his brain. But he had his doubts about how he would get from Brampton, in the centre of England, to northern Poland, which even before the outbreak of war would be a very arduous journey. Having spent so long in Brampton, Tony was not so sure that he could endure eight more years of hardship, travelling half way across a war torn Europe.

'Even if I did manage it and was then able to reverse my original paradox by stopping Jakub and the others ambushing Herman Swartz, what would I come back to?' he considered.

Presumably, Europe would once again be controlled by the Germans. He didn't have a problem with that. But he knew that he could never return to his original time-line, since his history had already happened and wherever he goes back to will be from this point in history and from this time-line. Therefore, once he had created the Paradox of saving Herman Swartz, he would no doubt find himself back here, in whatever building the Germans had built on this spot. With no clothes, no money, no documents and therefore, once again, no evidence of ever existing.

Even though he would prefer things to be back the way they were, he guessed that a person with no identification, money, friends, relatives etc in his original 'German' England, would have just as difficult a time with the authorities, if not worse than those he had encountered in this time-line. Besides, Hannah and Karl would still not be his and he therefore concluded that he would be no better off.

He also questioned his motives for undoing what he had originally done in 1945, and the only one that really sprang to mind was revenge. Revenge on those that had made such a mess of this time-line and revenge on those that had ruined his life. The question was; could he really contemplate 'sacrificing' millions of

Jewish lives, purely for his own personal revenge? But then again, what about the countless lives that had been lost, in the many wars and genocides in this new time-line? By not reverting the time-line, wouldn't he be condemning them to die? Tony was getting to the point that he didn't really know what to think.

He tried to look at it on a personal level, and his thoughts went back to Halina in Kosalin. She had been so kind to him in Poland and he was not sure that he could justify, in his own mind, condemning her to never have existed.

Another option was to try and find Kaska and save her life, but at the end of the day, finding her in the countryside of Poland would be like trying to find a needle in a haystack. Even if he did find her, knowing how stubborn and determined she was, why would she listen to or believe a word Tony said. He concluded that his chances were slim and therefore crossed it off as a viable option.

He even contemplated going back to before Hannah met the 'other' Tony. The one he had stabbed to death! Tony dreamt that maybe he could get her to fall in love with him once again, instead of her 'husband'. However, he knew that this was wishful thinking.

He didn't know how or when they met, so how could he stop them meeting?

He also had to face facts. Tony was now 45 and if he was honest to himself, the last few years hadn't exactly been kind to him. With all the sleeping rough and excessive drinking, plus the fact he'd been locked up in Brampton for so long, he now looked closer to 55 than 45. The further he went back to ensure she hadn't yet fallen for this 'other' Tony, the younger she would be. So why would such a young beautiful women, like Hannah, be interested in an 'old' man like Tony. He knew deep down that the simple answer was that she wouldn't, and if he thought otherwise then he would be deluding himself. As much as he would have liked to, Tony knew that he could never have Hannah, or Karl, for that matter, back. It broke his heart, but he decided that he had done them enough harm and therefore promised to himself that wherever or whenever he went back to, he would not interfere with their lives ever again, and therefore that they would not be part of his plans.

So what was he going to do? As much as he'd like to undo the damage he had done, he knew deep down that it was not practical. And, as much as the thought of wreaking his revenge on this time-line was appealing, he had to think of the consequences to himself. Although he felt that he was being selfish Tony decided that whatever his plans entailed, that the outcome had to be a better future for one person, and one person only, him!

So, after much deliberation, he finally decided to start a new life for himself in the 1970's. It was a great time for innovations and inventors. Tony considered that he could go back and invent a million and one things. Each one, long before they had ever been thought of. To finance it, and to make sure that he didn't fall in to the same poverty trap, as in this time-line, he had a simple, but brilliant, idea. Tony decided to utilize every available minute when he was not re-programming the time machine or writing his 'autobiography' by spending it in the library. One thing Brampton can boast about is its excellent library facility. By reading every sports book in there, Tony determined that he could cram his brain full of every sporting statistic from over the last thirty years. He had never really been much of a gambler or even into sport at all for that matter. But it will hardly be gambling when he knew he couldn't lose! 'By the time I've finished in the library I will know which horses will win all the big races, especially those at long odds. Which football teams will win all the big matches. Boxers, the big fights, and so on.' Tony contemplated smiling to himself.

'You never know I might even get to enjoy sport knowing that I can never back a loser.' he thought. Not that he intended to be greedy or draw attention to himself, but he knew he could ensure that he earned enough money to guarantee himself a decent life. For the first time in as long as he could remember Tony now felt confident about his future. At last he had something he could genuinely look forward to.

Tony had a really good feeling that his life would be so much better in the 1970's. Given his current circumstances, it couldn't be much worst. Could it?

Tony could kick himself for changing his mind after all his hard work, but faced with such a moral dilemma, it seemed like the appropriate thing to do. He decided that despite being a pain, having to re-calculate his data to take him back to 1970 instead of 1937, that this is the right decision.

'Why should I put myself through all the stress of trying to change the World, when I can create such a cosy life for myself'. Tony smiled as he contemplated that he had made the right decision.

His mind was made up. Tomorrow he would start the change to 1970.

'I just hope I have the time to complete the amendments before the bastards try and take away my machine!' he thought to himself.

Chapter 24 - Where the bloody hell is Tony Smith?

Although, it was getting late, I felt I owed it to Tony to tell him straight away, that he had already worked on TESS2 for the last time. So, with a certain amount of trepidation, I made my way to his room. As I walked along the corridor and approached his room I could see Tony sat on the edge of his bed reading a book. I knocked gently as I walked in through the opened door.

"Tony" I said, attracting his attention.

He looked up from the book he was busily reading.

"Sports Statistics of the Twentieth Century" I said out-loud, after getting a glimpse of the cover of his book. "I didn't know you were into sport" I said, surprised at his choice.

"I'm not" he replied. "But I've had a brilliant idea about making a decent life for myself when I use TESS2 to get out of here."

"I'm sure it is a brilliant idea, but I'm afraid it is about your machine that I wanted to see you about" I told him rather apprehensively. "You see, I've just come from the finance meeting and its not good news I'm sorry to say. I tried, honestly I tried, but I got out voted seven to one, so I'm afraid they are taking away TESS2." I informed him.

"Two weeks, that's all I need, just two more weeks, then they can have it." he replied unaware of just how imminent its removal was.

"I'm sorry Tony, but you haven't got two weeks, or even two days for that matter. It's being removed first thing in the morning." I told him grimly.

"They can't do that….10 days, that's all I'll need, just get me 10 more days" Tony pleaded, getting somewhat agitated.

"I'm sorry Tony, but they've finally run out of patience. TESS2 is being removed first thing in the morning and there is nothing that I, or anyone else, can do about it!"

"You must stop them" he pleaded once more. "If they remove it, I swear I will kill myself. I mean it!" threatened Tony.

"Tony, I can understand your frustration, but for Christ's sake please don't do this to me. If I go back to the committee and tell them you are threatening to commit suicide over a stupid computer, then all the progress I've made getting them to consider your release under license will be thrown out of the window. The chances are remote in any case, but I can guarantee that they would not review your situation in a month of Sundays if they thought for one minute that you were still that unstable." I reasoned with him.

"I don't sodding care if I get released or not. Don't you understand - I don't want to get out of here, not in this fucked up time-line. There is nothing for me out there. I need to go back to a different time, where I can start my life afresh"

"Tony, you know time travel is not possible! The sooner you realise this the better. You promised me that once you had failed to build a time-machine that you would stop all this nonsense about time travel. Well, it's now time to admit that you have failed" I said tersely.

"It is possible…..and I can prove it" he snapped back.

"Tony, you've had well over a year to prove that it is possible and we are no closer to whizzing through time now, than we were when you first started building the bloody contraption!" I argued back. I was disappointed with myself for getting drawn in to a confrontational situation with Tony, but he continued to argue.

"TESS2 is fully working and ready to go" he told me surprisingly.

"So what happened to the 10 more days you said you needed a few moments ago?" I questioned him without trying to sound too condescending.

"I do need 10 more days if I want to go back to 1970, but I could go back to 1937 now if I wanted to. AND I can prove it!"

"Let's get this straight. You are telling me that your time machine is fully functional and ready to send you back in time to 1937?" I asked rather intrigued by this sudden turn of events.

"Yes, it is. Given the option I would prefer to go back to 1970, but with the choice between having TESS2 taken away from me and being stuck in this place or taking my chances back in 1937, I know which one I will take" Tony said resolutely.

This was turning out better than I thought as I realised that I might yet get my opportunity to finalise my 'therapy' after all. If I could get him to his machine and he proved to himself that TESS2 was nothing more than a supped up computer and not a time-machine, or a Temporal Energy Separation System, as he calls it, then my decision to let him build it in the first place would be fully justified.

"If I take you to TESS2 now, will you promise that once you have had your shot at going back in time, if by any chance whatsoever you are not successful, then you will drop all this nonsense about time travel once and for all? Plus, if that is the case, agree that TESS2 can be removed in the morning? Without any fuss?" I added.

"Yes, I promise" he assured me.

Brampton is a very secure facility and since it was after 6 o'clock Tony's computer room was now off limits and through a number of restricted access doors and corridors. Even though I have access to all areas I didn't fancy having to explain what I was doing, if challenged by any of the duty doctors or security. I'm not normally the type of person to take risks, but since this was going to be my one and only opportunity to bury this notion of time-travel, I decided it was worth it. I could have waited until morning and explained to Dr Jones that we could now conclude my experiment. However, he was such a stubborn git that I doubted that he'd listen. Besides he wasn't due in until later in the day and by that time the machine would be in bits and my opportunity lost.

I concluded that it was therefore now or never!

"Come on then. Let's do it!" I said jubilantly.

Tony jumped from his bed eagerly, with a celebratory "Yessss," as I beckoned him to follow me out of his room. I must admit that I felt a nervous apprehension as we 'sneaked' through the mazelike corridors of the institution. Each time we approached a CCTV camera I ensured that my clothing was pulled up over my head, and instructed Tony to do the same. All was looking good until our luck finally ran out and we literally ran into Dr Yates.

"Hello Dave, I wasn't expecting to see you down this end of the building at this time of night. Are you lost?" he laughed."Arrrh, I certainly didn't expect to see you here at this time of night Mr Smith" he added, noticing my companion. "You do realise that you could be in serious trouble for being down here?" he reminded us both.

"Look Bob, I just need 10 minutes access to Tony's computer, he's got some personal files he wants to retrieve before they take it away in the morning" I lied rather unconvincingly. "You know I wouldn't normally ask, but he has worked so hard on this machine of his. How would you feel if they destroyed everything that you'd been working on for the last 18 months? It's the least we can do for him" I pleaded.

"I suppose so, but this isn't really appropriate. This is a top security mental institution, not a holiday camp. We can't have people, doctors or patients, roaming around at will. There are proper procedures for this type of request. You know that old man Jones would do his nut if he caught you?" he lectured.

"Sorry Bob, I know you're right. I promise it won't happen again, but if you can just turn your back for 10 minutes then we'll be out of here before you know it, OK?"

"I suppose so, but I'm not very happy about it!" he agreed reluctantly.

"Thanks Bob, you're a gentleman. And don't worry, we'll keep this our little secret." I reassured him.

"Just make it quick" he said "before we all end up in the shit!"

Bob Yates was a rather tall and gangly sort of chap. He wore a pair of dark rimmed glasses and was generally rather unassuming. He had only been at Brampton for around nine months and, put in this situation, I guess he would have felt slightly intimidated by my senior position to his own. I was nevertheless grateful for his 'turning a blind eye', since he was undoubtedly taking a bit of a risk. He was right, old man Jones would blow a gasket if he got wind of it. I thanked him and opened the door to the computer room.

Tony thanked me for the way I had managed to get us past Bob Yates and for giving him this opportunity 'to get out of here'. I assured him that I was doing it for my good as much as his. As fascinating as his stories had always been, I told him that they were now getting a little tedious and that I felt the only way we could both move on, was for him to have this opportunity 'to fail'.

He thanked me nevertheless.

"You do realise what I intend to do back in 1937?" Tony asked me as we sat in front of TESS2.

"Let me guess? You intend to save us all from this evil world we live in, rescue the woman and live happily ever after" I joked.

"Something like that." laughed Tony.

"I am going to stop Herman Swartz being killed in 1945 and make sure the blue-prints for the Atomic bomb end up in their rightful place. In the hands of the Nazis. By doing so, I will no doubt change the outcome of the war and will condemn millions of people to death or to have never existed at all. In all probability this will include you. From the 25th April 1945 onwards, all events in the world will take a different direction and unless you are confident that your parents will meet and conceive you in the same circumstances, as they did in this timeline, then you will not be alive today. Understand?" he questioned.

"I understand, I understand – now get on with it" I replied rather dismissively.

259

"You're a good man Dave, I just want you to know that I've enjoyed all our talks over the years and I'm sorry that what I'm about to do will have such a devastating effect on you." said Tony apologetically. "There is an alternative you know" he added.

"Which is?" I questioned.

"To give me ten more days. Then I will reset my calculations to go back to 1970, where the effects on the time-line will be insignificant and no one needs to suffer."

"You know that's not possible" I told him, "and if we don't hurry now you might not get the opportunity to go anywhere"

"Any time." Tony corrected me.

"Whatever." I said beckoning him to get a move on.

"Very well" said Tony. "I had a moral dilemma about going back to 1937 and changing the face of the world. However, if you now give me no option, I will have no qualms about doing what I have to do. I promise you now, that I will do everything in my power to ensure that Germany will once again rule much of the world and life as you know it will no longer exist. I just wanted to make sure that you fully understand the consequences of your decision" he reiterated.

"Look for the last time, I understand, just get on with it," I snapped impatiently.

"If I no longer exist then I guess it's something I'll just have to live with" I added as a half-hearted attempt at a joke. "Now get a move on, before I change my mind."

Tony nodded and started to strip off.

"What the hell are you doing?" I asked him somewhat alarmed.

"I've told you many times that you have to be naked for the Temporal Energy Separation to take place" he reminded me.

"OK, OK, just make it as quick as possible" I said rather grudgingly. I wasn't liking this one bit. It was starting to get bizarre and I was worried what it might look like if Dr Yates was to walk in.

Once naked, Tony started to 'wire himself up' - attaching a dozen, or so electrodes that were coming out of the back of his machine, to various points on his body. When he had finally completed the process he looked at me.

"There is a file called "TimeShift" on this computer. Please read it when I've gone and let the world know that I wasn't mad after all. You need to let people know what their future holds, so they can live life to the full in the short time they will have left. Or it will at least give them the opportunity to repent their sins if they feel that more appropriate." he laughed.

"Thank you David" he said, smiling as he activated a count down on the computer screen.

I don't know why but I suddenly felt very apprehensive. I still had no doubt in my mind that time travel was an impossibility and nothing was actually going to happen, but how was Tony going to react when he finds that such a big part of his life has just been a delusion. How on earth would he pick up the pieces? Tony was so convinced that he was about to be transported back in time, I feared that as soon as he realises that he has failed miserably he will not be able to face reality and he will go into meltdown! Maybe this 'therapy' wasn't such a good idea after all!

In the background the screen counted down….3….2…1….0.

As the screen hit zero there was a sudden hum of noise as the electrodes on Tony's body started lighting up. One after another they started to connect to each other, through what looked like low voltage beams of fluorescent light arcing across Tony's skin. Once the electrodes were all linked, the gaps in between them also started to connect to each other with more and more strands of light. This process started to gather speed, as Tony's body started to look like an illuminated road map. The glow of light started to intensify as the outline of Tony's body began to disappear behind the brilliant light. It looked like a fantastic visual effect from a sci-fi movie - but this was for real.

I then started to panic. I feared that Tony was in the process of killing himself! Being burnt to death by the intense heat now being given off by the glow of light. I made a grab for the plug, but as I pulled it, there was a whooshing noise and suddenly the light was gone. More alarmingly, so was Tony!

As I stood there shaking, with my jaw down by my knees the door flung open. It was Bob Yates. "What the hell are you doing in here? The corridor just lit up like the Blackpool Illuminations" he yelled. Before I could say anything and realising that I was alone in the room he added "Tony Smith, where the bloody hell is Tony Smith?."

"I think the question maybe when is Tony Smith, not where." I answered, still mesmerised by what I had just witnessed.

"My God you've vaporised him" he shouted.

"I...I....I didn't touch him" I argued weakly.

"Oh my God, Oh my God, you've killed him" he started repeating to himself as he scurried around panicking.

I felt like slapping him around his face and telling him to get a grip of himself, but I was still routed to the spot, shocked and dazed at what had just happened.

Then, my own panic starting to set in. What if Doctor Yates was right, maybe I had just helped Tony kill himself! What if he has just been vaporised into nothingness by the shear heat of the light? I started to shake uncontrollably and then it was my turn to start repeating "Oh my God, Oh my God!."

"Come on, pull yourself together. Tell me what happened" demanded Bob Yates as he managed to compose himself and seeing my state of distress.

Although I was a bit of a gibbering wreck I explained the best I could what we were really doing here and what I had just witnessed.

"You're not telling me you believe he's actually gone back in time?" said Bob, bemused by what I had told him.

"I'm not sure what I believe. But I know what I've just seen and I know Tony Smith is no longer here!"

"He's been vaporised. I've read it before, how someone can just disappear into thin air, if the heat is that intense." he said despairingly and looking around the floor for signs of ash or other remnants of Tony Smith. I repeated that I didn't know what to believe, but the simple fact was, that I'd lost a patient who was in my care, and furthermore in a restricted area of the unit. I knew I could be in deep trouble.

"Look, Tony Smith said there was a file on the computer, which would explain everything in more detail. Let's have a look to see if that gives us any clues." I said hopefully. So we re-booted the machine and searched for the file in question.

"Here it is – 'TimeShift'," I pointed out to Bob, as I opened the file and started to read its contents.

Much of it was an elaboration of what Tony had already told me in our many conversations. It was a step by step account of his time-travel experiences, including accounts of all the experiments he had conducted in the early days. One in particular left me dumbfounded. I read it out loud to Bob.

'Having travelled back in time I was able to witness myself, that is, the me that was already in the past, going back in time even further. At the first instant of the temporal reaction the electro-conductors arc light to each other, as if creating a fluorescent spiders web or road map all over my body. As the quantum calculations escalate, the light strands start to bridge the areas between the main arcs, until such a time as these smaller 'veins' themselves start to branch out into smaller, yet more numerous tributaries.

This reaction is accompanied with an ever increasing radiation of light, which continues to intensify until it is finally converted into the ultra condensed light energy. At this point the light generated becomes so intense that it is almost blinding to the eye. This acute intensity only lasts a matter of seconds as the condensed matter finally implodes and is forced to go 4ᵗʰ dimensionally.

At the exact point of the time-shift there is a loud whooshing sound and the light is extinguished instantly.'

"My God. If this isn't proof that I've witnessed the reality of time travel, then I don't know what is!" I said excitedly.

"This proves nothing" said Bob

"But, this is precisely what I've just witnessed. It's exactly how I've just described it to you - Is it not? How would Tony Smith be able to describe what I have just witnessed, in such detail, unless he has seen it for himself?" I asked.

"Look, I don't know what to think, but I do know that if you start going round telling everyone you believe in time-travel, they'll lock you up! How do you think old man Jones is going to react when you tell him Tony Smith has just disappeared to another dimension? If you take my advice, you go home and forget that any of this has happened" Bob advised me sternly.

"How can I forget that I've just seen a naked man disappear in front of my very eyes? And more importantly, how the hell do I explain Tony's disappearance?" I responded despairingly.

"Who saw you come down here?" he asked.

"No one. Why?"

"So why do you have to explain his disappearance? You're not on duty are you?"

"No I suppose not." I responded, realising where this was going.

"Then it'll be up to that dopey prat Kevin Whitmore to explain how he lost a patient on his shift!" he laughed.

"My God you're right. Other than the two of us, and Tony Smith I suppose, no one else knows that any of this has just happened." I knew Bob was talking sense, but was intrigued why he would help me in this way.

"Why would you do this for me?" I asked sceptically.

"I'm not doing it for you? How do you think it will look on me? I'm the idiot who allowed you in here. As far as I'm concerned I've not seen you tonight and you've not seen me! If you say otherwise I'll deny it" he said defiantly.

"Look, Dave, you're a half decent bloke and I don't want either of us to get in any trouble. If you know what's good for you, you will go home now and say nothing" he advised strongly.

I must admit it did make sense. I didn't much fancy getting the third degree from Arnold Jones and whatever we did now was not going to bring back Tony Smith. I nodded in agreement to Bob and we agreed that no one needed to know what had gone on this evening. Before leaving, I asked that he gave me one minute to collect my thoughts. As Bob left the room I quickly downloaded Tony's 'Time-shift' file on to a floppy disc. I knew that if my involvement in Tony Smith disappearance ever did get out and I got accused of any wrong doing, then at least this file would add some weight to my version of events. Once the download was complete I gathered up Tony's clothes and quickly and quietly made my way out of the building and headed to my car.

On the way home the enormity of what I had just witnessed started to dawn on me. If Tony Smith had not just vaporised himself, then I had to face the fact that there was a real likelihood that time travel was possible! As if that fact wasn't enough to take in, I now had to give real consideration to Tony's version of an alternate time-line and the fact that he was already back in 1937 with the intension of wiping out my existence!

The drive home was a blur, with my mind trying to take in all that had happened that evening. Despite what I had witnessed I was still struggling to comprehend that time travel could be possible. I wondered if there could be another explanation and hoped that the answer may be on the disc.

As I arrived at my house, I very quickly loaded Tonys file onto my laptop and printed out a copy. As I read it to myself, and given what I had just witnessed, it all now started to sound very feasible. Before, when Tony had explained things to me in our many conversations, I was always listening from a negative point of view. Never believing a word of what he was saying, I was only listening for points that I could question him about, or aspects that I could challenge. Always trying to disprove what he was saying. Now reading from a different perspective it made compelling reading and I now started to have severe doubts about my future. As these thoughts played on my mind, I knew that to remove the few lingering doubts which I still had, I needed further evidence and so I continued to read late into the night. I hoped that somewhere in the text there might be a clue that would help convince me, one way or the other, as to the fate of Tony Smith.

Having read nearly two thirds of the print-out I was struggling to keep my eyes open and I reluctantly decided that I would be better off continuing in the morning after a good nights sleep. Not that there was a remote possibility of a good nights sleep, with all that was going on in my head. Begrudgingly I got ready for bed, but just as I was about to turn off the lights I had a quick flick through the remaining pages to see how much I had left to read. As I flicked through the pages, there towards the end of the sheets of paper was something that jumped out and hit me. My Name. 'David Rose'.

Seeing my own name in print I quickly read the relevant section. It continued.

'David Rose, if you are reading this then no doubt you have just witnessed my departure to 1937. I hope you agree that it was quite an incredible spectacle? I don't like to say 'I told you so.', but now do you believe that time-travel is possible? Knowing you, I bet you're still not convinced and won't even believe your own eyes! Just in case you still need convincing I intend to send you a little proof from 1937.I take it that, even you, will believe where and when I am when you read the following message

'David Rose – Time is the essence of life, so don't waste it!! – from your friend Tony Smith'.

You will find it in the personal message section of the Yorkshire Post edition, for the 1st March 1937, in a few days time.

By the way, if you didn't already know they have them on microfiche in the institute library.

Finally, once you realise that I have been telling the truth all along, then you will also realise that I am serious about creating this almighty paradox. You must understand that it's nothing personal, but your time-line was never meant to be.

I had no right to change the lives of so many millions of people and therefore I owe it to all mankind to undo what I did back in 1945.

History is not something that can be messed with – I now know that.

I am sincerely sorry that this will mean the end of the world as you know it and will probably mean that you will never have existed, but it is something I must do. It's not as though you will feel any pain or even have any consciousness of what has happened, but please forgive me nevertheless. I have set my calculations to take me to the 25th February 1937. Since time travels faster in the past than the present, I've calculated that you have 756 days left, between now and my day of reckoning with Herman Swartz, in eight years of my time. All I can do is suggest you spend the next two years of your time-line living life to the full. Goodbye and good luck.

Your 'delusional' time-travelling patient (and friend). Tony Smith.'

I was gob smacked by what I had just read, but at least I now knew that if Tony was telling the truth, I would have incontrovertible proof that time travel is possible. If the message appears in the Yorkshire Post on the 1st March 1937, as Tony suggests that it will, then I will have to accept that time-travel is a reality. More alarmingly, I will have to face the fact that my days and those of many millions of people throughout the world may be numbered. Needless to say I hardly slept a wink that night.

Chapter 25 - Countdown to Oblivion

It was with a certain amount of trepidation that I drove to work the next day. I was on the late shift, which started at 3.00 pm. This gave me a bit of extra time to compose myself for the inevitable questions, that I was bound to face, once they realise that one of my 'high risk' patients had disappeared. As I approached the building I could see a fair amount of activity outside the building and it was soon apparent that there were a large number of reporters milling around the main entrance. Tony Smith's case had made all the front pages at the time, so if news got out about him 'escaping' then it was bound to be big news.

Judging by the commotion outside it was evident that the news had already leaked out. Two burly policemen greeted me as I got to the entrance. After a careful inspection of my pass they let me enter the building. My intension was to keep a low profile and if questioned, follow Dr Yates advice and deny all knowledge of Tony's disappearance; but as I entered the building I was greeted by Arnold Jones.

"I assume you have heard the news?" he asked me, before I had even got through the door.

"What news?" I unconvincingly replied, trying to act dumb.

"Your man, Tony Smith, is nowhere to be seen. We've had the building searched three times with no joy; so I've had no option but to call the police. They're inside at the moment with their sniffer dogs. They think he may be hiding in here since their review of all the external CCTV tapes have not shown him leaving the building. If he is hiding then he's doing a bloody good job of it, since we have searched everywhere"

"I don't suppose you know anything about his disappearance, do you?" he added.

"No, why should I know anything about it?" I lied.

"Well, he was your patient and I know you were pretty close to him" he answered.

"I'm sorry, but I know nothing about it" I lied once again, rather unconvincingly.

"That's funny" he said, "It's not quite what Bob Yates told me just 10 minutes ago!"

'Oooh shit' I thought to myself, as he continued.

"Whilst the police were reviewing the external tapes, I took the liberty of taking a look at the internal ones.

"I think you had better come with me" he said moving his arm to beckon me towards his office. I followed him in, and once there he sat at his large desk and pressed a number of buttons on the tape machine in front of him.

"Does this look familiar?" he asked as the tape machine started to play.

On the screen were two people, one wearing the white coat of a doctor and the other the casual clothes of a patient.

"That could be anyone" I argued feebly.

"I suggest you let me continue, before you embarrass yourself further" said Dr Jones tersely.

I nodded at him nervously.

"It could be anyone, I suppose" he continued, "but why do you think they would be wearing a jacket with your name badge on it?" he said smugly. To emphasize the point he froze the picture on the screen and by pressing a few gadgets on the tape machine zoomed in on the picture. There, clear as day, was the name 'Dr David Rose' on the badge of the jacket pulled up over my head.

How stupid could I have been, I thought to myself as he continued.

"It could, I suppose, be someone wearing your jacket, so I also took the liberty to check the internal security pass logs, and surprise surprise, at the same time this video footage was taken, we have a record of your pass being used to access three restricted areas."

"You could try and claim someone had stolen your jacket and your pass, but before you do and no doubt embarrass yourself further, I suggest you let me finish first" he said rather sharply.

I just nodded in agreement, as he continued.

"Since Dr Yates was in charge of this area last night, I also took the liberty, to ask him a few questions. At first he denied all knowledge. However, once I reminded him of the fact that he was responsible for security in the area where two unauthorised people had roamed about unchallenged, I gave him the ultimatum - either tell me what you know or face disciplinary action for gross incompetence and neglect of duty. Strangely enough after this bit of 'career advice' he suddenly remembered bumping into you and our missing friend. He stated that he left you alone in the computer room for about 10 minutes with Tony Smith, and that when he returned, the said Mr Smith had gone. He stated that you came out with some crap about him disappearing 'back in time'.

"Bob Yates might be a fool, but I'm not. Now cutting out the bullshit, would you please be so kind as to explain to me where the fucking hell he is?" he asked abruptly.

"It's like this…" I started. "You know that we have always assumed that Tony Smith was a psychotic delusionist, and that his time-travel stories were all part of his delusions… well, I'm afraid we need to think again."

I couldn't believe I was telling old man Jones, but I told him every last detail of what had happened the night before.

"….and so I'm afraid that Bob Yates isn't a fool after all – Tony Smith has actually travelled back in time!

After I had finished he just sat there staring at me.

At last he spoke. "And you expect me to believe this crock of shit?"

"I'm not asking you to believe anything" I told him. "But it is the truth!"

He looked at me again without saying a word and then started laughing loudly.

"I'm not sure what I would find more embarrassing - admitting to the police that we have had our first patient escape in 22 years or telling them that we actually let him build a bloody time-machine so that he could escape from here to a different dimension!"

"So you believe me?" I asked naively.

"Of course I don't bloody well believe you – you blithering idiot! Even if I did, I wouldn't admit it. Imagine the furore if the press got hold of that one. They would think that the lunatics have taken over the bloody asylum and they'd be right." he exclaimed.

"Now, I don't suppose you are going to tell me what really happened?" he asked hopefully.

"I've told you the truth. As far as I'm concerned Tony Smith is in 1937 and the destiny of mankind is in his hands!"

"You do realise that they will think that you're mad if you go around saying this, don't you?"

"I suppose they will, but I know what I saw last night" I told him stubbornly.

"Whatever you think you saw, I can tell you now it wasn't a time-machine. There is no such thing as time-travel and if you know what's good for you, you'll keep this story to yourself"

It was ironic that I had spent years arguing the exact same thing with Tony Smith, only this time I was on the opposite side of the argument.

"I'm not prepared to have the good name of this institute ridiculed, which will happen if you go around telling everyone this nonsense" stated Dr Jones.

"What about his time machine, come and see it for yourself" I pleaded with him.

"The hard drive of his 'time machine' was formatted this morning and the rest of it is being dismantled as we speak. By now it should be in a thousand pieces. As I have said, there is no time-machine. There never was and there never will be! Now I'm going to offer you an ultimatum" he said in a serious tone.

"Keep this story to yourself and I will make sure the police never see this tape or the security pass logs. Insist on telling the world and the police will see it all. Plus I will tell them of your friendly relationship with Tony Smith, and that it is of my opinion that you have collaborated with him to help him escape. The choice is yours, but either way I expect your resignation on my desk by tomorrow morning."

"What? You're sacking me!" I said despondently.

"No, you're resigning. If I have to sack you, then I'll make sure you never work again" he said threateningly.

"You can't treat me like this" I argued weakly, but it was to no avail. Old Man Jones told me to leave the building and think long and hard about what I do next. I knew he could be a bastard, but I didn't think he would stoop quite so low as to fire me!

I met Bob Yates on the way out.

"I'm sorry Dave" he told me.

"I have a wife and two kids to support you know. He threatened that I'd never work again if I didn't tell him!"

"Has he sacked you too?" I asked.

"No, but he told me that if I mentioned anything about time-machines that he'd make sure I'd…."

"Don't tell me, 'never work again.'" I said, finishing his sentence.

"You've got it" he laughed. I told Bob that I didn't blame him and we parted company with a shake of hands.

Outside I was stopped by a couple of the reporters, but I gave them the customary 'No comment', before getting back in my car. On the way back to my house it occurred to me that I hadn't used

273

my trump card – the message in the Yorkshire Post! I had worked out from Tony's notes that the time differential meant that the message in the Post, would not appear until tomorrow. This was the evidence I needed, not only to convince 'old man Jones', but also to remove the lingering doubts from my own mind.

Back at my house, I wasn't sure what to do with myself. I finished reading Tony's notes, and then read them again from cover to cover. All I could do now was sit and wait. Needless to say it seemed like an eternity waiting for the next day to arrive.

The next day, when it finally arrived, I knew I would have to go to the offices of the Yorkshire Post, since I was no longer allowed in the library of the Institute.

The staff at the Post were kind enough to let me view their papers, which were filed neatly in leather bound folders.

Here it was; 1st March 1937.

I eagerly started flicking through the pages. I was desperately disappointed when I got to the personal message section in the paper and Tony's message wasn't there. I went through it with a fine toothcomb, but there was definitely no message. Had I been a fool all along?

If I hadn't witnessed him going back in time what had I seen? Maybe Tony hadn't managed to place the message yet. Maybe it would appear another day, after all he would have had to beg, borrow or steal the money to pay for it, back in 1937. Since he went back with no money, or any clothes for that matter, maybe he's finding the task of placing the ad a little more difficult than he had envisaged. Maybe he's even got himself arrested for wandering around naked? I was starting to make up excuses for Tony, when suddenly the letters on the page I was reading started to go slightly blurry. I rubbed my eyes, but as I opened them again, I saw the makeup of the page change right in front of me! It was as though the messages already on the page were shifting up, to make room for a new message. The words were incredibly re-arranging themselves and appeared to be dancing around the page. It was all over in the blink of an eye, but as I now scanned the new layout there it was, right in the middle of the page.

'David Rose – Time is the essence of life, so don't waste it! – from your friend Tony Smith'.

I rubbed my eyes again - just to make sure my mind wasn't playing tricks on me. But sure as daylight, there was the message, just as Tony had promised. I let out a celebratory "Yes!" My God, he had done it! I thought to myself. I felt elated that I now had proof that I wasn't losing my own mind and I had actually witnessed a man travelling back in time. I was also relieved and pleased that Tony had not been vaporised by the intense heat, although when it actually sank in, I realised I had no reason to be pleased, since what I had just witnessed quite probably meant my eventual death sentence!

With this new evidence, Dr Jones would have to believe me and give me my job back. Luckily the Yorkshire post could sell you a print of any page from their archived papers. The normal waiting time was one week, but when I told them it was a matter of life and death, they agreed to do it there and then. Actually I had to pay an extra twenty quid, but I thought it was worth it just to be able to get one over 'Old man Jones'. However, I hadn't counted on Jones being such a stubborn old git.

At first he accused me of mocking up the page and getting it printed myself. However, after I told him that he could check the microfiche in his own library if he didn't believe me, he eventually accepted my word. Although, it was probably more to do with the fact that he was too lazy to walk to his own library to confirm that what I was saying was the truth. Despite this evidence he still insisted that it proved nothing. He said that Tony Smith, could have seen this message years ago. It could even have been the message that planted the seed in his mind for his delusional idea of time-travel in the first place.

"After all, how do we know his real name is Tony Smith?" he questioned.

"He could have seen the message and changed his name as part of his elaborate hoax to be someone or something he isn't - i.e. a time-traveller. Remember, we know little about Tony Smith prior to him committing that murder and coming here."

"What about the name David Rose? He didn't make that one up." I challenged.

"I admit that is a bit of a coincidence, but it still isn't evidence of time-travel. He remembered the name and therefore latched on to you."

"He was my patient. He didn't just latch on to me! Besides, I saw it for myself! I actually saw the page change right in front of my eyes and this message appear from nowhere." I reiterated.

"Yes, like you saw him disappear right in front of your eyes." he said sarcastically.

"Let us just say that I did believe you, not that I do, but how many other people do you think would? It's bad enough losing a high security patient, but if I went public with ludicrous stories of time-travel I'd be out of here quicker than a rat off a sinking ship and kissing goodbye to my pension. If you have helped him escape, then just come clean and admit it, but please do not question my intelligence with this nonsense. Now, do you have your letter of resignation or not?" he asked sternly.

I was about to start to plead for my job, when the realisation of the situation hit me. Even if Jones didn't believe me, I was now one hundred percent convinced that Tony Smith was in 1937. Having just watched the words on a page of newsprint dance around in front of my very eyes, was pretty compelling evidence. As far as I am concerned it was as conclusive proof that I could conceive that time travel was a reality. With that in mind and therefore the possibility that I only had two years to live anyway, why would I want to waste it working for this miserable old fool anyway?

So with a certain amount of gusto, which even surprised me, instead of pleading for my job back I told him in no uncertain terms where he could stick it! I called him a cantankerous old fart

276

and a blinkered fool, amongst other things. In fact I got quite carried away. By the time I had finished there was quite a gathering of staff, who, although I doubt would admit it, were getting a great deal of satisfaction watching Jonesy getting an ear bashing. Poor old Arnold's face was so red by the time I'd relented that I thought his head was about to explode! Quite predictably he had me escorted from the building. He was ranting and raving, as I was led out. I'm not certain, but I'm sure he mentioned something about me 'never working again.' as I left the building. Frankly, I didn't care if I didn't work again!

If I am to disappear in to nothingness, then I fully intend to live what time I have left to the full. However, I must admit that I also felt obliged to warn as many people as possible of their pending fate. I started with my family and friends, but soon realised that I was never going to convince them. They all thought it was a fascinating story, but said if I went around telling it to everyone I met they'd think I was stark raving mad! Some of them already thought I was mad anyway, for telling Dr Jones to stick my job up his arse.

I was about to give up on the whole idea as a lost cause - If I couldn't convince my own family how would I convince others? - When one of my friends suggested that I walked around with a sandwich board, saying 'The End is Nigh'. I laughed half heartedly at his suggestion, but then he added, "Or you could always write a book I suppose."

I think he said it as a bit of a joke, but I thought that it wasn't such a bad idea. Why not use the notes from Tony Smith to write a book? Then it's up to people whether they believe it or not. I thought to myself.

I thanked my friend for the idea, and he in turn suggested I call it 'How to throw your Career down the drain by Ivor Timemachine', which I didn't find particularly funny, but at least he had given me hope that I may, after all, be able to get my message to you.

So, I used Tony's notes to draft this book. Of course I had to use a little bit of poetic license, but I am confident that after all the

277

conversations I've had with Tony over the years, that I've managed to convey his words pretty accurately.

I was introduced to a publisher through a mutual friend, and they, with a little persuasion, agreed to publish the book. The rest, as they say, is history. I wanted to make it a factual book, but the publisher insisted on categorizing it as science fiction. I agreed with him in the end to get it published, but believe me as far as I'm concerned this book is science fact, not fiction! And so now you know the shocking truth.

I am one hundred percent convinced that we are all on a countdown to oblivion and depending on when you are reading this, the chances are, that you may only have a few months, weeks or even days, left to live. My advice is make the most of them. There is little doubt in my mind that all of our lives, here and now, are as a result of Tony Smith's actions back in his original 1945 time-line. We should perhaps be thankful for the lives that he has given us, but how can we? Knowing that he is now trying to erase us from History!

Once again, I'm afraid that all of our futures are in his hands.

We may all get lucky. He may well fail in his quest to undo his original paradox. He has a long arduous task to get half way across Europe and be in the right place at the right time – anything could happen to him along the way. He might even have second thoughts.

Once he is back there he could find a decent life for himself, and decide against having to turn the world upside down once again.

He might....., well at the end of the day, he might do anything. Whatever he is going to do, we can do nothing to stop him! The one thing that is for sure, is that if he succeeds then I doubt whether any of us will even realise it. I guess that we will feel no pain, instead we will just cease to exist. In fact, we would have never existed.

I guess that there are still plenty of you reading this book, who are still not convinced? In your shoes, perhaps I would be the same, but, if you had seen what I have seen, then believe me, you would be just as convinced as I am. If you're still sceptical, then you could always get hold of a copy of the 1st March 1937 issue of the Yorkshire Post. You can see it there for yourself, in black and white on page 27! At the end of the day I don't really care whether you believe me or not. I've done my bit and warned you of your pending fate. It's now up to you what you do with this information.

You could warn others, even talk them in to buying this book – well, I might as well at least have some income, whilst I await my fate. Or on the other hand you may choose to bury your head in the sand and continue your life in the same mundane way, and hope that I am wrong. Perhaps nothing will happen and we all get lucky!

But are you prepared to take the risk?

Time is one of the most valuable commodities we have. Ask anyone who has had a brush with death and they will tell you that they now appreciate every single day of their life and live it to the full. Why wait for your brush with death?

As a good friend of mine once said, '*Time is the essence of life, so don't waste it!*'.

Whether you have days, weeks or even years to live, follow Tony's advice and live life to the full – none of us know which day is going to be our last!

I wish you good luck and sincerely hope that I'm wrong.

If not, the clock is ticking and we are all now on **BORROWED TIME!**

17123427R00164

Printed in Great Britain
by Amazon